UNIVERSE 14

UNIVERSE 14

Edited by TERRY CARR

DOUBLEDAY & COMPANY, INC.
GARDEN CITY, NEW YORK

1984

Library of Congress Cataloging in Publication Data
Main entry under title: Universe 14.

Contents: The Lucky Strike/Kim Stanley Robinson
Gate of Horn, Gate of Ivory/Robert Silverberg
Passing as a Flower in the City of the Dead/Sharon N. Farber—[etc.]
1. Science fiction, American. I. Carr, Terry.
II. Title: Universe Fourteen.
PS648.S3U535 1984   813′.0876′08

ISBN: 0-385-19134-0
Library of Congress Catalog Card Number 83–20785
Copyright © 1984 by TERRY CARR
All Rights Reserved
Printed in the United States of America

First Edition

CONTENTS

UNIVERSE 14

Stories of alternative worlds, in which history was changed because a single thing happened differently, have fascinated science fiction readers for many decades. They can be thoughtful and evocative, as in Keith Roberts's Pavane, which tells how our world might have been if the Spanish Armada had won the victory, or humorous, like Somtow Sucharitkul's The Aquiliad, which tells what might have happened if the Romans had conquered the New World.

"The Lucky Strike" focuses on a much more recent, and "smaller," change in history . . . but one that could have effected changes just as great.

Kim Stanley Robinson's stories have appeared in the last four volumes of Universe, as well as in the sf magazines. "Venice Drowned" was nominated for a Nebula Award; "To Leave a Mark" received a Hugo nomination. His first novel, The Wild Shore, was recently published as an Ace Science Fiction Special.

THE LUCKY STRIKE

KIM STANLEY ROBINSON

War breeds strange pastimes. In July of 1945 on Tinian Island in the North Pacific, Captain Frank January had taken to piling pebble cairns on the crown of Mount Lasso—one pebble for each B-29 takeoff, one cairn for each mission. It was a mindless pastime, but so was poker. The men of the 509th had played a million hands of poker, sitting in the shade of a palm around an upturned crate, sweating in their skivvies, swearing and betting all their pay and cigarettes, playing hand after hand, until the cards got so soft and dog-eared you could have used them for toilet paper. Captain January had gotten sick of it, and after he lit out for the hilltop a few times some of his crew mates started trailing him. When their pilot, Jim Fitch, joined them it became an official pastime, like throwing flares into the compound or going hunting for stray Japs. What Captain January thought of the development he didn't say.

The others grouped near Captain Fitch, who passed around his battered flask. "Hey, January," Fitch called. "Come have a shot."

January wandered over and took the flask. Fitch laughed at his pebble. "Practicing your bombing up here, eh, Professor?"

"Yeah," January said sullenly. Anyone who read more than the funnies was Professor to Fitch. Thirstily January knocked back some rum. He passed the flask on to Lieutenant Matthews, their navigator.

"That's why he's the best," Matthews joked. "Always practicing."

Fitch laughed. "He's best because I make him be best, right, Professor?"

January frowned. Fitch was a bulky youth, thick-featured, pig-eyed—a thug, in January's opinion. The rest of the crew were all in their mid-twenties, like Fitch, and they liked the captain's bossy roughhouse style. January, who was thirty-seven, didn't go for it. He wandered away, back to the cairn he had been building. From Mount Lasso they had an overview of the whole island, from the harbor at Wall Street to the north field in Harlem. January had observed hundreds of B-29s roar off the four parallel runways of the north field and head for Japan. The last quartet of this particular mission buzzed across the width of the island, and January dropped four more pebbles, aiming for crevices in the pile. One of them stuck nicely.

"There they are!" said Matthews. "They're on the taxiing strip."

January located the 509th's first plane. Today, the first of August, there was something more interesting to watch than the usual Superfortress parade. Word was out that General LeMay wanted to take the 509th's mission away from it. Their commander, Colonel Tibbets, had gone and bitched to LeMay in person, and the general had agreed the mission was theirs, but on one condition—one of the general's men was to make a test flight with the 509th to make sure they were fit for combat over Japan. The general's man had arrived, and now he was down there in the strike plane with Tibbets and the whole first team. January sidled back to his mates to view the takeoff with them.

"Why don't the strike plane have a name, though?" Haddock was saying.

Fitch said, "Lewis won't give it a name because it's not his plane, and he knows it." The others laughed. Lewis and his crew were naturally unpopular, being Tibbets's favorites.

"What do you think he'll do to the general's man?" Matthews asked.

The others laughed at the very idea. "He'll kill an engine at takeoff, I bet you anything," Fitch said. He pointed at the wrecked B-29s that marked the end of every runway. "He'll want to show that he wouldn't go down if it happened to him."

"Course he wouldn't!" Matthews said.

"You hope," January said under his breath.

"They let those Wrights out too soon," Haddock said seriously. "They keep busting under the takeoff load."

"Won't matter to the old bull," Matthews said. Then they all started in about Tibbets's flying ability, even Fitch. They all thought Tibbets was the greatest. January, on the other hand, liked Tibbets even less than he liked Fitch. That had started right after he was assigned to the 509th. He had been told he was part of the most important group in the war and then given a leave. In Vicksburg a couple of fliers just back from England had bought him a lot of whiskeys, and since January had spent several months stationed near London they had talked for a good long time and gotten pretty drunk. The two were really curious about what January was up to now, but he had stayed vague on it and kept returning the talk to the blitz. He had seen an English nurse, for instance, whose flat had been bombed, family killed . . . But they had really wanted to know. So he had told them he was onto something special, and they had flipped out their badges and told him they were Army Intelligence, and that if he ever broke security like that again he'd be transferred to Alaska. It was a dirty trick. January had gone back to Wendover and told Tibbets so to his face, and Tibbets had turned red and threatened him some more. January despised him for that. During their year's training he had bombed better than ever, as a way of showing the old bull he was wrong. Every time their eyes had met it was clear what was going on. But Tibbets never backed off no matter how precise January's bombing got. Just thinking about it was enough to cause January to line up a pebble over an ant and drop it.

"Will you cut that out?" Fitch complained.

January pointed. "They're going."

Tibbets's plane had taxied to runway Baker. Fitch passed the flask around again. The tropical sun beat on them, and the ocean surrounding the island blazed white. January put up a sweaty hand to aid the bill of his baseball cap.

The four props cut in hard, and the sleek Superfortress quickly trundled up to speed and roared down Baker. Three quarters of the way down the strip the outside right prop feathered.

"Yow!" Fitch crowed. "I told you he'd do it!"

The plane nosed off the ground and slewed right, then pulled back on course to cheers from the four young men around January. January pointed again. "He's cut number three, too."

The inside right prop feathered, and now the plane was pulled up by the left wing only, while the two right props windmilled uselessly. "Holy smoke!" Haddock cried. "Ain't the old bull something?"

They whooped to see the plane's power and Tibbets's nervy arrogance.

"By God, LeMay's man will remember this flight," Fitch hooted. "Why, look at that! He's banking!"

Apparently taking off on two engines wasn't enough for Tibbets; he banked the plane right until it was standing on its dead wing, and it curved back toward Tinian.

Then the inside left engine feathered.

War tears at the imagination. For three years Frank January had kept his imagination trapped, refusing to give it any play whatsoever. The dangers threatening him, the effects of the bombs, the fate of the other participants in the war—he had refused to think about any of it. But the war tore at his control. That English nurse's flat. The missions over the Ruhr. The bomber just below him blown apart by flak. And then there had been a year in Utah, and the viselike grip that he had once kept on his imagination had slipped away.

So when he saw the number two prop feather, his heart gave a little jump against his sternum, and helplessly he was up there with Ferebee, the first-team bombardier. He would be looking over the pilots' shoulders . . .

"Only one engine?" Fitch said.

"That one's for real," January said harshly. Despite himself he *saw* the panic in the cockpit, the frantic rush to power the two right engines. The plane was dropping fast and Tibbets leveled it off, leaving them on a course back toward the island. The two right props spun, blurred to a shimmer. January held his breath. They needed more lift; Tibbets was trying to pull it over the island. Maybe he was trying for the short runway on the south half of the island.

But Tinian was too tall, the plane too heavy. It roared right into the jungle above the beach, where Forty-second Street met their East River. It exploded in a bloom of fire. By the time the sound of it struck them they knew no one in the plane had survived.

Black smoke towered into white sky. In the shocked silence on Mount Lasso, insects buzzed and creaked. The air left January's lungs with a gulp. He had been with Ferebee, he had heard the desperate shouts, seen the last green rush, been stunned by the dentist-drill-all-over pain of the impact.

"Oh my God," Fitch was saying. "Oh my God." Matthews was sitting. January picked up the flask, tossed it at Fitch.

"C-come on," he stuttered. He hadn't stuttered since he was sixteen. He led the others in a rush down the hill. When they got to Broadway a jeep careened toward them and skidded to a halt. It was Colonel Scholes, the old bull's exec. "What happened?"

Fitch told him.

"Those damned Wrights," Scholes said as the men piled in. This time one had failed at just the wrong moment; some welder in the States had kept flame to metal a second less than usual—or something equally minor, equally trivial—and that had made all the difference.

They left the jeep at Forty-second and Broadway and hiked east over a narrow track to the shore. A fairly large circle of trees was burning. The fire trucks were already there.

Scholes stood beside January, his expression bleak. "That was the whole first team," he said.

"I know," said January. He was still in shock, his imagination crushed, incinerated, destroyed. Once as a kid he had tied sheets to his arms and waist, jumped off the roof, and landed right on his chest; this felt like that had. He had no way of knowing what would come of this crash, but he had a suspicion that he had indeed smacked into something hard.

Scholes shook his head. A half hour had passed, the fire was nearly out. January's four mates were over chattering with the Seabees. "He was going to name the plane after his mother," Scholes said to the ground. "He told me that just this morning. He was going to call it *Enola Gay.*"

At night the jungle breathed, and its hot wet breath washed over the 509th's compound. January stood in the doorway of his Quonset barracks hoping for a real breeze. No poker tonight.

Noises were hushed, faces solemn. Some of the men had helped box up the dead crew's gear. Now most lay on their bunks. January gave up on the breeze, climbed onto his top bunk to stare at the ceiling.

He observed the corrugated arch over him. Cricket song sawed through his thoughts. Below him a rapid conversation was being carried on in guilty undertones, Fitch at its center. "January is the best bombardier left," he said. "And I'm as good as Lewis was."

"But so is Sweeney," Matthews said. "And he's in with Scholes."

They were figuring out who would take over the strike. January scowled. Tibbets and the rest were less than twelve hours dead, and they were squabbling over who would replace them.

January grabbed a shirt, rolled off his bunk, put the shirt on.

"Hey, Professor," Fitch said, "where you going?"

"Out."

Though midnight was near, it was still sweltering. Crickets shut up as he walked by, started again behind him. He lit a cigarette. In the dark the MPs patrolling their compound were like pairs of walking armbands. Forcefully January expelled smoke, as if he could expel his disgust with it. They were only kids, he told himself. Their minds had been shaped in the war, by the war, and for the war. They knew you couldn't mourn the dead for long; carry around a load like that and your own engines might fail. That was all right with January. It was an attitude that Tibbets had helped to form, so it was what he deserved. Tibbets would *want* to be forgotten in favor of the mission; all he had lived for was to drop the gimmick on the Japs, and he was oblivious to anything else—men, wife, family, anything.

So it wasn't the lack of feeling in his mates that bothered January. And it was natural of them to want to fly the strike they had been training a year for. Natural, that is, if you were a kid with a mind shaped by fanatics like Tibbets, shaped to take orders and never imagine consequences. But January was not a kid, and he wasn't going to let men like Tibbets do a thing to his mind. And the gimmick . . . the gimmick was not natural. A chemical bomb of some sort, he guessed. Against the Geneva convention. He stubbed his cigarette against the sole of his sneaker, tossed the butt over the fence. The tropical night breathed over him. He had a headache.

For months now he had been sure he would never fly a strike. The dislike Tibbets and he had exchanged in their looks (January was acutely aware of looks) had been real and strong. Tibbets had understood that January's record of pinpoint accuracy in the runs over the Salton Sea had been a way of showing contempt. The record had forced him to keep January on one of the four second-string teams, but with the fuss they were making over the gimmick January had figured that would be far enough down the ladder to keep him out of things.

Now he wasn't so sure. Tibbets was dead. He lit another cigarette, found his hand shaking. The Camel tasted bitter. He threw it over the fence at a receding armband and regretted it instantly. A waste. He went back inside.

Before climbing onto his bunk he got a paperback out of his footlocker. "Hey, Professor, what you reading now?" Fitch said, grinning.

January showed him the blue cover. *Winter's Tales,* by an Isak Dinesen. Fitch examined the little wartime edition. "Pretty racy, eh?"

"You bet," January said heavily. "This guy puts sex on every page." He climbed onto his bunk, opened the book. The stories were strange, hard to follow. The voices below bothered him. He concentrated harder.

As a boy on the farm in Arkansas, January had read everything he could lay his hands on. On Saturday afternoons he would race his father down the muddy lane to the mailbox (his father was a reader too), grab *The Saturday Evening Post,* and run off to devour every word of it. That meant he had another week with nothing new to read, but he couldn't help it. It was a way off the farm, a way into the world. He had become a man who could slip between the covers of a book whenever he chose.

But not on this night.

The next day the chaplain gave a memorial service, and on the morning after that Colonel Scholes looked in the door of their hut right after mess. "Briefing at eleven," he announced. His face was haggard. "Be there early." He looked at Fitch with bloodshot eyes, crooked a finger. "Fitch, January, Matthews—come with me."

January put on his shoes. The rest of the men sat on their bunks and watched them wordlessly. January followed Fitch and Matthews out of the hut.

"I've spent most of the night on the radio with General LeMay,"

Scholes said. He looked them each in the eye. "We've decided you're to be the first crew to make a strike."

Fitch was nodding, as if he had expected it.

"Think you can do it?" Scholes said.

"Of course," Fitch replied. Watching him, January understood why they had chosen him to replace Tibbets. Fitch was like the old bull, he had that same ruthlessness. The young bull.

"Yes sir," Matthews said.

Scholes was looking at him. "Sure," January said, not wanting to think about it. "Sure." His heart was pounding directly on his sternum. But Fitch and Matthews looked serious as owls, so he wasn't going to stick out by looking odd. It was big news, after all; anyone would be taken aback by it. Nevertheless, January made an effort to nod.

"Okay," Scholes said. "McDonald will be flying with you as copilot." Fitch frowned. "I've got to go tell those British officers that LeMay doesn't want them on the strike with you. See you at the briefing."

"Yes sir."

As soon as Scholes was around the corner Fitch swung a fist at the sky. "Yow!" Matthews cried. He and Fitch shook hands. "We did it!" Matthews took January's hand and wrung it, his face plastered with a goofy grin. "We did it!"

"Somebody did it, anyway," January said.

"Ah, Frank," Matthews said. "Show some spunk. You're always so cool."

"Old Professor Stoneface," Fitch said, glancing at January with a trace of amused contempt. "Come on, let's get to the briefing."

The briefing hut, one of the longer Quonsets, was completely surrounded by MPs holding carbines. "Gosh," Matthews said, subdued by the sight. Inside, it was already smoky. The walls were covered by the usual maps of Japan. Two blackboards at the front were draped with sheets. Captain Shepard, the naval officer who worked with the scientists on the gimmick, was in back with his assistant Lieutenant Stone, winding a reel of film onto a projector. Dr. Nelson, the group psychiatrist, was already seated on a front bench near the wall. Tibbets had recently sicced the psychiatrist on the group—another one of his great ideas, like the spies in the bar. The man's questions had struck January as stupid. He hadn't even been able to figure out that Easterly was a flake, something that was clear to anybody who flew with him or even played him in a single round of poker. January slid onto a bench beside his mates.

The two Brits entered, looking furious in their stiff-upper-lip way. They sat on the bench behind January. Sweeney's and Easterly's crews filed in, followed by the other men, and soon the room was full. Fitch and the rest pulled out Lucky Strikes and lit up; since they had named the plane only January had stuck with Camels.

Scholes came in with several men January didn't recognize and went to the front. The chatter died, and all the smoke plumes ribboned steadily into the air.

Scholes nodded, and two intelligence officers took the sheets off the blackboards, revealing aerial reconnaissance photos.

"Men," Scholes said, "these are the target cities."

Someone cleared his throat.

"In order of priority they are Hiroshima, Kokura, and Nagasaki. There will be three weather scouts—*Straight Flush* to Hiroshima, *Strange Cargo* to Kokura, and *Full House* to Nagasaki. *The Great Artiste* and *Number 91* will be accompanying the mission to take photos. And *Lucky Strike* will fly the bomb."

There were rustles, coughs. Men turned to look at January and his mates, and they all sat up straight. Sweeney stretched back to shake Fitch's hand, and there were some quick laughs. Fitch grinned.

"Now listen up," Scholes went on. "The weapon we are going to deliver was successfully tested stateside a couple weeks ago. And now we've got orders to drop it on the enemy." He paused to let that sink in. "I'll let Captain Shepard tell you more."

Shepard walked to the blackboard slowly, savoring his entrance. His forehead was shiny with sweat, and January realized he was excited or nervous. He wondered what the psychiatrist would make of that.

"I'm going to come right to the point," Shepard said. "The bomb you are going to drop is something new in history. We think it will knock out everything within four miles."

Now the room was completely still. January noticed that he could see a great deal of his nose, eyebrows, and cheeks; it was as if he were receding back into his body, like a fox into its hole. He kept his gaze rigidly on Shepard, steadfastly ignoring the feeling. Shepard pulled a sheet back over a blackboard while someone else turned down the lights.

"This is a film of the only test we have made," Shepard said. The film started, caught, started again. A wavery cone of bright cigarette smoke speared the length of the room, and on the sheet sprang a dead gray landscape—a lot of sky, a smooth desert floor, hills in the distance. The projector went *click-click-click-click, click-click-click-click.* "The bomb is on top of the tower," Shepard said, and January focused on the pinlike object sticking out of the desert floor, off against the hills. It was between eight and ten miles from the camera, he judged; he had gotten good at calculating distances. He was still distracted by his face.

Click-click-click-click, click—then the screen went white for a second, filling even their room with light. When the picture returned the desert floor was filled with a white bloom of fire. The fireball coalesced, and then quite suddenly it leaped off the earth all the way into the *stratosphere*, by God, like a tracer bullet leaving a machine gun, trailing a whitish pillar of smoke behind it. The pillar gushed up, and a growing ball of smoke billowed outward, capping the pillar. January calculated the size of the cloud but was sure he got it wrong. There it stood. The picture flickered, and then the screen went white again, as if the camera had melted or that part of the world had come apart. But the flapping from the projector told them it was the end of the film.

January felt the air suck in and out of his open mouth. The lights came on in the smoky room, and for a second he panicked. He struggled to shove his features into an accepted pattern—the psychiatrist would be looking around at them all—and then he glanced around and realized he needn't have worried, that he wasn't alone. Faces were bloodless, eyes were blinky or bugged out with shock, mouths hung open or were clamped whitely shut. For a few moments they all had to acknowledge what they were doing. January, scaring himself, felt an urge to say, "Play it again, will you?" Fitch was pulling his curled black hair off his thug's forehead uneasily. Beyond him January saw that one of the Limeys had already reconsidered how mad he was about missing the flight. Now he looked sick. Someone let out a long *whew*, another whistled. January looked to the front again, where Dr. Nelson watched them, undisturbed.

Shepard said, "It's big, all right. And no one knows what will happen when it's dropped from the air. But the mushroom cloud you saw will go to at least thirty thousand feet, probably sixty. And the flash you saw at the beginning was hotter than the sun."

Hotter than the sun. More licked lips, hard swallows, readjusted baseball caps. One of the intelligence officers passed out tinted goggles like welder's glasses. January took his and twiddled the opacity dial.

Scholes said, "You're the hottest thing in the armed forces, now. So no talking, even among yourselves." He took a deep breath. "Let's do it the way Colonel Tibbets would have wanted us to. He picked every one of you because you were the best, and now's the time to show he was right. So—so let's make the old man proud."

The briefing was over. Men filed out into the sudden sunlight. Into the heat and glare. Captain Shepard approached Fitch. "Stone and I will be flying with you to take care of the bomb," he said.

Fitch nodded. "Do you know how many strikes we'll fly?"

"As many as it takes to make them quit." Shepard stared hard at all of them. "But it will only take one."

War breeds strange dreams. That night, January writhed over his sheets in the hot, wet, vegetable night, in that frightening half sleep when you sometimes know you are dreaming but can do nothing about it, and he dreamed he was walking . . .

. . . *walking through the streets when suddenly the sun swoops down, the sun touches down and everything is instantly darkness and smoke and silence, a deaf roaring. Walls of fire. His head hurts and in the middle of his vision is a blue-white blur as if God's camera went off in his face. Ah—the sun fell, he thinks. His arm is burned. Blinking is painful. People stumbling by, mouths open, horribly burned—*

He is a priest, he can feel the clerical collar, and the wounded ask him for help. He points to his ears, tries to touch them but can't. Pall of black smoke over everything, the city has fallen into the streets. Ah, it's the end of the world. In a park he finds shade and cleared ground. People crouch under bushes like animals. Where the park meets the river, red and black figures crowd into steaming water. A figure gestures from a copse of bamboo. He enters it, finds five or six faceless soldiers huddling. Their eyes have melted, their mouths are holes. Deafness spares him their words. The sighted soldier mimes drinking. The soldiers are thirsty. He nods and goes to the river in search of a container. Bodies float downstream.

Hours pass as he hunts fruitlessly for a bucket. He pulls people

*from the rubble. He hears a bird screeching, and he realizes that
his deafness is the roar of the city burning, a roar like the blood in
his ears, but he is not deaf, he only thought he was because there
are no human cries. The people are suffering in silence. Through
the dusky night he stumbles back to the river, pain crashing
through his head. In a field, men are pulling potatoes out of the
ground that have been baked well enough to eat. He shares one
with them. At the river everyone is dead—*

—and he struggled out of the nightmare drenched in rank
sweat, the taste of dirt in his mouth, his stomach knotted with
horror. He sat up, and the wet, rough sheet clung to his skin. His
heart felt crushed between lungs desperate for air. The flowery
rotting-jungle smell filled him, and images from the dream flashed
before him so vividly that in the dim hut he saw nothing else. He
grabbed his cigarettes and jumped off the bunk, hurried out into
the compound. Trembling, he lit up, started pacing around. For a
moment he worried that the idiot psychiatrist might see him, but
then he dismissed the idea. Nelson would be asleep. They were all
asleep. He shook his head, looked down at his right arm, and
almost dropped his cigarette—but it was just his stove scar, an old
scar. He'd had it most of his life, since the day he'd pulled the
frypan off the stove and onto his arm, burning it with oil. He could
still remember the round O of fear that his mother's mouth had
made as she rushed in to see what was wrong. Just an old burn scar,
he thought, let's not go overboard here. He pulled his sleeve
down.

For the rest of the night he tried to walk it off, cigarette after
cigarette. The dome of the sky lightened until all the compound
and the jungle beyond it was visible. He was forced by the light of
day to walk back into his hut and lie down as if nothing had
happened.

Two days later Scholes ordered them to take one of LeMay's
men over Rota for a test run. This new lieutenant colonel ordered
Fitch not to play with the engines on takeoff. They flew a perfect
run, January put the dummy gimmick right on the aiming point,
and Fitch powered the plane down into the violent bank that
started their 150-degree turn and flight for safety. Back on Tinian
the lieutenant colonel congratulated them and shook each of their
hands. January smiled with the rest, palms cool, heart steady. It
was as if his body were a shell, something he could manipulate

from without, like a bombsight. He ate well, he chatted as much as
he ever had, and when the psychiatrist ran him to earth for some
questions, he was friendly and seemed open.

"Hello, Doc."

"How do you feel about all this, Frank?"

"Just like I always have, sir. Fine."

"Eating well?"

"Better than ever."

"Sleeping well?"

"As well as I can in this humidity. I got used to Utah, I'm afraid."
Dr. Nelson laughed. Actually January had hardly slept since his
dream. He was afraid of sleep. Couldn't the man see that?

"And how do you feel about being part of the crew chosen to
make the first strike?"

"Well, it was the right choice, I reckon. We're the b—— the best
crew left."

"Do you feel sorry about Tibbets's crew's accident?"

"Yes sir, I do." You better believe it.

After the jokes that ended the interview, January walked out
into the blaze of the tropical noon and lit a cigarette. He allowed
himself to feel how much he despised the psychiatrist and his blind
profession at the same time he was waving good-bye to the man.
Ounce brain. Why couldn't he have seen? Whatever happened it
would be his fault . . . With a rush of smoke out of him January
realized how painfully easy it was to fool someone if you wanted
to. All action was no more than a mask that could be perfectly
manipulated from somewhere else. And all the while in that somewhere else, January lived in a *click-click-click* of film, in the silent
roaring of a dream, struggling against images he couldn't dispel.
The heat of the tropical sun—ninety-three million miles away,
wasn't it?—pulsed painfully on the back of his neck.

As he watched the psychiatrist collar their tail gunner, Kochenski, he thought of walking up to the man and saying *I quit.* I don't
want to do this. In imagination he saw the look that would form in
the man's eye, in Fitch's eye, in Tibbets's eye, and his mind re-
coiled from the idea. He felt too much contempt for them. He
wouldn't for anything give them a means to despise him, a reason
to call him coward. Stubbornly he banished the whole complex of
thought. Easier to go along with it.

And so a couple of disjointed days later, just after midnight of
August 9, he found himself preparing for the strike. Around him

Fitch and Matthews and Haddock were doing the same. How odd were the everyday motions of getting dressed when you were off to demolish a city! January found himself examining his hands, his boots, the cracks in the linoleum. He put on his survival vest, checked the pockets abstractedly for fishhooks, water kit, first-aid package, emergency rations. Then the parachute harness, and his coveralls over it all. Tying his bootlaces took minutes; he couldn't do it when watching his fingers so closely.

"Come on, Professor!" Fitch's voice was tight. "The big day is here."

He followed the others into the night. A cool wind was blowing. The chaplain said a prayer for them. They took jeeps down Broadway to runway Able. *Lucky Strike* stood in a circle of spotlights and men, half of them with cameras, the rest with reporters' pads. They surrounded the crew; it reminded January of a Hollywood premiere. Eventually he escaped up the hatch and into the plane. Others followed. Half an hour passed before Fitch joined them, grinning like a movie star. They started the engines, and January was thankful for their vibrating, thought-smothering roar. They taxied away from the Hollywood scene, and January felt relief for a moment, until he remembered where they were going. On runway Able the engines pitched up to their twenty-three-hundred-RPM whine, and looking out the clear windscreen, he saw the runway paint marks move by ever faster. Fitch kept them on the runway till Tinian had run out from under them, then quickly pulled up. They were on their way.

When they got to altitude, January climbed past Fitch and Mc-Donald to the bombardier's seat and placed his parachute on it. He leaned back. The roar of the four engines packed around him like cotton batting. He was on the flight, nothing to be done about it now. The heavy vibration was a comfort, he liked the feel of it there in the nose of the plane. A drowsy, sad acceptance hummed through him.

Against his closed eyelids flashed a black eyeless face, and he jerked awake, heart racing. He was on the flight, no way out. Now he realized how easy it would have been to get out of it. He could have just said he didn't want to. The simplicity of it appalled him. Who gave a damn what the shrink or Tibbets or anyone else thought, compared to this? Now there was no way out. It was a comfort, in a way. Now he could stop worrying, stop thinking he had any choice.

Sitting there with his knees bracketing the bombsight, January dozed, and as he dozed he daydreamed his way out. He could climb the step to Fitch and McDonald and declare he had been secretly promoted to major and ordered to redirect the mission. They were to go to Tokyo and drop the bomb in the bay. The Jap War Cabinet had been told to watch this demonstration of the new weapon, and when they saw that fireball boil the bay and bounce into heaven they'd run and sign surrender papers as fast as they could write, kamikazes or not. They weren't crazy, after all. No need to murder a whole city. It was such a good plan that the generals were no doubt changing the mission at this very minute, desperately radioing their instructions to Tinian, only to find out it was too late . . . so that when they returned to Tinian, January would become a hero for guessing what the generals really wanted and for risking all to do it. It would be like one of the Hornblower stories he had read in *The Saturday Evening Post*.

Once again January jerked awake. The drowsy pleasure of the fantasy was replaced with desperate scorn. There wasn't a chance in hell that he could convince Fitch and the rest that he had secret orders superseding theirs. And he couldn't go up there and wave his pistol around and *order* them to drop the bomb in Tokyo Bay, because he was the one who had to actually drop it, and he couldn't be down in front dropping the bomb and up ordering the others around at the same time. Pipe dreams.

Time swept on, slow as a second hand. January's thoughts, however, matched the spin of the props; desperately they cast about, now this way now that, like an animal caught by the leg in a trap. The crew was silent. The clouds below were a white scree on the black ocean. January's knee vibrated against the bombsight. He was the one who had to drop the bomb. No matter where his thoughts lunged, they were brought up short by that. He was the one, not Fitch or the crew, not LeMay, not the generals and scientists back home, not Truman and his advisors. Truman—suddenly January hated him. Roosevelt would have done it differently. If only Roosevelt had lived! The grief that had filled January when he learned of Roosevelt's death reverberated through him more strongly than ever. It was unfair to have worked so hard and then not see the war's end. And FDR would have ended it differently. Back at the start of it all he had declared that civilian centers were never to be bombed, and if he had lived, if, if, if. But he hadn't. And now it was smiling bastard Harry Truman, ordering *him*, Frank January, to drop the sun on two hundred thousand women and children. Once his father had taken him to see the Browns play before twenty thousand, a giant crowd— "I never voted for you," January whispered viciously and jerked to realize he had spoken aloud. Luckily his microphone was off. And Roosevelt would have done it differently, he *would have*.

The bombsight rose before him, spearing the black sky and blocking some of the hundreds of little cruciform stars. *Lucky Strike* ground on toward Iwo Jima, minute by minute flying four miles closer to their target. January leaned forward and put his face in the cool headrest of the bombsight, hoping that its grasp might hold his thoughts as well as his forehead. It worked surprisingly well.

His earphones crackled and he sat up. "Captain January." It was Shepard. "We're going to arm the bomb now, want to watch?"

"Sure thing." He shook his head, surprised at his own duplicity. Stepping up between the pilots, he moved stiffly to the roomy cabin behind the cockpit. Matthews was at his desk taking a navigational fix on the radio signals from Iwo Jima and Okinawa, and Haddock stood beside him. At the back of the compartment was a small circular hatch, below the larger tunnel leading to the rear of the plane. January opened it, sat down, and swung himself feetfirst through the hole.

The bomb bay was unheated, and the cold air felt good. He stood facing the bomb. Stone was sitting on the floor of the bay; Shepard was laid out under the bomb, reaching into it. On a rubber pad next to Stone were tools, plates, several cylindrical blocks. Shepard pulled back, sat up, sucked a scraped knuckle. He shook his head ruefully. "I don't dare wear gloves with this one."

"I'd be just as happy myself if you didn't let something slip," January joked nervously. The two men laughed.

"Nothing can blow till I change those wires," Stone said.

"Give me the wrench," Shepard said. Stone handed it to him, and he stretched under the bomb again. After some awkward wrenching inside it he lifted out a cylindrical plug. "Breech plug," he said, and set it on the mat.

January found his skin goose-pimpling in the cold air. Stone handed Shepard one of the blocks. Shepard extended under the bomb again. Watching them, January was reminded of auto me-

chanics on the oily floor of a garage, working under a car. He had
spent a few years doing that himself, after his family moved to
Vicksburg. Hiroshima was a river town. One time a flatbed truck
carrying bags of cement powder down Fourth Street hill had lost
its brakes and careened into the intersection with River Road,
where, despite the driver's efforts to turn, it smashed into a passing
car. Frank had been out in the yard playing and heard the crash
and saw the cement dust rising. He had been one of the first there.
The woman and child in the passenger seat of the Model T had
been killed. The woman driving was okay. They were from Chi-
cago. A group of folks subdued the driver of the truck, who kept
trying to help at the Model T, though he had a bad cut on his head
and was covered with white dust.

"Okay, let's tighten the breech plug." Stone gave Shepard the
wrench. "Sixteen turns exactly," Shepard said. He was sweating
even in the bay's chill, and he paused to wipe his forehead. "Let's
hope we don't get hit by lightning." He put the wrench down,
shifted onto his knees, and picked up a circular plate. Hubcap,
January thought. Stone connected wires, then helped Shepard
install two more plates. Good old American know-how, January
thought, goose pimples rippling across his skin like cat's-paws over
water. There was Shepard, a scientist, putting together a bomb
like he was an auto mechanic changing oil. January felt a tight rush
of rage at the scientists who had designed the bomb. They had
worked on it for over a year. Had none of them in all that time
ever stopped to think what they were doing?

But none of them had to drop it. January turned to hide his face
from Shepard, stepped down the bay. The bomb looked like a big
long trash can, with fins at one end and little antennae at the other.
Just a bomb, he thought, damn it, it's just another bomb.

Shepard stood and patted the bomb gently. "We've got a live
one now." Never a thought about what it would do. January hurried by the man, afraid that hatred would crack his shell and give
him away. The pistol strapped to his belt caught on the hatchway,
and he imagined shooting Shepard—shooting Fitch and McDonald and plunging the controls forward so that *Lucky Strike* tilted
and spun down into the sea like a spent tracer bullet, like a plane
broken by flak, following the arc of all human ambition. Nobody
would ever know what had happened to them, and their trash can
would be dumped to the bottom of the Pacific. He could even

shoot everyone, parachute out, and perhaps be rescued by one of the Superdumbos following them . . .

The thought passed, and remembering it January squinted with disgust. But another part of him agreed that it was a possibility. It could be done. It would solve his problem.

"Want some coffee?" Matthews asked.

"Sure," January said, and took a cup. He sipped—hot. He watched Matthews and Benton tune the loran equipment. As the beeps came in, Matthews took a straightedge and drew lines from Okinawa and Iwo Jima. He tapped a finger on the intersection. "They've taken the art out of navigation," he said to January. "They might as well stop making the navigator's dome," thumbing up at the little Plexiglas bubble over them.

"Good old American know-how," January said.

Matthews nodded. With two fingers he measured the distance between their position and Iwo Jima. Benton measured with a ruler.

"Rendezvous at five thirty-five, eh?" Matthews said. They were to rendezvous with the two trailing planes over Iwo.

Benton disagreed. "I'd say five-fifty."

"What? Check again, guy, we're not in no tugboat here."

"The wind—"

"Yeah, the wind. Frank, you want to add a bet to the pool?"

"Five thirty-six," January said promptly.

They laughed. "See, he's got more confidence in me," Matthews said with a dopey grin.

January recalled his plan to shoot the crew and tip the plane into the sea, and he pursed his lips, repelled. Not for anything would he be able to shoot these men, who, if not friends, were at least companions. They passed for friends. They meant no harm.

Shepard and Stone climbed into the cabin. Matthews offered them coffee. "The gimmick's ready to kick their ass, eh?" Shepard nodded and drank.

January moved forward, past Haddock's console. Another plan that wouldn't work. What to do? All the flight engineer's dials and gauges showed conditions were normal. Maybe he could sabotage something? Cut a line somewhere?

Fitch looked back at him and said, "When are we due over Iwo?"

"Five forty, Matthews says."

"He better be right."

A thug. In peacetime Fitch would be hanging around a pool table giving the cops trouble. He was perfect for war. Tibbets had chosen his men well—most of them, anyway. Moving back past Haddock, January stopped to stare at the group of men in the navigation cabin. They joked, drank coffee. They were all a bit like Fitch—young toughs, capable and thoughtless. They were having a good time, an adventure. That was January's dominant impression of his companions in the 509th; despite all the bitching and the occasional moments of overmastering fear, they were having a good time. His mind spun forward, and he saw what these young men would grow up to be like as clearly as if they stood before him in businessmen's suits, prosperous and balding. They would be tough and capable and thoughtless, and as the years passed and the great war receded in time they would look back on it with ever-increasing nostalgia, for they would be the survivors and not the dead. Every year of this war would feel like ten in their memories, so that the war would always remain the central experience of their lives—a time when history lay palpable in their hands, when each of their daily acts affected it, when moral issues were simple, and others told them what to do—so that as more years passed and the survivors aged, bodies falling apart, lives in one rut or another, they would unconsciously push harder and harder to thrust the world into war again, thinking somewhere inside themselves that if they could only return to world war then they would magically be again as they were in the last one—young and free and happy. And by that time they would hold the positions of power, they would be capable of doing it.

So there would be more wars, January saw. He heard it in Matthews's laughter, saw it in their excited eyes. "There's Iwo, and it's five thirty-one. Pay up! I win!" And in future wars they'd have more bombs like the gimmick, hundreds of them no doubt. He saw more planes, more young crews like this one, flying to Moscow, no doubt, or to wherever, fireballs in every capital. Why not? And to what end? To what end? So that the old men could hope to become magically young again. Nothing more sane than that. It made January sick.

They were over Iwo Jima. Three more hours to Japan. Voices from *The Great Artiste* and *Number 91* crackled on the radio. Rendezvous accomplished, the three planes flew northwest, toward Shikoku, the first Japanese island in their path. January

manuevered down into the nose. "Good shooting," Matthews
called after him.

Forward it seemed quieter. January got settled, put his headphones on, and leaned forward to look out the ribbed Plexiglas.

Dawn had turned the whole vault of the sky pink. Slowly the
radiant shade shifted through lavender to blue, pulse by pulse a
different color. The ocean below was a glittering blue plane, mar-
bled by a pattern of puffy pink cloud. The sky above was a vast
dome, darker above than on the horizon. January had always
thought that dawn was the time when you could see most clearly
how big the earth was and how high above it they flew. It seemed
they flew at the very upper edge of the atmosphere, and January
saw how thin it was, how it was just a skin of air really, so that even
if you flew up to its top the earth still extended away infinitely in
every direction. The coffee had warmed January, he was sweating.
Sunlight blinked off the Plexiglas. His watch said six. Plane and
hemisphere of blue were split down the middle by the bombsight.
His earphones crackled, and he listened in to the reports from the
lead planes flying over the target cities. Kokura, Nagasaki, Hiroshima, all of them had six-tenths cloud cover. Maybe they would
have to cancel the whole mission because of weather. "We'll look
at Hiroshima first," Fitch said. January peered down at the fields of
miniature clouds with renewed interest. His parachute slipped
under him. Readjusting it, he imagined putting it on, sneaking
back to the central escape hatch under the navigator's cabin,
opening the hatch . . . He could be out of the plane and gone
before anyone noticed. They could bomb or not but it wouldn't be
January's doing. He could float down onto the world like a puff of
dandelion, feel cool air rush around him, watch the silk canopy
dome hang over him like a miniature sky, a private world.

An eyeless black face. January shuddered; it was as though the
nightmare could return any time. If he jumped nothing would
change, the bomb would still fall—would he feel any better, float-
ing on his Inland Sea? Sure, one part of him shouted; maybe,
another conceded; the rest of him saw that face . . .

Earphones crackled. Shepard said, "Lieutenant Stone has now
armed the bomb, and I can now tell you all what we are carrying.
Aboard with us is the world's first atomic bomb."

Not exactly, January thought. Whistles squeaked in his earphones. The first one went off in New Mexico. Splitting atoms.
January had heard the term before. Tremendous energy in every

atom, Einstein had said. Break one, and—he had seen the result on film. Shepard was talking about radiation, which brought back more to January. Energy released in the form of X rays. Killed by X rays! It would be against the Geneva convention if they had thought of it.

Fitch cut in. "When the bomb is dropped Lieutenant Benton will record our reaction to what we see. This recording is being made for history, so watch your language." Watch your language! January choked back a laugh. Don't curse or blaspheme God at the sight of the first atomic bomb incinerating a city with X rays!

Six-twenty. January found his hands clenched together on the headrest of the bombsight. He felt as if he had a fever. In the harsh wash of morning light the skin on the backs of his hands appeared slightly translucent. The whorls in the skin looked like the delicate patterning of waves on the sea's surface. His hands were made of atoms. Atoms were the smallest building blocks of matter. It took billions of them to make those tense, trembling hands. Split one atom and you had the fireball. That meant that the energy contained in even one hand . . . He turned up a palm to look at the lines and the mottled flesh under the transparent skin. A person was a bomb that could blow up the world. January felt that latent power stir in him, pulsing with every hard heart knock. What beings they were, and in what a blue expanse of a world! And here they spun on to drop a bomb and kill a hundred thousand of these astonishing beings.

When a fox or raccoon is caught by the leg in a trap, it lunges until the leg is frayed, twisted, perhaps broken, and only then does the animal's pain and exhaustion force it to quit. Now in the same way January wanted to quit. His mind hurt. His plans to escape were so much crap—stupid, useless. Better to quit. He tried to stop thinking, but it was hopeless. How could he stop? As long as he was conscious he would be thinking. The mind struggles longer than any fox.

Lucky Strike tilted up and began the long climb to bombing altitude. On the horizon the clouds lay over a green island. Japan. Surely it had gotten hotter. The heater must be broken, he thought. Don't think. Every few minutes Matthews gave Fitch small course adjustments. "Two seventy-five, now. That's it." To escape the moment, January recalled his childhood. Following a mule and plow. Moving to Vicksburg (rivers). For a while there in Vicksburg, since his stutter made it hard to gain friends, he had played a game with himself. He had passed the time by imagining that everything he did was vitally important and determined the fate of the world. If he crossed a road in front of a certain car, for instance, then the car wouldn't make it through the next intersection before a truck hit it, and so the man driving would be killed and wouldn't be able to invent the flying boat that would save President Wilson from kidnappers, so he had to wait for that car, oh damn it, he thought, damn it, think of something *different.* The last Hornblower story he had read—how would *he* get out of this? The round O of his mother's face as she ran in and saw his arm— The Mississippi, mud-brown behind its levees— Abruptly he shook his head, face twisted in frustration and despair, aware at last that no possible avenue of memory would serve as an escape for him now; for now there was no part of his life that did not apply to the situation he was in, and no matter where he cast his mind it was going to shore up against the hour facing him.

Less than an hour. They were at thirty thousand feet, bombing altitude. Fitch gave him altimeter readings to dial into the bombsight. Matthews gave him wind speeds. Sweat got in his eye and he blinked furiously. The sun rose behind them like an atomic bomb, glinting off every corner and edge of the Plexiglas, illuminating his bubble compartment with a fierce glare. Broken plans jumbled together in his mind, his breath was short, his throat dry. Uselessly and repeatedly he damned the scientists, damned Truman. Damned the Japanese for causing the whole mess in the first place, damned yellow killers, they had brought this on themselves. Remember Pearl. American men had died under bombs when no war had been declared; they had started it and now it was coming back to them with a vengeance. And they deserved it. And an invasion of Japan would take years, cost millions of lives. End it now, end it, they deserved it, they deserved it, steaming river full of charcoal people silently dying, damned stubborn race of maniacs!

"There's Honshu," Fitch said, and January returned to the world of the plane. They were over the Inland Sea. Soon they would pass the secondary target, Kokura, a bit to the south. Seventhirty. The island was draped more heavily than the sea by clouds, and again January's heart leaped with the idea that weather would cancel the mission. But they did deserve it. It was a mission like any other mission. He had dropped bombs on Africa, Sicily, Italy, all Germany . . . He leaned forward to take a look through the sight. Under the X of the cross hairs was the sea, but at the lead edge of the sight was land. Honshu. At two hundred and thirty miles an hour that gave them about a half hour to Hiroshima. Maybe less. He wondered if his heart could beat so hard for that long.

Fitch said, "Matthews, I'm giving over guidance to you. Just tell us what to do."

"Bear south two degrees," was all Matthews said. At last their voices had taken on a touch of awareness.

"January, are you ready?" Fitch asked.

"I'm just waiting," January said. He sat up so Fitch could see the back of his head. The bombsight stood between his legs. A switch on its side would start the bombing sequence—the bomb would not leave the plane immediately upon the flick of the switch but would drop after a fifteen-second radio tone warned the following planes. The sight was adjusted accordingly.

"Adjust to a heading of two sixty-five," Matthews said. "We're coming in directly upwind." This was to make any side-drift adjustments for the bomb unnecessary. "January, dial it down to two hundred and thirty-one miles per hour."

"Two thirty-one."

Fitch said, "Everyone but January and Matthews, get your goggles on."

January took the darkened goggles from the floor. One needed to protect one's eyes or they might melt. He put them on, put his forehead on the headrest. They were in the way. He took them off. When he looked through the sight again there was land under the cross hairs. He checked his watch. Eight o'clock. Up and reading the papers, drinking tea.

"Ten minutes to AP," Matthews said. The aiming point was Aioi Bridge, a T-shaped bridge in the middle of the delta-straddling city. Easy to recognize.

"There's a lot of cloud down there," Fitch noted. "Are you going to be able to see?"

"I won't be sure until we try it," January said.

"We can make another pass and use radar if we need to," Matthews said.

Fitch said, "Don't drop it unless you're sure, January."

"Yes sir."

Through the sight a grouping of rooftops and gray roads was just visible between broken clouds. Around it green forest. "All right,"

Matthews exclaimed, "here we go! Keep it right on this heading, Captain! January, we'll stay at two thirty-one."

"And same heading," Fitch said. "January, she's all yours. Everyone be ready for the turn."

January's world contracted to the view through the bombsight. A stippled field of cloud and forest. Over a small range of hills and into Hiroshima's watershed. The broad river was mud brown, the land pale hazy green, the growing network of roads flat gray. Now the tiny rectangular shapes of buildings covered almost all the land, and swimming into the sight came the city proper, narrow islands thrusting into a dark blue bay. Under the cross hairs the city moved island by island, cloud by cloud. January had stopped breathing. His fingers were rigid as stone on the switch. And there was Aioi Bridge. It slid right under the cross hairs, a tiny T right in a gap in the clouds. January's fingers crushed the switch. Deliberately he took a breath, held it. Clouds swam under the cross hairs, then the next island. "Almost there," he said calmly into his microphone. "Steady." Now that he was committed his heart was humming like the Wrights. He counted to ten. Now flowing under the cross hairs were clouds alternating with green forest, leaden roads. "I've turned the switch, but I'm not getting a tone!" he croaked into the mike. His right hand held the switch firmly in place. Behind him Fitch was shouting something; Matthews's voice cracked across it. "Flipping it b-back and forth," January shouted, shielding the bombsight with his body from the eyes of the pilots. "But *still*—wait a second—"

He pushed the switch down. A low hum filled his ears. "That's it! It started!"

"But where will it land?" Matthews cried.

"Hold steady!" January shouted.

Lucky Strike shuddered and lofted up ten or twenty feet. January twisted to look down, and there was the bomb, flying just below the plane. Then with a wobble it fell away.

The plane banked right and dove so hard that the centrifugal force threw January against the Plexiglas. Several thousand feet lower, Fitch leveled it out and they hurtled north.

"Do you see anything?" Fitch cried.

From the tail gun Kochenski gasped, "Nothing." January struggled upright. He reached for the welder's goggles, but they were no longer on his head. He couldn't find them. "How long has it been?" he said.

"Thirty seconds," Matthews replied.

January shut his eyes.

The blood in his eyelids lit up red, then white.

On the earphones a clutter of voices—"Oh my God. Oh my God." The plane bounced and tumbled, metallically shrieking. January pressed himself off the Plexiglas. " 'Nother shock wave!" Kochenski yelled. The plane rocked again. This is it, January thought, end of the world, I guess that solves my problem.

He opened his eyes and found he could still see. The engines still roared, the props spun. "Those were the shock waves from the bomb," Fitch called. "We're okay now. Look at that! Will you look at that son of a bitch go!"

January looked. The cloud layer below had burst apart, and a black column of smoke billowed up from a core of red fire. Already the top of the column was at their height. Exclamations of shock hurt January's ears. He stared at the fiery base of the cloud, at the scores of fires feeding into it. Suddenly he could see past the cloud, and his fingernails cut into his palms. Through a gap in the clouds he saw it clearly, the delta, the six rivers, there off to the left of the tower of smoke—the city of Hiroshima, untouched.

"We missed!" Kochenski yelled. "We missed it!"

January turned to hide his face from the pilots; on it was a grin like a rictus. He sat back in his seat and let the relief fill him.

Then it was back to it. "Goddamn it!" Fitch shouted down at him. McDonald was trying to restrain him. "January, get up here!"

"Yes sir." Now there was a new set of problems.

January stood and turned, legs weak. His right fingertips throbbed painfully. The men were crowded forward to look out the Plexiglas. January looked with them.

The mushroom cloud was forming. It roiled out as if it might continue to extend forever, fed by the inferno and the black stalk below it. It looked about two-miles wide and half-a-mile tall, and it extended well above the height they flew at, dwarfing their plane entirely. "Do you think we'll all be sterile?" Matthews said.

"I can taste the radiation," McDonald declared. "Can you? It tastes like lead."

Bursts of flame shot up into the cloud from below, giving a purplish tint to the stalk. There it stood—lifelike, malignant, sixty-thousand-feet tall. One bomb. January shoved past the pilots into the navigation cabin, overwhelmed.

"Should I start recording everyone's reactions, Captain?" asked Benton.

"To hell with that," Fitch said, following January back. But Shepard got there first, descending quickly from the navigation dome. He rushed across the cabin, caught January on the shoulder. "You bastard!" he screamed as January stumbled back. "You lost your nerve, coward!"

January went for Shepard, happy to have a target at last, but Fitch cut in and grabbed him by the collar, pulled him around until they were face to face.

"Is that right?" Fitch cried, as angry as Shepard. "Did you screw up on purpose?"

"No," January grunted, and knocked Fitch's hands away from his neck. He swung and smacked Fitch on the mouth, caught him solid. Fitch staggered back, recovered, and no doubt would have beaten January up, but Matthews and Benton and Stone leaped in and held him back, shouting for order. "Shut up! Shut up!" Mc-Donald screamed from the cockpit, and for a moment it was bedlam. But Fitch let himself be restrained, and soon only McDonald's shouts for quiet were heard. January retreated to between the pilot seats, right hand on his pistol holster.

"The city was in the cross hairs when I flipped the switch," he said. "But the first couple of times I flipped it nothing happened—"

"That's a lie!" Shepard shouted. "There was nothing wrong with the switch, I checked it myself. Besides the bomb exploded *miles* beyond Hiroshima, look for yourself! That's *minutes*." He wiped spit from his chin and pointed at January. "You did it."

"You don't know that," January said. But he could see the men had been convinced by Shepard, and he took a step back. "You just get me to a board of inquiry, quick. And leave me alone till then. If you touch me again," glaring venomously at Fitch and then Shepard, "I'll shoot you." He turned and hopped down to his seat, feeling exposed and vulnerable, like a treed raccoon.

"They'll shoot *you* for this," Shepard screamed after him. "Disobeying orders—treason—" Matthews and Stone were shutting him up.

"Let's get out of here," he heard McDonald say. "I can taste the lead, can't you?"

January looked out the Plexiglas. The giant cloud still burned and roiled. One atom . . . Well, they had really done it to that forest. He almost laughed but stopped himself, afraid of hysteria. Through a break in the clouds he got a clear view of Hiroshima for the first time. It lay spread over its islands like a map, unharmed. Well, that was that. The inferno at the base of the mushroom cloud was eight or ten miles around the shore of the bay and a mile or two inland. A certain patch of forest would be gone, destroyed— utterly blasted from the face of the earth. The Japs would be able to go out and investigate the damage. And if they were told it was a demonstration, a warning—and if they acted fast—well, they had their chance. Maybe it would work.

The release of tension made January feel sick. Then he recalled Shepard's words, and he knew that whether his plan worked or not he was still in trouble. In trouble! It was worse than that. Bitterly he cursed the Japanese. He even wished for a moment that he *had* dropped it on them. Wearily he let his despair empty him.

A long while later he sat up straight. Once again he was a trapped animal. He began lunging for escape, casting about for plans. One alternative after another. All during the long, grim flight home he considered it, mind spinning at the speed of the props and beyond. And when they came down on Tinian he had a plan. It was a long shot, he reckoned, but it was the best he could do.

The briefing hut was surrounded by MPs again. January stumbled from the truck with the rest and walked inside. He was more than ever aware of the looks given him, and they were hard, accusatory. He was too tired to care. He hadn't slept in more than thirty-six hours and had slept very little since the last time he had been in the hut, a week before. Now the room quivered with the lack of engine vibration to stabilize it, and the silence roared. It was all he could do to hold on to his plan. The glares of Fitch and Shepard, the hurt incomprehension of Matthews, they had to be thrust out of his focus. Thankfully he lit a cigarette.

In a clamor of question and argument the others described the strike. Then the haggard Scholes and an intelligence officer led them through the bombing run. January's plan made it necessary to hold to his story. ". . . and when the AP was under the cross hairs I pushed down the switch, but got no signal. I flipped it up and down repeatedly until the tone kicked in. At that point there was still fifteen seconds to the release."

"Was there anything that may have caused the tone to start when it did?"

"Not that I noticed immediately, but—"

"It's impossible," Shepard interrupted, face red. "I checked the switch before we flew and there was nothing wrong with it. Besides, the drop occurred over a minute—"

"Captain Shepard," Scholes said. "We'll hear from you presently."

"But he's obviously lying—"

"Captain Shepard! It's not at all obvious. Don't speak unless questioned."

"Anyway," January said, hoping to shift the questions away from the issue of the long delay, "I noticed something about the bomb when it was falling that could explain why it stuck. I need to discuss it with one of the scientists familiar with the bomb's design."

"What was that?" Scholes asked suspiciously.

January hesitated. "There's going to be an inquiry, right?"

Scholes frowned. "This is the inquiry, Captain January. Tell us what you saw."

"But there will be some proceeding beyond this one?"

"It looks like there's going to be a court-martial, yes, Captain."

"That's what I thought. I don't want to talk to anyone but my counsel, and some scientist familiar with the bomb."

"*I'm* a scientist familiar with the bomb," Shepard burst out. "You could tell me if you really had anything, you—"

"I said I need a scientist!" January exclaimed, rising to face the scarlet Shepard across the table. "Not a g-goddamned mechanic." Shepard started to shout, others joined in, and the room rang with argument. While Scholes restored order January sat down, and he refused to be drawn out again.

"I'll see you're assigned counsel and initiate the court-martial," Scholes said, clearly at a loss. "Meanwhile you are under arrest, on suspicion of disobeying orders in combat." January nodded, and Scholes gave him over to MPs.

"One last thing," January said, fighting exhaustion. "Tell General LeMay that if the Japs are told this drop was a warning, it might have the same effect as—"

"I told you!" Shepard shouted, "I told you he did it on purpose!"

Men around Shepard restrained him. But he had convinced

most of them, and even Matthews stared at him with surprised anger.

January shook his head wearily. He had the dull feeling that his plan, while it had succeeded so far, was ultimately not a good one. "Just trying to make the best of it." It took all of his remaining will to force his legs to carry him in a dignified manner out of the hut.

His cell was an empty NCO's office. MPs brought his meals. For the first couple of days he did little but sleep. On the third day he glanced out the office's barred window and saw a tractor pulling a tarpaulin-draped trolley out of the compound, followed by jeeps filled with MPs. It looked like a military funeral. January rushed to the door and banged on it until one of the young MPs came.

"What's that they're doing out there?" January demanded.

Eyes cold and mouth twisted, the MP said, "They're making another strike. They're going to do it right this time."

"No!" January cried, "No!" He rushed the MP, who knocked him back and locked the door. *"No!"* He beat the door until his hands hurt, cursing wildly. "You don't *need* to do it, it isn't *necessary."* Shell shattered at last, he collapsed on the bed and wept. Now everything he had done would be rendered meaningless. He had sacrificed himself for nothing.

A day or two after that the MPs led in a colonel, an iron-haired man who stood stiffly and crushed January's hand when he shook it. His eyes were a pale icy blue.

"I am Colonel Dray," he said. "I have been ordered to defend you in court-martial." January could feel the dislike pouring from the man. "To do that I'm going to need every fact you have, so let's get started."

"I'm not talking to anybody until I've seen an atomic scientist."

"I am your *defense* counsel—"

"I don't care who you are," January said. "Your defense of me depends on you getting one of the scientists *here.* The higher up he is, the better. And I want to speak to him alone."

"I will have to be present."

So he would do it. But now January's counsel, too, was an enemy.

"Naturally," January said. "You're my counsel. But no one else. Our atomic secrecy may depend on it."

"You saw evidence of sabotage?"

"Not one word more until that scientist is here."

Angrily the colonel nodded and left.

Late the next day the colonel returned with another man. "This is Dr. Forest."

"I helped develop the bomb," Forest said. He had a crew cut and was dressed in fatigues, and to January he looked more Army than the colonel. Suspiciously he stared back and forth at the two men.

"You'll vouch for this man's identity on your word as an officer?" he asked Dray.

"Of course," the colonel said stiffly, offended.

"So," Dr. Forest said. "You had some trouble getting it off when you wanted to. Tell me what you saw."

"I saw nothing," January said harshly. He took a deep breath; it was time to commit himself. "I want you to take a message back to the scientists. You folks have been working on this thing for years, and you must have had time to consider how the bomb should have been used. You know we could have convinced the Japs to surrender by showing them a demonstration—"

"Wait a minute," Forest said. "You're saying you didn't see anything? There wasn't a malfunction?"

"That's right," January said, and cleared his throat. "It wasn't *necessary*, do you understand?"

Forest was looking at Colonel Dray. Dray gave him a disgusted shrug. "He told me he saw evidence of sabotage."

"I want you to go back and ask the scientists to intercede for me," January said, raising his voice to get the man's attention. "I haven't got a chance in that court-martial. But if the scientists defend me then maybe they'll let me live, see? I don't want to get shot for doing something every one of you scientists would have done."

Dr. Forest had backed away. Color rising, he said, "What makes you think that's what we would have done? Don't you think we considered it? Don't you think men better qualified than you made the decision?" He waved a hand. "Goddamn it—what made you think you were competent to decide something as important as that!"

January was appalled at the man's reaction; in his plan it had gone differently. Angrily he jabbed a finger at Forest. "Because *I* was the man doing it, *Doctor* Forest. You take even one step back from that and suddenly you can pretend it's not your doing. Fine for you, but *I was there.*"

At every word the man's color was rising. It looked like he might pop a vein in his neck. January tried once more. "Have you ever tried to imagine what one of your bombs would do to a city full of people?"

"I've had enough!" the man exploded. He turned to Dray. "I'm under no obligation to keep what I've heard here confidential. You can be sure it will be used as evidence in Captain January's court-martial." He turned and gave January a look of such blazing hatred that January understood it. For these men to admit he was right would mean admitting that they were wrong—that every one of them was responsible for his part in the construction of the weapon January had refused to use. Understanding that, January knew he was doomed.

The bang of Dr. Forest's departure still shook the little office. January sat on his cot, got out a smoke. Under Colonel Dray's cold gaze he lit one shakily, took a drag. He looked up at the colonel, shrugged. "It was my best chance," he explained. That did something—for the first and only time the cold disdain in the colonel's eyes shifted, to a little, hard, lawyerly gleam of respect.

The court-martial lasted two days. The verdict was guilty of disobeying orders in combat and of giving aid and comfort to the enemy. The sentence was death by firing squad.

For most of his remaining days January rarely spoke, drawing ever further behind the mask that had hidden him for so long. A clergyman came to see him, but it was the 509th's chaplain, the one who had said the prayer blessing the *Lucky Strike*'s mission before they took off. Angrily January sent him packing.

Later, however, a young Catholic priest dropped by. His name was Patrick Getty. He was a little pudgy man, bespectacled and, it seemed, somewhat afraid of January. January let the man talk to him. When he returned the next day January talked back a bit, and on the day after that he talked some more. It became a habit.

Usually January talked about his childhood. He talked of plowing mucky black bottomland behind a mule. Of running down the lane to the mailbox. Of reading books by the light of the moon after he had been ordered to sleep. And of being beaten by his mother for it with a high-heeled shoe. He told the priest the story of the time his arm had been burned, and about the car crash at the bottom of Fourth Street. "It's the truck driver's face I remember, do you see, Father?"

"Yes," the young priest said. "Yes."

And he told him about the game he had played in which every action he took tipped the balance of world affairs. "When I remembered that game I thought it was dumb. Step on a sidewalk crack and cause an earthquake—you know, it's stupid. Kids are like that." The priest nodded. "But now I've been thinking that if everybody were to live their whole lives like that, thinking that every move they made really was important, then . . . it might make a difference." He waved a hand vaguely, expelled cigarette smoke. "You're accountable for what you do."

"Yes," the priest said. "Yes, you are."

"And if you're given orders to do something wrong, you're still accountable, right? The orders don't change it."

"That's right."

"Hmph." January smoked a while. "So they say, anyway. But look what happens." He waved at the office. "I'm like the guy in a story I read—he thought everything in books was true, and after reading a bunch of westerns he tried to rob a train. They tossed him in jail." He laughed shortly. "Books are full of crap."

"Not all of them," the priest said. "Besides, you weren't trying to rob a train."

They laughed at the notion. "Did you read that story?"

"No."

"It was the strangest book—there were two stories in it, and they alternated chapter by chapter, but they didn't have a thing to do with each other! I didn't get it."

"Maybe the writer was trying to say that everything connects to everything else."

"Maybe. But it's a funny way to say it."

"I like it."

And so they passed the time, talking.

So it was the priest who was the one to come by and tell January that his request for a presidential pardon had been refused. Getty said awkwardly, "It seems the President approves the sentence."

"That bastard," January said weakly. He sat on his cot.

Time passed. It was another hot, humid day.

"Well," the priest said. "Let me give you some better news.

Given your situation I don't think telling you matters, though I've been told not to. The second mission—you know there was a second strike?"

"Yes."

"Well, they missed too."

"What?" January cried, and bounced to his feet. "You're kidding!"

"No. They flew to Kokura but found it covered by clouds. It was the same over Nagasaki and Hiroshima, so they flew back to Kokura and tried to drop the bomb using radar to guide it, but apparently there was a . . . a genuine equipment failure this time, and the bomb fell on an island."

January was hopping up and down, mouth hanging open, "So we n-never—"

"We never dropped an atom bomb on a Japanese city. That's right." Getty grinned. "And get this—I heard this from my superior—they sent a message to the Japanese Government telling them that the two explosions were warnings, and that if they didn't surrender by September 1 we would drop bombs on Kyoto and Tokyo, and then wherever else we had to. Word is that the Emperor went to Hiroshima to survey the damage, and when he saw it he ordered the Cabinet to surrender. So . . ."

"So it worked," January said. He hopped around, "It worked, it worked!"

"Yes."

"Just like I said it would!" he cried, and hopping in front of the priest he laughed.

Getty was jumping around a little too, and the sight of the priest bouncing was too much for January. He sat on his cot and laughed till the tears ran down his cheeks.

"So—" He sobered quickly. "So Truman's going to shoot me anyway, eh?"

"Yes," the priest said unhappily. "I guess that's right."

This time January's laugh was bitter. "He's a bastard, all right. And proud of being a bastard, which makes it worse." He shook his head. "If Roosevelt had lived . . ."

"It would have been different," Getty finished. "Yes. Maybe so. But he didn't." He sat beside January. "Cigarette?" He held out a pack, and January noticed the green wrapper, the round bull's-eye. He frowned.

"You haven't got a Camel?"

"Oh. Sorry."

"Oh well. That's all right." January took one of the Lucky Strikes, lit up. "That's awfully good news." He breathed out. "I never believed Truman would pardon me anyway, so mostly you've brought good news. Ha. They *missed*. You have no idea how much better that makes me feel."

"I think I do."

January smoked the cigarette.

"So I'm a good American after all. I *am* a good American," he insisted, "no matter what Truman says."

"Yes," Getty replied, and coughed. "You're better than Truman any day."

"Better watch what you say, Father." He looked into the eyes behind the glasses, and the expression he saw there gave him pause. Since the drop every look directed at him had been filled with contempt. He'd seen it so often during the court-martial that he'd learned to stop looking; and now he had to teach himself to see again. The priest looked at him as if he were . . . as if he were some kind of hero. That wasn't exactly right. But seeing it . . .

January would not live to see the years that followed, so he would never know what came of his action. He had given up casting his mind forward and imagining possibilities, because there was no point to it. His planning was ended. In any case he would not have been able to imagine the course of the post-war years. That the world would quickly become an armed camp pitched on the edge of atomic war, he might have predicted. But he never would have guessed that so many people would join a January Society. He would never know of the effect the Society had on Dewey during the Korean crisis, never know of the Society's successful campaign for the test-ban treaty, and never learn that, thanks in part to the Society and its allies, a treaty would be signed by the great powers that would reduce the number of atomic bombs year by year, until there were none left.

Frank January would never know any of that. But in that moment on his cot looking into the eyes of young Patrick Getty, he guessed an inkling of it—he felt, just for an instant, the impact on history.

And with that he relaxed. In his last week everyone who met him carried away the same impression—that of a calm, quiet man, angry at Truman and others, but in a withdrawn, matter-of-fact way. Patrick Getty, a strong force in the January Society ever

after, said January was talkative for some time after he learned of
the missed attack on Kokura. Then he got quieter, as the day
approached. On the morning that they woke him at dawn to
march him out to a hastily constructed execution shed, his MPs
shook his hand. The priest was with him as he smoked a final
cigarette, and they prepared to put the hood over his head. January looked at him calmly. "They load one of the guns with a blank
cartridge, right?"

"Yes," Getty said.

"So each man in the squad can imagine he may not have shot
me?"

"Yes. That's right."

A tight, unhumorous smile was January's last expression. He
threw down the cigarette, ground it out, poked the priest in the
arm. "But I *know*." Then the mask slipped back into place for
good, making the hood redundant, and with a firm step January
went to the wall. One might have said he was at peace.

GATE OF HORN,
GATE OF IVORY

ROBERT SILVERBERG

Often at night on the edge of sleep I cast my mind toward the abyss of time to come, hoping that I will tumble through some glowing barrier and find myself on the shores of a distant tomorrow. I strain at the moorings that hold me to this time and this place and yearn to break free. Sometimes I feel that I *have* broken free, that the journey is at last beginning, that I will open my eyes in the inconceivable dazzling future. But it is only an illusion, like that fluent knowledge of French or Sanskrit or calculus which is born in dreams and departs by dawn. I awaken and it is the year 1983 and I am in my own bed with the striped sheets and the blue coverlet and nothing has changed.

But I try again and again and still again, for the future calls me and the bleak murderous present repels me, and again the illusion that I am cutting myself loose from the time line comes over me, now more vivid and plausible than ever before, and as I soar and hurtle and vanish through the permeable membranes of the eons I wonder if it is finally in truth happening. I hover suspended somewhere outside the fabric of time and space and look down upon the Earth, and I can see its contours changing as though I watch an accelerated movie: roads sprout and fork and fork once more; villages arise and exfoliate into towns and then into cities and then are overtaken by the forest; rivers change their courses and deliver their waters into great mirror-bright lakes that shrivel and become meadows. And I hover, passive, a dreamer, observing. There are two gates of sleep, says Homer, and also Virgil. One is fashioned of horn, and one of ivory. Through the gate of horn pass the visions that are true, but those that emerge from the gate of ivory are deceptive dreams that mean nothing. Do I journey in a dream of the ivory gate? No, no, this is a true sending, this has the solidity and substance of inexorable reality. I have achieved it this time. I have crossed the barrier. Hooded figures surround me; somber eyes study me; I look into faces of a weird sameness, tawny skin, fleshless lips, jutting cheekbones that tug the taut skin above them into drumheads. The room in which I lie is high-vaulted and dark but glows with a radiance that seems inherent in the material of its walls. Abstract figurings, like the ornamentation of a mosque, dance along those walls in silver inlay; but this is no mosque, nor would the tribe of Allah have loved those strange and godless geometries that restlessly chase one another like lustful squirrels over the wainscoting. I am there; I am surely there.

"I want to see everything," I say.

"See it, then. Nothing prevents you."

One of them presses into my hand a shining silver globe, an orb of command that transports me at the tiniest squeeze of my hand. I fly upward jerkily and in terror, rising so swiftly that the air grows cold and the sky becomes purple, but in a moment I regain control and come to govern my trajectory more usefully. At an altitude of a few dozen yards I pass over a city of serene cubical buildings of rounded corners, glittering with white Mediterranean brilliance in the gentle sunlight. I see small vehicles, pastel-hued, teardrop-tapered, in which citizens with the universal face of the era ride above crystalline roadbeds. I drift over a garden of plants I cannot recognize, perhaps new plants entirely, with pink succulent leaves and great, mounding, golden inflorescences, or ropy stems like bundles of coaxial cable, or jagged green thorns tipped with tiny blue eyes. I come to a pond of air where serene naked people swim with minimal motions of their fingertips. I observe a staircase of some yielding rubbery substance that vanishes into a glowing nimbus of radiance, and children are climbing that staircase and disappearing into that sparkling place at its top. In the zoological gardens I look down on creatures from a hundred worlds, stranger than any protozoan made lion-sized.

For days I tour this place, inexhaustibly curious, numb with awe. There is no blade of grass out of place. There is no stain nor blemish. The sounds I hear are harmonious sounds, and no other. The air is mild and the winds are soft. Only the people seem stark and austere to me, I suppose because of their sameness of features and the hieratic Egyptian solemnity of their eyes, but after a while I realize that this is only my poor archaic sensibility's misunderstanding, for I feel their love and support about me like a harness as I fly, and I know that these are the happiest, most angelic of all the beings that have walked the earth. I wonder how far in time I have traveled. Fifty thousand years? Half a million? Or perhaps— perhaps, and that possibility shrivels me with pain—perhaps much less than that. Perhaps this is the world of a hundred fifty years from now, eh? The post-apocalyptic era, the coming utopia that lies just on the farther shore of our sea of turbulent nightmares. Is it possible that our world can be transformed into this so quickly? Why not? Miracles accelerate in an age of miracles. From the wobbly thing of wood and paper that flew a few seconds at Kitty Hawk to the gleaming majesty of the transcontinental jetliner was only a bit more than fifty years. Why not imagine that a world like this can be assembled in just as little time? But if that is so—

The torment of the thought drives me to the ground. I fall; they are taken by surprise, but ease my drop; I land on the warm moist soil and kneel, clutching it, letting my head slacken until my forehead touches the ground. I feel a gentle hand on my shoulder, just a touch, steadying me, soothing me.

"Let go," I say, virtually snarling. "Take your hand off!"

The hand retreats.

I am alone with my agony. I tremble, I sob, I shiver. I am aware of them surrounding me, but they are baffled, helpless, confused. Possibly they have never seen pain before. Possibly suffering is no part of their vocabulary of spirit.

Finally one of them says softly, "Why do you weep?"

"Out of anger. Out of frustration."

They are mystified. They surround me with shining machinery, screens and coils and lights and glowing panels, that I suspect is going to diagnose my malady. I kick everything over. I trample the intricate mechanisms and shove wildly at those who reach for me, even though I see that they are reaching not to restrain me but to soothe me.

"What is it?" they keep asking. "What troubles you?"

"I want to know what year this is."

They confer. It may be that their numbering system is so different from ours that they are unable to tell me. But there must be a way: diagrams, analogies, astronomical patterns. I am not so primitive that I am beyond understanding such things.

Finally they say, "Your question has no meaning for us."

"No meaning? You speak my language well enough. *I need to know what year this is.*"

"Its name is Eiligorda," one of them says.

"Its *name?* Years don't have names. Years have numbers. My year is numbered 1983. Are we so far in my future that you don't remember the years with numbers?" I begin stripping away my clothing. "Here, look at me. This hair on my body—do you have hair like that? These teeth—see, I have thirty-two of them, arranged in an arc." I hold up my hands. "Nails on my fingers! Have fingernails evolved away?" I tap my belly. "In here, an appendix dangling from my gut! Prehistoric, useless, preposterous! How long ago did that disappear? Look at me! See the ape-man, and tell me how ancient I am!"

"Our bodies are just like yours," comes the quiet reply. "Except that we are healthier and stronger and resistant to disease. But we have hair. We have fingernails. We have the appendix." They are naked before me, and I see that it is true. Their bodies are lean and supple, and there is a weird and disconcerting similarity of physique about them all, but they are not alien in any way; these could be twentieth-century bodies.

"I want you to tell me," I say, "how distant in time your world is from mine."

"Not very," someone answers. "But we lack the precise terminology for describing the interval."

"Not very," I say. "Listen, does the Earth still go around the sun?"

"Of course."

"The time it takes to make one circuit—has that changed?"

"Not at all."

"How many times, then, do you think the Earth has circled the sun since my era?"

They exchange glances. They make quick rippling gestures—a

kind of counting, perhaps. But they seem unable to complete the calculation. They murmur, they smile, they shrug. At last I understand their problem, which is not one of communication but one of tact. They do not want to tell me the truth for the same reason that I yearn to know it. The truth will hurt me. The truth will split me with anguish.

They are people of the epoch that immediately succeeds yours and mine. They are, quite possibly, the great-great-grandchildren of some who live in our world of 1983; or it may be that they are only grandchildren. The future they inhabit is not the extremely distant future. I am positive of that. But time stands still for them, for they do not know death.

Fury and frenzy return to me. I shake with rage; I taste burning bile; I explode with hatred, and launch myself upon them, scratching, punching, kicking, biting, trying in a single outpouring of bitter resentment to destroy the entire sleek epoch into which I have fallen.

I harm several of them quite seriously.

Then they recover from their astonishment and subdue me, without great effort, dropping me easily with a few delicate musical tones and holding me captive against the ground. The casualties are taken away.

One of my captors kneels beside me and says, "Why do you show such hostility?"

I glare at him. "Because I am so close to being one of you."

"Ah. I think I can comprehend. But why do you blame us for that?"

The only answer I can give him is more fury; I tug against my invisible bonds and lunge as if to slaughter him with sheer energy of rage; from me pours such a blaze of madness as to sear the air, and so intense is my emotion that it seems to me I am actually breaking free, and seizing him, and clawing at him, and smashing him. But I am only clutching at phantoms. My arms move like those of a windmill, and I lose my balance and topple and topple and topple, and when I regain my balance I am in my own bed once more, striped sheets, blue coverlet, the red eye of the digital clock telling me that it is 4:36 A.M. So they have punished me by casting me from their midst. I suppose that is no more than I deserve. But do they comprehend, do they really comprehend, my torment? Do they understand what it is like to know that those who will come just a little way after us will have learned how to live forever and to live in paradise, and that one of us, at least, has had a glimpse of it, but that we will all be dead when it comes to pass? Why should we not rage against the generations to come, aware that we are nearly the last ones who will know death? Why not scratch and bite and kick? An awful iron door is closing on us, and *they* are on the far side, safe. Surely they will begin to understand that, when they have given more thought to my visit. Possibly they understood it even while I was there. I suspect they did, finally. And that when they returned me to my own time I was given a gift of grace by those gilded futurians: that their mantle of immortality has been cast over me, that I will be allowed to live on and on until time has come round again and I am once more in their era, but now as one of them. That is their gift to me, and perhaps that is their curse on me as well, that I must survive through all the years of terrible darkness that must befall before that golden dawn, that I will tarry here until they come again.

*Because artificial satellites in space will be totally planned envi-
ronments, specifically designed to support human life, it follows
that some of these could be further refined for particular* kinds *of
human life . . . such as the medically designed colony in the
following story. People who can no longer live in the uncontrolled
environment of Earth—people who would have died if they didn't
have this colony as a refuge—make new lives in orbit around
Earth.*

*But altered living conditions inevitably cause changes in people
and society; and a new world whose physical environment is safe
might be hostile to some people in other ways.*

*Sharon N. Farber is currently serving her internship in St. Louis,
Missouri. Her stories have appeared in* Isaac Asimov's Science Fiction Magazine *and elsewhere.*

PASSING AS A FLOWER
IN THE CITY OF THE DEAD

SHARON N. FARBER

Henri hated parties; he was striding through the cocktail crowd,
his massive head down, shoulders back. Watching her husband,
Madeline wanted to laugh. This was "the pacing lion of the landscape"? What would that sycophantic art critic call him if she
could see him now, skeletal after months of untreated leukemia,
bald as a newborn from total body irradiation?

"The stalking scarecrow," Madeline thought.

She lost sight of her husband as he pushed through into the
house. Madeline put down her drink; it was adding to the steady-
state nausea she'd felt from the aseptic food and from the sight of
the colony ceiling far overhead. Her universe was a cylinder in
space, the overhead view one of land and houses, while Earth and
stars hid under her feet. Perhaps 180 degrees away another
woman stood in another party and watched Madeline spin by. A
treeless, grassless vista painted pastel blue.

"I'm Bob. How do you like Blues?" A man grinned at her. He had finely coiled gray hair, held a drink in each hand, and seemed more alive than anyone else at the party.

"It takes getting used to . . ."

"Of course," he boomed, and Madeline noticed that his presence had cleared an even wider space. They were alone, haloed by emptiness like a colony of hemolytic streptococci on a blood agar plate.

"We're pariahs, you 'n' I," he said, setting down one empty paper cup, draping that hand about her shoulder, and steering her effortlessly to the refreshments table. "Moses parting the Red Sea," he whispered, and Madeline laughed as the crowd melted away about them. He picked up a decanter, nestled in an arrangement of silk flowers, and poured full a pottery mug.

"Drink this. It'll settle your stomach and curdle your brain," he commanded. "The amnestic waters of the river Styx across which the dead must pass." He looked about with exaggerated movements, then whispered sotto voce, "Don't tell anyone. I've had a classical education."

"You aren't afraid?" she asked.

"Afraid of what? Parsing verbs?"

She giggled. "No, of me. I'm a newcomer." She ran one hand through her crew-cut-length hair. "Some bacterium may have snuck in with me.

"I'm a very dangerous woman," she added in her best villainess voice.

Bob chortled. "Not too observant, are we? Look at me!"

Studying him, she realized why he had seemed so different, so alive. Of all those standing in the crowded patio, he alone lacked the pallor of the bloodless. He held his hand beside hers, allowing her to compare his rosy pink hue, the blue veins like ropes, with her own clear veins in cadaver flesh.

"None of that fluorocarbon-soup artificial blood for me," he said. "I'm the last of the red-blooded men. At least on Blues."

Madeline nodded. "Your immune system is intact. You can laugh in the face of any pathogen."

"Right." He grinned, downing his drink. "I'm going to feel awful in the morning—I've got all my blood. Red, white, blue, you name it."

Madeline contrasted him to the others, to herself. A pale, bloodless lot. An O'Neill colony inhabited by those with leukemia, with

autoimmune disease, with transplanted organs. They had all stood
on the banks of the Styx, only to be saved by the killing of their
every blood cell—the treacherous cells that multiplied erratically,
or attacked their own organs, or fought the transplants. And the
innocent blood cells had died as well, the cells that carried oxygen,
fought invading microbes, stopped hemorrhages.

They were alive, locked in a hermetically sealed, sterile tin can
rotating in space.

The man intruded on her thoughts. "Yes, I'm that fiend incar-
nate, that villain of stage and screen, the Outsider."

"But why . . ."

"Was I invited? Giselle works in my department. Even she isn't
rude enough not to invite me. She just never thought I'd be rude
enough to come." His grin widened. "I've seen you in the hospital.
You're in the lab? Come see me. Respiratory." He put down his
cup and left, swiveling at the gate to face the crowd. "I'm leaving.
You can talk about me now," he yelled.

"Obnoxious, isn't he." Giselle was at Madeline's side, small and
dainty, with brown hair to her waist. Hair was a status symbol on
Blues. The longer the hair, the longer the head had been on Blues.
The longer the survival from the terminal disease.

"Loud, but amusing."

"You don't have to work with him."

The elderly man beside Giselle snarled. "Earthies. They come
in, work their stint, and leave, acting like they're so damn superior."

He gazed suspiciously at Madeline as if, she thought, he were
smelling pseudomonas. Or smelling anything. She was a woman
without colonizing bacteria—her sweat, her breath, even her fe-
ces were almost odorless.

He suspects, she thought, panicking. No, he could not suspect.
She was as much the Outsider as Bob, but she had the protective
discoloration of the bloodless.

Giselle clapped her hands. "Everybody!"

"Damn," the man said. "Must you go through with this?"

"Father, stop acting like it's indecent."

"You just like to shock people. It must be your genetics. It certainly wasn't your upbringing." He stormed into the house.

Giselle shrugged at Madeline. "Father's a bit traditional . . .
Everybody! May I have your attention—you too, you wastrel . . ."
The revelers paused in their various pursuits and looked to their

hostess. Henri, studying the flower bed with its plastic nasturtiums, glowered at Madeline.

"During the party, many of you have met our newcomers, Henri and Madeline. Madeline, it happens, is an actual relative of mine. A blood relative."

The audience chuckled, to Madeline's bewilderment. Henri merely looked as if he were trapped in an ethnographic film.

"She was my genetic mother's second cousin on Earth. Let's welcome these newcomers to Blues."

The audience clapped politely, all the while scrutinizing the strangers like laboratory specimens. Then they returned to their interrupted pastimes. A young man with a braided beard began to flirt with Giselle. Madeline moved away, finding herself before the girl's adoptive father.

"You don't approve of me."

He answered vehemently. "You had some nerve calling, introducing yourself."

Madeline sighed. *It's true*, she thought. *Civilization diminishes proportionally to the distance from Paris.* She decided to try again, smiling ingratiatingly.

"Giselle seems to have grown into a beautiful young lady—she looks just like her mother. Before I emigrated, Giselle's mother begged me to find her, to see what sort of woman she'd become—"

"Her mother! The woman who bore her? What claim has she? Who spent six months in quarantine with her, risking their lives to care for her? We did. Who raised her, taught her? We did, Hilda and me. And the whole time we're getting her through the traumas of growing up, especially growing up in this place—the whole time she keeps getting letters from that earthside bitch."

Forcing down her anger, she replied, "It's not easy for those who stay behind either. Giselle's parents—"

"Hilda was her mother! I am her father!" He stopped, shook his head. "I'm sorry. You're new, you don't understand yet.

"To come to Blues is to die and be reborn. You get some awful disease—myeloma. You?"

She paused a moment. "Lupus."

"You say good-bye to your family, write your will, dispose of all your belongings. You're shot into space, to the quarantine station. Six months alone in tiny rooms, while radiation and chemicals kill every blood cell, every germ in your body. Then, when you're positively bug free—because without our immune systems the common cold could wipe out the colony—when you're safe, you enter Blues. Hairless, like a baby. Reincarnated into a new world."

He grabbed her left hand, holding it up. "You wore a ring for many years. Where is your husband now?"

She barely choked back her answer.

He nodded. "He stayed on Earth. Do you still write him? Don't. You can never return to Earth. Let go of the past. 'Until death do us part.' Blues is a city of the dead."

Madeline asked hesitantly, "And if my husband had come with me?"

"Come with you?" His face would have flushed livid, had he had any blood. "Fidoes. Faithful spouses following their loved ones into hell. Virtuous little toads. Don't let me near one. I'd show him a bit of hell."

"I don't understand. How can you hate someone so full of love for her husband—or wife—that she—they'd follow them here?"

He snarled and stalked away.

Giselle came up and put a hand on Madeline's shoulder. Her other hand was resting loosely on Henri's forearm. "God—what's Father yelling about this time?"

"Fidoes."

"Them again? Well, of course we all hate Fidoes."

"Why." Henri always stated his questions.

"Because they remind us of what we've lost. We're under life sentences, unable to see Earth or relatives. (Not that I, personally, have any memories of either.) But we're all unified in that respect. Then Fidoes come, like it's a big joke, play the self-righteous martyr for a few years, then return to Earth. Father says the only way to survive here is to sever all ties with your past."

Madeline said, "And that's why you don't write your mother?"

Giselle rolled her eyes at the mere thought.

"Don't judge. Annette is a lovely woman," Henri said.

Giselle pulled her hand away, regarding him with narrowed eyes. "How do you know? I thought you two met in quarantine."

Madeline said hastily, "We knew each other before, in art school." She felt her entire past slipping away, negated by words that blithely tossed out memories of marriage, career, friends, love —Anything to avoid the truth. She was a Fido.

"Henri and I, meeting again. It was quite a coincidence."

"Quite," Giselle agreed.

Henri slept with the corner of his mouth twitching, making an occasional soft moan. Madeline lay propped up on one arm. Despite the months, he still seemed alien to her, her now bald and thin husband merging in her mind's eye with her grandfather. Even the venous catheter high on Henri's chest, closed except during the bimonthly infusion of artificial blood, reminded her of *Grandpere*'s central-line venous access when his peripheral veins could no longer sustain an intravenous line.

Her grandfather had been only fifty-six when they diagnosed lymphoma, and he'd refused the standard treatment.

"Let them clean me out like a rat in a lab, replace my blood with cream, send me to outer space? Never. If I must die, I shall do so with my family around me."

He'd done well for a while, then gone downhill with a vengeance. And so to the special hospital in America, where he'd suffered through six-drug chemotherapy, radiation, interferon, debulking operations. Madeline remembered him wasting away, shriveling, his final days a contest to see which would kill him first —the disease or the treatment, the pain of the invading lymphocytes or the pain of the poisons that fought the cells.

She remembered Dr. Elbein, though she found it impossible to picture him without his entourage of fellows, residents, and medical students. He'd stood outside the door, unaware how his voice carried in the stillness. "This is a rare opportunity to relive medical history," he'd said, his voice unexpectedly gentle from a face that sharp and sardonic. "We called them 'hot leuks,' though lymphoma's really just 'leuk equivalent.' We'd drug them until the white count dropped into the basement, then hope it would crawl back up before they died of infection."

"Why 'hot leuks'?" a student asked.

"Because leukemics are hot. They look fine one minute and crump the next. Every night on call they'd spike and you'd have to do a complete fever workup—you kids can't imagine how much time that ate up. And if they didn't spike they'd need blood or platelets—and they never had any veins.

"You think it's awful with this guy, watching him puke and get septic and waste away?" He laughed. "We had wards full of them. Now we just shoot them into space, like atomic waste."

"Waste," Madeline whispered, and tried to sleep.

She dreamed of the hospital, air sweet with bouquets and bodily decay. Her husband seemed as pale as his sheets. Watching Henri sleep had always given her a feeling of security; she'd been safe from all harm with her lion beside her. Now she was watching him, anticipating every harsh breath, afraid that the next might not come.

He woke screaming.

"I'm here," she said.

He clutched her. "Don't leave me."

"Of course not."

"Never. I—I'm afraid. Don't ever leave me." And he began to cry.

She'd never seen him cry before. "I'll stay with you," she promised, and woke.

She rose, made coffee, and sat quietly in the studio. The coffee was bland, artificial—real coffee might stimulate too much gastric acid secretion, causing ulcers that would bleed. People without blood platelets cannot afford to bleed. Hence the boring food, the soft-edged furniture, the dull knives. Hence Madeline's inability to sculpt.

Internal bleeding—a bruise—stops by the action of clotting factors made in the liver. But cuts, scrapes, open wounds—bleeding from them stops due to platelets. And platelets come from the same stem cells which give rise to the white and red blood cells, the stem cells which had been diligently destroyed in almost all the inhabitants of Blues. The artificial clotting aids could not completely replace platelets. Thus there was no more chance of Madeline getting a sculpting tool than of her getting fresh fruit or a potted palm.

She surveyed the studio. It was so different from their studio back home, with the north window facing the garden. Here the one small window faced another building, pastel blue. Paintings in every stage of completion—here the canvases were either blank or turned to face the wall. Her sculptures on every shelf—here were only photographs of her statues, too heavy to bring from Earth.

"They don't understand your work," Henri had always said, "because they're fools."

She looked at the shelf of paints and her one attempt at sculpture since arrival, a clay sphere with little tendrils reaching out—a sun sending out plumes of gas, or a macrophage ready to engulf. It was covered in the fine powder that passed for dust on Blues.

She reached for it scornfully. Clay had no life, no soul, so unlike wood. Wood contained the sculpture already; she had only to find it and release it from its covering. But clay was like all of Blues, a bland mediocre world, as devoid of ugliness as it was of beauty. People, though—people were still the same . . .

The sphere slipped from her fingers, pancaking on the floor.

Henri entered, rubbing at his scalp to push back the mane that no longer existed. "What . . ."

"Found art," she said. "It's an egg."

He adopted his nasal art-critic voice. "The egg, symbol of life and new beginnings." When Madeline failed to laugh at the imitation, he picked up a canvas, stared at it, turned it back to face the wall again, and began pacing.

Madeline sipped her coffee. "It was an awful party."

He paused, a strange smile on his face. "Your cousin doesn't believe we're living together. She says we don't act like lovers. She says we act like an old married couple." He laughed once, a staccato bark, and resumed pacing.

Madeline ran into Giselle in the line at the hospital cafeteria as the older woman tried to choose a meal. The plastic-looking food had many strikes against it. It was shipped from Earth fully processed. It was digestible by people lacking normal bowel flora and with their gastric acid secretion diminished by drugs. As if that were not enough, it was also hospital food.

Madeline made some polite comments about Giselle's party.

"How do you like Blues?"

"It's—different. Hard to adjust to. My job is, too. I'm a medical technician. My specialties are bacteriology and hematology—not much demand for either. Now all I do is plate specimens; I haven't seen a single rod or coccus to reward my efforts."

"Thank God," Giselle said.

"Well, at least I'm working with culture." Giselle did not get the joke, so Madeline continued. "It's worse for Henri. He's a painter."

"An artist?" Giselle became enthusiastic. "Lord knows we need more art up here. What does he paint?"

"He began in landscapes. But"—she caught herself from saying "we"—"he had to live in cities, to lecture and teach and such. Have you heard of the microlandscape school? Henri was one of the founders. It's easy to find grandeur in the country, with the vistas of trees, mountains, sky . . ." She was falling back into her standard explanation, culled almost directly from the exhibit pamphlets she'd helped write.

"Those are just concepts in textbooks," Giselle said. "Maybe . . . is it like Out-there? Space is huge and black and wonderful. It just keeps going, with stars like spots of fire . . ." She pushed at the remnants of her sandwich, her mind somewhere else.

"The Group decided to paint city landscapes," Madeline continued dreamily. "A flower in the sidewalk, tree leaves against the sky . . . Beauty is ubiquitous in the country. The challenge is to find it in the city." Like searching for bacteria in the pus of a sterile abscess.

"Unfortunately, there's no sky here, no trees, no flowers. Henri is without inspiration. He can't paint."

Giselle's face lit up. "But there's beauty in Blues."

"Ah, you were raised here."

"No, it's there for everyone. The arc of a roof against a support strut, the glint of a house far overhead, the way the stars smear out underfoot in the observation deck . . ."

Madeline was thoughtful. "Do you think you could get someone else to see this beauty? Henri?"

"I can try."

They received a letter from Bertrand, a glorious collage of pictures and words that began, *"Mon cher* Henri, *ma belle* Madeline," appellations that made Henri bristle.

"He's got something planned," Henri muttered. "While the cat's away the mice shall play."

Madeline put the letter on hold. "Bertrand's not so bad."

"The man's an upstart. The only thing that held him back was his inability to decide which he'd rather do—steal my school or seduce my wife."

Madeline shrugged, half smiling, and switched the letter back on. "The prices for your paintings have already skyrocketed, my dear Henri, to a height almost worthy of your present surroundings. Also, may I opine, to a degree undreamed of in your earthly days."

"The rodent."

"He's just trying to be poetic."

"Even the sculptures of your lovely wife are coveted and much sought after."

"Vultures," Henri growled.

A new picture came on. "Our latest exhibit. Marcel's *Flowers in the Crosswalk I.*" It was a good example of their school—austere brushwork, unpretentious realism.

"Flowers in the Crosswalk II." Now the flowers were buffeted in the airstream of rushing traffic. There was a cartoonlike simplicity to the art. Henri sat rigid.

"Flowers in the Crosswalk III." The final item in the triptych blinked into being, the flowers transformed into metal, the trucks and motorbikes into elephants, typewriters, musical notes.

"Surrealism!" Henri bellowed, banging his fist onto the console. Paintings began to flash by rapidly, each sillier than the last, each more of a parody of the circle's previous work, of Henri's life work.

Henri rose and left the room, his massive shoulders slumped. Madeline stopped the letter at the last of the art and slowly read the title.

"Dancing on My Grave Before I'm Even Dead."

Madeline had not seen much of Henri for the last few days. He set out early each morning, led by Giselle or one of her friends, returning each evening with an armful of charcoal roughs. The house began to fill with students, trying to convert their own crude sketches into full canvases. They painted into the night, falling asleep on the couch or rug, working and lying underfoot until Madeline would wake and send them to their own homes as she left for the lab.

While Henri had found beauty in a tree thrusting out of pavement, Madeline had found it in the microscope. She'd given up her own art studies—one of them had to bring home a salary—but the aesthetics of a Wright's-stained blood smear had eased her through the workaday world. The delicate lobulations of a PMN, no two cells alike. The frothy purple lacework of a platelet. The sweet blue of a lymphocyte's cytoplasm. Even when she'd gone to the lab to see the slide that spelled Henri's doom, even as she'd scanned field after field of leukemic myelocytes, she'd thought, *How can they be bad? They're too beautiful.*

"Why so quiet?"

She looked around. Bob, the stranger from the party, was leaning against an incubator. A stethoscope peeked out of one pocket of his very loud suit.

She put down her pipette. "You'll think I'm crazy. I was remembering the beauty of a good peripheral blood smear."

"Not crazy—just a little weird. One of my path teachers was artsy. Wanted to be an architect, became a pathologist instead. He always said, 'The worst cancer looks gorgeous in hematoxylin and eosin.' He'd show us a slide of, say, lung with its fine mesh of purple and pink, and he'd say, 'Go on, show me anything in art nouveau that can beat this.' Frankly, I didn't think it was so hot. Not that it kept me from getting the top grade in the class."

"No," Madeline said. "One does not need a sense of aesthetics to be successful."

"What's wrong," Henri demanded, putting down his brush. The studio was now full of paintings by Henri and his new pupils. Views of stars, of houses, of women lying in artificial flowers or standing in the metallic sheen of the oxygen equipment. Works in progress lay propped everywhere and hung on the walls, covering the photos of Madeline's sculptures. "You've been unhappy all evening."

"Don't you know what today is?"

"It's our anniversary. Well, we can't very well celebrate it, can we. They don't even know we're married."

"But we could . . ."

"Let's choose a new anniversary, Madeline, one appropriate to our life here. I know! We can have a party for the day when they told me I was dying." Laughing bitterly, he turned back to the canvas.

As Henri was becoming engrossed in his painting and his teaching, Madeline was making friends at work. They gossiped as she plated a seemingly infinite number of specimens from people, places, things in the never-ending war to keep the colony germ-free. She joined a chess club. She went to a party to bid a temporary farewell to a co-worker who had won the adoption lottery and was going on leave to help her new three-year-old immunosuppressed son through the terrors of quarantine.

She occasionally met Giselle at lunch. They would begin by gossiping—had X sliced her finger on a broken window and bled to death by accident, or was it suicide or murder; did Y's newly adopted daughter have brain damage; would Z wed yet again?

But, perhaps because of her own lung damage from recurrent pneumonia as an infant, lunch with Giselle always ended up a bitter catalog of the disasters that walked into the Pulmonary Functions Lab—chronic lungers incapacitated by smoking, by radiation fibrosis, by bronchiectasis from infection.

After yet another description of yet another pulmonary cripple, Giselle changed her subject. "I got another letter from your cousin today."

"Annette? How is she?"

"I don't know. I just erase them as they come through the computer."

"Giselle! How can you!"

"That woman inundates me with her unwanted attention!"

"You can hardly call a few letters a year an inundation."

"She gave me up to Blues—why can't she give me up completely? I didn't ask to be born. I don't owe her—"

Madeline had had enough dramatics. "Calm down, Giselle. Don't you ever wonder about your family? You had an older brother. Antoine. The colds started at three months. Then pneumonia. Meningitis. Constant diarrhea. He didn't respond to immunoglobulin replacement. He died before his first birthday.

"The geneticists said there was only a one-in-four chance the next child would also have an immunodeficiency. Annette and Pierre wanted children, and they took the chance. They treated you as if you were made of jewels. Then at three months, when the maternal antibodies begin to disappear, you sneezed . . .

"They didn't have a third child. Don't you see—allowing you to leave Earth, to live, was an act of love. Your mother loves you, Giselle, though she hasn't seen you for twenty years."

The girl stared into her coffee cup.

Madeline said softly, "Read the next letter you receive. Please."

"Well, hello ladies."

Giselle groaned as Bob sat down. "Lucky women, lunching with the last of the red-blooded men. Who could ask for more?"

Giselle rose. "I have to get back to work."

Bob waited until she was gone. "At last. We're alone." The other diners within range of his booming voice turned in astonishment.

Madeline stifled a giggle. "At last."

"I brought you a gift." He handed her a slide, folded in lens paper. Madeline unwrapped it, rotating it into the light.

"Notice the perfect feather edge," Bob said. "Haven't done a smear in twenty years, but I haven't lost my touch. Nothing's beyond the last of the red-blooded men."

"But what . . ."

"Blood. My own, of course, with just the right amount of Wright's stain. A nostalgic voyage to a world where people have hot, pulsing red stuff in their arteries."

Smiling, she pocketed the slide. "Thank you, Bob. As I revel in each red cell, each delightful leukocyte, each marvelous monocyte, I'll think of you."

He shuddered. "If you find anything strange on the diff—do me a favor. Don't tell me."

The great and near great of Blues were there. Administrators, store owners, journalists. They looked at the paintings, drank the bland wine, argued politics.

"We're nothing but a company store, existing on Earth's sufferance."

"Look, they won't run something this expensive if it isn't worth their while. Why shouldn't we tend the satellites and factories. We aren't invalids . . ."

Madeline moved along making sure everyone had a glass of wine, a piece of cheese. She felt almost at home. She'd had years of practice running art shows.

A man grabbed her arm as she passed. "Do you play cello?"

"Sorry."

"Damn. We've almost got an entire orchestra. All we need is another cellist."

She bit back the temptation to suggest he hire one. She knew how the few hired personnel from Earth were ostracized, despised. Instead, she smiled devilishly. "Sooner or later some cellist down there will need a kidney transplant. You just have to be patient."

As she wandered, she looked at the paintings—a few starscapes, but mostly scenes of the station itself. Henri's contributions easily stood out, with their mastery of perspective, their confident brush strokes. The students' contributions were remarkable only for their odd viewpoints. The school had drawn from Giselle's peers, Earth children uprooted by disease and raised on Blues. One student—the boy with the braided beard—showed promise. His paintings were a tangle of intersecting levels that gave Madeline vertigo, the same feeling she got whenever she looked above her at the other side of the colony.

She paused before a final picture, a sentimental still life of silken flowers. Giselle's. It was the most amateurish of all, and Madeline resented its presence.

She heard Giselle's laughter. The girl was entertaining some journalist, translating Henri's dour phrases into an artistic manifesto. That had always been Madeline's job back home. But here— Madeline was deluding herself. If anyone was the hostess of the art show, it was Giselle.

One of the daring young artists accepted a refill of his glass, then pointed to Giselle. "Isn't she grand tonight?"

"She appears to be in her element." She noticed Giselle's father buttonholing people and forcing them to confront his daughter's still life.

"I was an artist," she said.

"You?"

The boy obviously thought of her as a drudge who existed only to support Henri. *The juvenile form of the PMN is called a stab,* Madeline thought. *How appropriate.*

"Me. I gave up my career to support—my husband. But I still sculpted, even showed."

"Sculpture. You mean, pottery and plastic and stuff?"

"Wood. I miss it. The feel of a good knife, the search for the right pattern in the grain . . ."

"Well, miss away," he said. "I'd like to see you find a knife on Blues. They'd have a fit."

"Would they?" She watched him move deeper into the room of harsh design but rounded edges, an environment to minimize trauma.

"Ah, for a knife as sharp as a child's tongue."

Hearing applause, Madeline watched the young artist with the braided beard present Giselle with a bouquet. His ringlets of hair reminded her of a cluster of staphylococci. She shook her head and looked away, turning back at the shriek.

Giselle had dropped the plastic flowers and was clutching her hand. Clear liquid, like viscous water, ran from her hand and onto the floor.

"Oh no I'm sorry I'm sorry, I don't know how . . ." the man

babbled. The others stood, horrified. Giselle's father began to berate the young man. "You've killed her," he screamed.

Madeline felt like a character out of *Alice in Wonderland.* She pushed through the crowd to Giselle, grabbing her hand, feeling the slippery fluid. She raised Giselle's hand high, holding pressure over the artery in the upper arm.

Giselle was wide-eyed and shaking. She would have been pale were she not already the sickly yellow of the bloodless. "It's going to be all right," Madeline said, and from the corner of her eye noticed Henri.

He was as wide-eyed as Giselle. He stared at the younger woman, looking almost ready to faint.

Madeline's heart missed a beat.

"Call an ambulance," she said.

"It's ludicrous; everyone is overreacting. You'd think she was Camille, coughing out her lungs. Not a cut finger." Madeline gazed in the window of the emergency room cubicle. Giselle had a liter of artificial blood hung in her central line. Henri clutched her free hand as a doctor sutured up the other.

Bob, who had heard the commotion and come to the emergency room to offer advice, said, "People bleed to death frequently here. Well, bleed isn't the best description."

"As good as 'blood relative,' " Madeline said.

"Who's the wimp cutting off her circulation?"

"The man I live with." So easily was Henri relegated to a bloodless description.

"Oh." Bob put an arm about Madeline's shoulder, ushered her upstairs to his office, and materialized two cups of coffee. They nursed the coffee in silence. She stared at the decorations on the wall, the diplomas and certificates, the framed portraits. In one, a dozen men and women in formal attire faced the camera; Bob wore blue jeans. In another, he was the one beard in a sea of clean-shaven faces.

Bob said finally, "My place is pretty nice. Lots of posters of trees and all. The bed is big, too."

She said, "Thanks. I'll keep it in mind."

"No commitments or anything. I can't get caught; it would leave too many broken hearts from Boise to Mars. Just temporary quarters, you know?"

She nodded. "We wouldn't want to upset your girlfriends."

"Right. God, I love the French. You understand things so well."

"You're a good man, Bob."

"Hey, what do you expect from the last of the red-blooded men? Are you going to fight for him?"

"I'm not sure yet."

"Then keep this in mind about Giselle. She has a combined immunodeficiency."

"So?"

"So that means that only her lymphocytes were useless. She still had stem cells that became perfectly good red cells and platelets and polys."

Madeline put down her coffee. "You mean—"

"Yeah. Giselle grew up as rosy and healthy as me. She looked like an Outsider, an Earthie. She took elective chemo, wiped out her stem cells voluntarily. Just to look 'normal.'"

Standing, he kissed Madeline's hand. "Be careful. Giselle is a very determined young lady."

Henri haunted the hospital, sleeping in the lounge, pacing cat-like through the halls, until Giselle went home. Then he moved to the couch in his studio. Whenever Madeline passed the open door he would jump before a canvas, holding the brush poised as if in decision. But the painting never progressed.

And finally, one morning when Madeline went in to work, her friends did not speak to her. When she sat down to lunch, her neighbors moved to another table. Returning to the lab, she found her white coat shredded, her locker opened, and its contents smashed.

"Why are you doing this?" she screamed. The others kept to their tasks, plating samples, staring into microscopes. She grabbed a co-worker and spun him around. "Why!"

"Fido," he said, wrenching loose. "Bow wow." The others in the lab took up the barking call.

She fled to the transport, running the final quarter kilometer home. The front door was unlocked, Henri's studio vacant. The painting had progressed since morning.

She went to the bedroom and flung open the door. Henri looked at her guiltily. Giselle sat up, long hair ebony against her yellow-ivory skin, and smiled. "Woof woof."

"You told them!"

"It was your cousin's latest letter. I'm glad you persuaded me to read it. She hoped we'd be good friends, you and I, and talked about your long, idyllic marriage to a famous painter. Henri confirmed it. Can't keep a secret, can you, my angel?" She leaned over and kissed him, then looked back at Madeline. Henri's expression was as blank as unsculpted marble.

"You would stoop so low . . ."

Giselle said, "You have no rights here. Outsider."

"Henri!"

He didn't answer.

"Henri—you as well? All right, she's young and pretty and amusing, but Henri, it's empty glamour. It's the sparkle of a castle in a fishbowl."

He spoke at last. "They have your marrow frozen in the lab. You can return to Earth. I—I'm the fish; I can't leave the fishbowl. So I'll settle for the castle."

She fled.

She clung to the spoke, in the still center without gravity. Near her a father and daughter played with fighting kites. She could see the entirety of the O'Neill module below her, curving up and above her. With ponds, forests, meadows, it might have been beautiful. Instead it was all shiny metal and muted pastels.

"Get me," the father urged. "That's it," and they giggled.

Madeline remembered the oncologist, a large-boned woman with eyes that crinkled when she smiled. She had not been smiling then. "Don't do it," she'd said.

"Henri's afraid to go alone."

"I'm begging you—stay on Earth."

"He's my husband."

The doctor had shrugged. "All right; you won't be the first. But you'll do it our way. You'll need a cover story to fit in—lupus. We haven't used that before. We'll say your mother died from SLE. When you developed it you decided to emigrate early, before the steroid side effects. You'll undergo the same treatments your husband does—we'll kill every blood cell in your body. But there'll be one difference. We'll keep some of your marrow, for when you change your mind and decide to come home. It will be in the freezer, waiting for you."

"Then it will wait forever."

"Forever," Madeline repeated now. She could push off from the tower, glide slowly to her doom. And when she landed—there would be no telltale red spot on the pavement.

She looked down at the colony, people visible only as abstractions. She'd thought of it as a colony, like a colony of bacteria growing on an artificial medium, but from this height it seemed more like a body. A cylinder full of life, in pieces so small the individual components were meaningless. And herself? The Outsider. The infective particle.

The people without individual immune systems had formed a larger, more potent immune system to reject her. What could she do? Stay, like Bob, and become an abscess walled off by hate? Or let them win. The short flight downward . . .

The body cannot tolerate an invader. One or the other must die.

She left everything for Henri and Giselle, taking only the old brandy—Napoleon fleeing the winter. She knocked and entered, carrying the bottle. Bob, wearing only a pair of jeans, stood staring into a hologram of a redwood forest.

"For you," she said, and put down the bottle.

He spoke to the wall. "A going away present?"

She took one step forward, then stopped. "Bob, come with me. Choose life. Why stay and be destroyed?"

Laughing, he turned to face her. She saw the large, hasty scar of an emergency laparotomy bisecting his abdomen.

He grinned. "Drunk driver. My spleen looked like hamburger."

"After the splenectomy—"

"Yeah. Recurrent pneumococcal infections."

"Antibiotics—"

He cut her off. "I'm allergic to sulfa and the beta-lactams. The others were too toxic for long-term prophylaxis."

"Then—you're immunocompromised; Earth would kill you. You belong on Blues."

He laughed again. "Belong? I'm the last of the red-blooded men. I never belong."

The art show was the expected babble of voices, clink of glasses. She left the paintings and let the crowd drift her toward the sculptures in the center. She paused before the crenulated sphere engulfing the small rod, both carved out of heart of cedar. She'd become very fond of hues of red.

A ruddy-faced young man was studying the piece carefully. "Looks real symbolic," he said.

"It's a macrophage, phagocytosing a salmonella."

The man chuckled. "Come on. It's obviously some sort of Jungian allegory about the female swallowing the male or something. I'm a photographer; I can't understand anything more symbolic than a traffic sign. What do you do?"

"I sculpt," she said and pointed to her name on the stand.

He barely blushed, then examined her name and looked pointedly at her unadorned fingers.

"Weren't you married?"

She shrugged. "I'm a widow. More wine?"

Science fiction is about change, or so goes one of the many defini-
tions of this genre. Here's a story about a radical change that
comes over the world—not a new ice age or the disappearance of
the ozone layer, but something basic, *something* important.

Damon Knight, critic, teacher, and editor of science fiction, has
always had a gift for the logic of the absurd, as those who have
read "To Serve Man," "The Great Cow Pat Boom," and "Forever,"
among other Damonic stories, will recall.

O

DAMON KNIGHT

One day everybody in the world whose name began with the
letter *o* abruptly disappeared. Marina Oswald, who was then living
in Chevy Chase, went away and never came back; so did Mr. and
Mrs. Robert F. Otto, of Binghamton, New York, and all their children; so did Barry Outka and Lynn Overall, both of Austin, Texas;
so did Aram Ouzounian of the Armenian SSR and Jean-Luc Ouel-
lette of France and Tetsu Okuma of Japan. All the O'Haras,
O'Gradys, O'Flahertys, and O'Keefes vanished like smoke, along
with the Owens, the Ortegas, and the Oppenheims.

A good deal of real estate came on the market, especially in
Ireland. Suddenly there was elbowroom in cities that had been
overcrowded. The tempo of life relaxed; people had time to smile
at each other on the street.

The next thing that happened was that all animals, birds, fish,
and reptiles whose names began with the letter *o* disappeared—
ocelots, octopuses, okapis, opossums, orangutans, orioles, ostriches,
otters, owls, and oxen, together with whole orders and suborders
such as the Ophidia, the Orthoptera, and the Ostracoda. As a
general thing, nobody missed them.

Oak trees, oats, okra, olives, oranges, and other plants also vanished, but there were lots of substitutes—barley, for instance, pick-
les, and tangerines.

So far, so good; but when whole cities, states, and other geographical features turned up missing, there was widespread unease. Ohio, Oklahoma, and Oregon were gone, no one knew where; so were Omaha, Omsk, Ontario, Osaka, Oshkosh, Oslo, and Oxford, along with a host of lesser-known places such as Oconomowoc, Odendaalsrus, Opa-locka, Opp, and Ouagadougou. The United Nations appointed a Commission of Inquiry into the Disappearance of Inhabited Places, but it bogged down because nobody could remember the names of the towns they were looking for.

On the whole, most people thought the changes were improvements. There was nothing between Toronto and Rochester but a large grassy plain suitable for agriculture or grazing. The main island of Hawaii was gone, but it had been all built up in condominiums anyway. The space between Indiana and Pennsylvania had closed up somehow, and Kansas was now bounded on the south by Texas.

A curious result was that people began to feel superstitious about using words that began with the missing letter. "Ah, hell," they said, and "Unlatch the door." Children, when they wanted to write something dirty on a wall, simply drew circles. Custodians went around behind them changing the circles into 8's.

Mathematicians began to use the symbol Z for a zero, thus: "The national debt amounts to $156,ZZZ,ZZZ,ZZZ." Multiples of one thousand became known as "zizzes," as in "We've got to come up with a megazizz in new funding by the end of January."

In dictianaries and in camman usage, the letter *a* ar *e* was used as a substitute far the missing and naw unspeakable letter. Ane spake ef gaing ta "the men's rum," ar "the tailet." The ultimate insult was "yeu asshale."

Manufacturers had ta change many ef their brand names, at great expense and sametimes with unfartunate results. Marlbara and Xerex were all right, but Caca-Cala suffered a nasedive in papularity.

The publishing industry was buming, and sign painters had mare wark than they cauld handle. In spite ef the glut ef hausing, canstructian warkers were busy tu, tearing dawn traffic circles and turning them inta squares. Eyeglasses were square, and sa were cups and saucers, drinking glasses, and battles, resulting in great ecanamies in shipping and starage. A labaratary in Califarnia perfected a chicken that laid square eggs. A few peaple tuk the wheels aff their cars, replacing them with skids ar runners, but mast falks were cantent ta caver the wheels with ruffled skirts.

As the new century dawned, peaple surveyed their warld and faund it gud. From pale ta pale, the square-shauldered Earth was cavered with the rectilinear warks ef man—square buildings, square intersecting streets, square traffic exchanges, square lakes, and square mauntains. Even peaple's faces were becaming square. Set free ef all their circularity and canfusian, faursquare to the sunrise, the peaple ef the warld cauld well say, with the paet Alexander Pape,

Let us, since life can little mare supply
Than just ta luk abaut us, and ta die,
Expatiate free a'er all this scene ef man;
A mighty maze! but nat withaut a plan . . .

A lot of people bridle when "the art of war" is mentioned—they feel that mass killing doesn't deserve to be described as anything so fine as art. But perhaps they underestimate the wide variety of uses to which art can be put. Imagine a future after widespread plagues have reduced the United States to a jumble of city-states, autonomous enclaves controlled by very different groups of people; if one of those cities were run by artists, and they should find themselves invaded by an army, what might they do?

Pat Murphy's first novel, published in 1982, was The Shadow Hunter. *She lives in San Francisco.*

ART IN THE WAR ZONE

PAT MURPHY

Jax watched through binoculars as the army from Sacramento crossed the Bay Bridge to invade San Francisco. She could see the figure of a woman sitting on the freeway sign just past the bridge's second tower. The Jaxdoll was waiting for the army to come to her.

"About two hundred of them, wouldn't you say?" asked Danny-boy. "No problem."

Jax took her eyes from her binoculars to frown at him. They were at the top of the Union 76 Tower, where they had the best view of the bridge. Danny-boy sat at the edge of the platform, legs dangling over the long drop to the street below. His khaki-colored cap was pushed back on his head, and his curly red hair was braided to keep it out of his way. He was Jax's lover and head of the War Council of the Artists Collective. His binoculars were trained on the army, and he did not see Jax frown.

Jax glanced at The Machine, the other artist in her fighting unit, and The Machine just shrugged. He was busy with his equipment —monitoring the radio, listening to reports from other groups scattered around the city, and preparing to communicate with the army through the Jaxdoll.

The Jaxdoll was what The Machine called an automatic sculpture. It was an automaton, built to look like Jax and mimic some of her gestures. When The Machine had given it to Jax for her birthday the year before, it had been wired to snap its fingers in a characteristic Jaxian gesture and say in Jax's voice, "If you're going to do it, do it now." Now, rigged with a radio transmitter and receiver, the Jaxdoll sat on a road sign above the freeway. The sign had once given directions to the Civic Center in downtown San Francisco. More recently, it had welcomed out of towners to the Summer Solstice Festival. Currently it held a banner that read "SACRAMENTO, GO HOME!"

Jax looked at the army again. Sunlight sparkled on burnished gun barrels. The army had ten battered jeeps loaded with troops and supplies, forty or so men on horseback, and a slow-moving transport truck. The soldiers were all dressed in green. The horses were nervous, and Jax watched the riders fight to keep them under control.

"What do you think?" Danny-boy asked her.

"I think this is going to be harder than you think," she said.

This was not a new conversation. This was a very old conversation. For months she had been trying to convince Danny-boy that a war could not be a work of art.

Danny-boy was a pacifist who specialized in organizing large art projects. When rumors of Sacramento's invasion plans had first reached the city, he had just finished two projects—wrapping the old Alcoa Building in aluminum foil, and repainting the Golden Gate Bridge in a lovely shade of sky blue. Danny-boy took on the war as a moral challenge worthy of an artist and called the first meeting of the War Council. At that meeting, the artists elected Danny-boy to head the War Council, put Jax in charge of weapons procurement and combat training, and put The Machine, a specialist in electronic gadgetry, in charge of electronic surveillance and espionage. With that, preparations for war began.

Three months later, the Government of Sacramento had sent the artists a message demanding that the City of San Francisco become a part of Unified California under the leadership of Sacramento, pay taxes, and generally stop making trouble—or face the consequences. By that time the artists had gathered or created weapons, stockpiled food enough for a two-month siege, and organized a military organization where none had existed before. The artists painted the messenger as blue as the Golden Gate Bridge and sent him home.

"I still say we should have blown up the bridge when they were halfway across. If they want to get you, then get them first," Jax said. She had said the same thing at the first meeting of the War Council, and she had been outvoted. Most people did not trust Jax. They considered her art and her temperament to be dark and violent, and the city was not a dark and violent place. Danny-boy had argued against her, and the War Council sided with Danny-boy. People liked Danny-boy. They trusted him.

"They're people," Danny-boy said. "Stupid people, but they shouldn't have to die just for being stupid. There aren't enough people around as it is. Maybe back before the Plagues you could justify killing people, but now . . ."

"I can justify it," she said. "They wouldn't mind killing us, so I don't mind killing them." She took her eyes away from the binoculars to scowl at him again. "You've been trying to convert me to someone with higher moral values for so long that sometimes you think you've succeeded. You haven't. I have only one rule to live by: I like to live. No higher moral values."

She returned to her study of the army. The foremost jeep carried no supplies. The driver was a young man, much the same as the men on horseback. The man beside him was another matter. His face looked like it had been chiseled from granite. His hair matched the gray of the gun barrels. The gold braid on his hat and the gold eagles on the shoulders of his green jacket glittered. His hat was cocked back, and he stared ahead with fearsome intensity.

A red, white, and blue flag flew from the jeep; it looked like a flag of the old United States, before the Plagues had decimated the population and divided the country. "Ugly flag," Jax commented.

When the army was within shouting distance of the Jaxdoll, one of the riders saw her and waved to the men in the jeep. The procession stopped, and the rider rode back to confer with the granite-faced man. Then the rider went forward alone. He reined his horse in under the Jaxdoll. The Machine fiddled with his controls and made the doll lean forward a little, as if it were watching the rider. The Machine handed Jax a microphone.

"Hi, soldier," she said confidently. "I'd like to talk to whoever's in charge of this invasion." The rider stared up at the doll, and Jax watched his face through the binoculars. He was young—maybe eighteen or nineteen.

"Who are you?" he called.

"My name's Jax," she said. "I'm here to speak for the Artists Collective. We run this city, remember? We've been running it since the Fourth Plague. And we don't like visitors unless they're invited. Who are you?"

"Come down from there, and I'll take you to the general." His voice was sharp. He sounded as young as he looked. An army of youngsters, recruited from the Central Valley, she thought.

"Tell the general to come here," Jax snapped back. She watched the rider frown and study the supports for the sign, looking for an easy way to climb up. "You'd look pretty silly trying to get me down. Just tell the general that I'm alone and harmless."

He wheeled his horse around and trotted back to the jeep for a lengthy conference with the general, the man with the stone face. The general frowned throughout the discussion. Then the rider backed off, and the jeep drove forward.

"Get down from there, woman," the general growled without hesitation.

Jax grinned. The Jaxdoll did not change expression. "I can talk to you just as well from up here," she said. "I'm here to give you a message from the Artists Collective: Go home. You aren't welcome here. We aren't open for a festival right now, and we aren't welcoming visitors."

The granitic lines of the general's face shifted; he smiled. "What do you plan to do if we don't go home?"

The Jaxdoll leaned further forward. "We'll declare war. And then we'll kill you one by one." The Jaxdoll shrugged. "We don't want to kill you, but we will."

"Get down from there," the general snapped. The Jaxdoll did not move.

"You've been warned," Jax said, and she turned the microphone off and looked at Danny-boy. "Well," she said. "Looks like we've got a war to fight." Danny-boy was watching the army through his binoculars and grinning.

She looked through the binoculars and saw two soldiers manhandling the Jaxdoll down from the sign. They loaded her into the back of the general's jeep and the procession moved on.

"There goes The Angel," Danny-boy said. She looked up in time to see the silver hang glider soar overhead. The Angel, the only member of the War Council's air force, did not wave. His gaze was focused on the army. He swooped over the soldiers gracefully, but not too low. He dropped three smoke bombs. As the bombs fell they left trails of smoke—red, yellow, and blue. The army scattered and the horses spooked. For a time the men were hidden by the clouds of smoke. The Angel soared away from the sound of rifle fire.

"Good shot," Jax said. She watched through the binoculars as the smoke cleared and the army regrouped. The soldiers moved on, following the freeway and watching the skies. They took the Civic Center off ramp, and Jax lost sight of them behind the skyscrapers of downtown.

The city was an unnerving place for a first-time visitor. San Francisco was as strange as the combined efforts of several hundred artists, working together for fifty or so years, could make it. Coit Tower was painted like a giant phallus, and the downtown area was a riot of abstract neon, powered by a wind generator atop one of the taller buildings. The Transamerica Pyramid was caught in a spiderweb of colorful climbing ropes (that was one of Danny-boy's first projects), and a giant spider was frozen in mid step halfway up one face of the building (that was one of The Machine's first projects). Near the Pyramid a group of artists who called themselves the Royal Order of Masons was constructing a sphinx. On the other side of town a group called the Secret Order of the Druids was building a replica of Stonehenge for the next Summer Solstice Festival.

At the Civic Center off ramp, where the army would exit the freeway, a neosurrealist group headed by an artist named Lily had set up a herd of plastic horses, scavenged from saddlery shops in the city and the suburbs. With great care Lily had mounted a human skeleton on each horse, wired in a riding posture. She had rigged the skeletons so that they moved in the slightest breeze, shaking their heads and moving their jaws with great animation. It was a very ominous, very effective display.

Just beyond the horses was a group of kinetic sculptures. A tyrannosaurus watched the street with tiny piggy eyes and opened and closed formidable jaws. A pterodactyl perched on a street-light, flexing its wings and making a strange rasping cry whenever the wind blew. Zatch, the artist who had sculpted these, had plans to reconstruct the entire history of the world in kinetic sculpture, starting with the age of reptiles.

Jax, Danny-boy, and The Machine listened to reports from the other artists. "The horses are spooking," said a voice from the radio. "They don't seem to like Lily's display. Hell, one guy just shot three of the horses."

"Everyone's a critic," said another voice, which Jax recognized as Lily's.

"They're heading for the Civic Center," continued the first speaker. "Someone just shot a hole in the pterodactyl, but he's still flapping his wings."

"They're in the plaza now," said a new voice. "Some of the guys on horses are scouting around. They're checking out some of the houses."

Jax could hear the sound of distant gunfire. "These guys shoot at everything that moves," said the voice on the radio. "Crazy."

"The flag on City Hall is coming down. They're putting up the ugliest flag I've ever seen. We'll have to do something about that." Jax recognized the voice—it was Catseye, a fiery young painter. He sounded ready to climb the roof of City Hall and remove the flag that moment.

"They're parking the jeeps in front of that ugly concrete build-ing on Golden Gate Avenue," someone was saying. "They don't have much taste in architecture. That's the ugliest building around."

"That's an easy building to defend," Jax commented to Danny-boy. "Smart move."

Danny-boy marked the army's position on the map he had fas-tened to a clipboard, then tucked his pencil behind his ear. He looked calm and confident. "Years from now," he said, "they'll remember this war. They'll tell about how a band of artists held off an army without firing a shot. We're making a legend, Jax. A project even bigger and better than repainting the Golden Gate." He grinned at her.

Jax leaned back on her elbows and wondered why he was not wearing the handgun she had issued him. "Hey, Danny-boy," she said. "Now that we're at war, do you suppose you could wear your gun? On the off chance that you might have to fire a shot?" His belt, holster, and gun lay with his water and other supplies on the far side of the roof. She brought him the gun.

He looked a little sheepish, but he did not lose his grin. "This is a war of symbols," he said, "not guns."

"Wear the gun," she said softly. "Please." He put it on, his grin a little crooked but still in place. "In case you've forgotten," she said, "you can't shoot anyone with a symbol. And there's a war on."

It was night. Fog crept through the wide streets and narrow alleys of the city. The tatters of foil that still clung to the Alcoa Building rustled in the gentle breeze from San Francisco Bay. Somewhere far away a fog horn bellowed.

The sentry on the corner of Turk and Market streets yawned and stretched.

Jax watched from the shadows behind him. He was looking out into the night, facing the outside world from which danger would come. Jax had come up through the sewers. She was alone. The Machine was in the van that served as their mobile headquarters, and Danny-boy had joined Catseye for the first evening of fighting. Jax preferred to work alone.

The sentry lit a cigarette. The flame cast a brief light on his face. He was young; he looked tired. Jax sympathized, just then, with Danny-boy and his insistence on minimal violence. She was glad she did not have to kill this youngster. He could have been one of her brothers, drafted to fight in a war. He did not deserve to die for that.

Jax slipped the dart into the blowgun and aimed at his neck, just above the collar of his shirt. She preferred the blowgun to the tranquilizer rifle; it was quieter and just as effective. She fired and ducked farther back in the shadows when he grabbed his neck. He was fumbling for his rifle, starting to lift it as the tranquilizer took effect, and he fell. He was down.

She stepped from the shadows and laid him carefully on his back. She crossed his arms neatly on his chest and snapped open the pouch of indelible skin paints that she carried on her belt. With her left hand she brushed the hair away from his forehead. She worked quickly and carefully, using the red paint and the black. Simplicity, she felt, was best at this point. In bold lettering across his forehead, she wrote DEAD in red. On his right cheek with black paint, she signed BY JAX. Between his folded hands she placed the death certificate, written by Danny-boy and lettered by Animal, a skilled calligrapher. The paper said:

CERTIFICATE OF DEATH

Please consider yourself removed from combat.
Look at it this way—we could have killed you.
If you don't quit fighting, we will.
Signed,

Danny-boy
War Chief
Artists Collective

Jax plucked the dart from the sentry's neck, picked up his rifle, and faded back into the shadows.

"Aces," Jax said to The Machine. "I got one."

He nodded. She had found the van at the planned rendezvous point. The Machine was wearing headphones and monitoring communications among the artists. Mama B, a stout older lady who painted murals on buildings, was also wearing headphones. She had been training with The Machine for the past four months.

"I've been listening to the men guarding the Jaxdoll," Mama B said softly to Jax. "She makes them real nervous."

"Good," Jax said. "They'll be even more nervous tomorrow." She was impatient, eager to leave the safety of the van for the darkness and excitement of the streets. "Where's Danny-boy?" she asked The Machine.

"Catseye and Danny-boy are still out. So far, they've taken two sentries out by the Pyramid. Lily's squad got the ones guarding the horses. She let the horses loose, and she's bringing one home with her. A white one, she said."

"Good," Jax said. "Real good." She sat on the floor of the van for a moment, then slipped out the door again, too restless to stay inside. She could hear the sound of distant gunfire, and she wondered what the soldiers were firing at. All day they had been firing at shadows, at their own reflections in windows, at moving sculptures, at nothing.

Jax heard the sound of running feet and faded into the shadows. Danny-boy ran from the shadows, two steps ahead of Catseye. Catseye was laughing as he ran, and the tiny drops of fog sparkled on his curly black hair. Jax stepped from the shadows, and Catseye ran to her. "They never knew what hit 'em," he said, still grinning, always grinning. "We got four."

All in all, on the first night of the war, the artists got fifteen soldiers—each one labeled DEAD, autographed, and left with a certificate of death. Among the artists, there were no casualties.

In the morning Jax talked to the general through the Jaxdoll. The Machine parked the van up by Twin Peaks, and Jax sat in the open doorway, looking out over the city. Puffs of red and black smoke rose near Market and Castro streets; she guessed that an ambush was underway. The morning sun glittered on the silver wings of The Angel's glider as it soared over the streets of downtown.

"Hey, soldier," Jax said into the microphone. "Get the general over here. I need to talk to him." She waited, watching the smoke drift over the city.

Over the headphones, she heard a door open. "That you, General?"

"You have something to say to me?" The general was not happy.

"I just thought I'd suggest that you leave town," she said. "This is your second warning."

"Another warning? Why would we leave now? Because you have painted the foreheads of a few of my men?" The general laughed—an abrupt, forced sound.

"We've killed fifteen of your men," Jax said. "You have only two hundred men. At this rate, in less than half a month you'll all be dead."

"You have killed no one. You've painted on the foreheads of a few men. My men are laughing today about these paintings. They are—"

"They are dead men," Jax said, and she made her voice cold. "Dead men, General. And war is nothing to laugh at." She could hear the rustling of clothing; someone in the room was moving restlessly. The guard perhaps.

"You fight a very stupid war," the general said.

"We've never fought a war before," Jax admitted. "We're improvising." Danny-boy grinned at her from across the van.

"My men have real bullets, woman," the general said. "When we kill a man, he's really dead."

"Are you suggesting we should do the same?" She raised her voice. "What do you think of that, soldier? Do you think that tonight we should really kill people?"

The soldier did not speak. "You have nothing more to say to me?" the general asked. She heard him stand.

"I guess not," she said. "The war goes on." She heard the general close the door behind him. "Hey, soldier," she said to the guard. "What do you think of all this?"

There was no answer.

After a moment she turned off the microphone and pulled off

the headphones. "I wish the soldier had said something," she said to Danny-boy. "I wonder if he's one of the ones we got last night." Danny-boy shrugged. They pulled the door of the van closed and drove off to set up temporary headquarters somewhere else.

The war went on. The Angel showered the city with leaflets. On one side of each leaflet was a prose poem by Ralston, head of propaganda; on the other side, it said SURRENDER BEFORE IT'S TOO LATE.

The Video Squad triggered a remote projector that displayed a pornographic movie on a white wall on one side of the Civic Center plaza. The movie was periodically interrupted by commercial announcements in which Danny-boy explained why the men should surrender.

Jax worked alone for the most part, finding soldiers who were alone or in pairs. At dusk on the third day of the war, she was prowling around the edge of downtown when she spotted a man sitting by himself at one side of a large plaza. She caught him from behind with a tranquilizer dart and went to label him DEAD. Beside one of his outstretched hands was a notepad and a pencil. He had been drawing the buildings of the city; his style was crisp and clean with sharp lines and hard edges.

She dragged him into the shadows, took his weapons, painted his forehead, and waited for him to wake up. "Hello," she said when his eyes blinked open. "I'm Jax."

His eyes opened wide. His hand went quickly for his gun, then came away from his empty holster slowly. His eyes focused first on the gun in her hand, then on her face.

"What . . . what do you want? Are you . . ." He stopped, struggling with the words, then reached up to his forehead.

"Yeah, you're dead," she said calmly.

He struggled to sit up, swaying just a little. She reached out to help him, but dropped her hand when his eyes widened and he tried to edge away. "What do you want?" he tried again.

She glanced down at the sketch pad. "You do much of this?"

The soldier chewed on his lip and looked down at his hands. He shook his head quickly, an unconvincing denial. His expression was panicky, and he did not meet her eyes.

"Good composition," she said. "Nice feeling to it. I like it." The soldier looked startled. "When the general gives up, come and join us."

"The general will never give up," he said.

"Well, then, when you give up on following the general."

"The general kills deserters."

She frowned at him. "If you desert, how can he kill you? He'd have to catch you." The soldier was watching her as if she were crazy. "He's just a man."

The soldier did not answer. She heard distant gunfire and the dull explosions of smoke bombs, and she stood up, taking his rifle with her. "Think about it," she said, and she ran away into the twilight shadows.

On the fifth day of the war, temporary headquarters were in the old Pacific Telephone building. Headquarters were wherever Danny-boy was, and they were always temporary. Before the fighting began the artists had set up living quarters in several different locations. All important facilities were scattered: the chemical warfare lab run by a skin painter named Tiger was on the other side of town; the repair shop for electronics was elsewhere; food was stored in a number of places.

Midway through the fifth day Gambit, a musician of the natural noise school, started his automatic bells. Gambit had spent months experimenting to find buildings with the best resonant quality and scavenging to find gongs and bells with the best tone. His favorite was a gong that he had scavenged from a Buddhist temple and hung in a brick warehouse with a high arched roof. The sledge-hammer that struck the gong was powered by the controlled fall of an old safe filled with sandbags, linked to the hammer by a complex set of pulleys. The hammer struck the gong every five minutes, and when the gong rang the entire city block reverberated with a sustained middle C. Gambit had scattered twenty or so bells throughout the city, set to ring according to a precise mathematical formula. Jax thought that the clash of notes sounded like nothing so much as distant explosions.

Jax came in from the street with her head aching from the constant clamor of the bells. In the basement room that served as headquarters the bells were muffled, but she could still hear them. She wondered what they sounded like in the general's rooms.

Danny-boy was studying a map that he had pinned to a wall. One hand was against the wall, propping him up. He smiled when he saw Jax, but his smile had a jittery look about it.

"They're getting worried," he said. "The soldiers are traveling in groups of two or three now."

"I know," said Jax.

"The general is mad and he's yelled at three men this morning so far. The guys that aren't dead yet don't trust the guys that are dead. They won't go on patrol with the dead ones."

"How do you know that?" She looked over his shoulder at the map and could make no sense of the marks he had made on it.

"Phone system," he said. "Wherever the lines are still up, The Machine can listen in on anything within earshot of a phone. There are still a few phones around." He turned from the map and put one arm around her shoulders. "Did you know that you're a ghost? You can make yourself invisible—that's how you manage to get so many men. And I'm some kind of god-hero too."

"We're starting to get to them."

Danny-boy nodded. "They seem to think we're immortal or invulnerable, since they still haven't shot or caught any of us."

"Yeah? Well, don't let them fool you into thinking the same thing. We've been real lucky so far."

"I thought that was skill," he said. He grinned, and for a moment he did not look as tired.

"Mostly luck. Those guys are good shots—I've seen them practicing. But the city spooks them, and they don't know where to aim." She shrugged. "All it will take is one stray shot, and someone on our side will be a casualty. Don't fool yourself."

"I know better," he said. "I know you aren't a ghost."

"Did you get any sleep last night?" she asked him.

He shrugged. "Not much. I went out with Catseye and Zatch. I wanted to keep an eye on Catseye."

"Get any sleep today?"

"A nap. It's hard to sleep with those bells going."

"Do you know how long it will take those damn things to run down?"

"Maybe a week," he said.

"Come on," she said, and she took his hand and led him away from the map down one flight of stairs to a room still deeper beneath the city. On the floor was a straw-tick mattress and a few blankets. She could still hear the bells, but they were a distant annoyance now. Danny-boy lay down beside her and put his arms around her. He was frowning.

"Something wrong?" she asked.

"Nothing new," he said.

"You worried now?"

He shrugged. "Just tired," he said. "That's all."

She kissed him and snuggled closer. "We'll be legendary," she said. "Now go to sleep."

She held him until he fell asleep in her arms.

The war went on.

Tiger, working alone in the war chemicals division, made three batches of a new kind of smoke bomb, one that released an hallucinogenic gas.

The Angel dropped a new set of leaflets: on one side was a picture of a group of pretty women; on the other side it said JOIN US.

Ralston began propaganda broadcasts through the system of loudspeakers left from the Summer Solstice Festival. Mama A, a blues singer with a rich contralto voice, was the main DJ. "Soldiers," she said in sweetly chiding tones. "Why do you keep fighting? There's no need for that, no need at all. Put down your rifles and come join us. We'd be glad to have you. Don't you understand that you're free men?" By the end of the second day of broadcasting, the soldiers had found all the speakers and destroyed them at the general's orders.

Jax, working with Zatch and Catseye, laid a trap near Mission Dolores Park. They made a convincingly gruesome open grave by dressing department store mannequins in army green, splashing them with red-brown paint, and tumbling them into a shallow trench. "Toss a little dirt on top," Catseye suggested. Zatch heaved a few shovelfuls of dirt over the dead mannequins, and Jax turned one dummy's head so that its eyes did not stare glassily skyward. The trench, which was left over from a fountain-building project abandoned in favor of the war, extended for about ten feet past the buried mannequins.

Jax stood over the grave. Her tranquilizer rifle was slung over one shoulder, the rifle taken from the soldier she had caught sketching over the other. "Looks convincing," she said.

Catseye waited in the tower of a nearby church. Jax and Zatch waited on the low rooftop of an old store, lying almost prone behind the high facade that faced the street. Jax lay her head on her arms and tried to relax. About ten of Gambit's bells were still ringing, but she had grown accustomed to their sound.

"You look tired," Zatch said. He folded his arms and rested them on the low facade. He was a burly man with strong hands and an unshakable confidence in himself.

She shrugged. "Everyone's tired," she said.

He nodded and kept an eye on the street. "Danny-boy's been looking bad."

"Yeah," she said, turning her head to stare at him. "And I'm sure the general is tired and the guys we're going to ambush are tired and you're tired." She shrugged. "Danny-boy's okay."

"There," Zatch said, pointing at Catseye's tower. Catseye was waving—a patrol was coming. He waved three times, indicating three men. Jax moved forward and came to a crouch just behind the high facade of the store. Zatch followed. Jax let the three soldiers pass the store, then fired a burst of bullets just behind them. They whirled and stopped in the center of the street. They could not see her.

"Drop your guns," Zatch said. His voice echoed and made his exact location impossible to pinpoint. The soldiers conferred, a small huddle of frightened young men. Jax could not hear what they were saying.

"Drop them," she said. "This is Jax and I'm getting impatient."

A thin youth with red hair was the first to place his rifle in the street, put his hands up, and back away. The other two followed. All three were marked DEAD.

Jax stood and covered the soldiers while Catseye climbed down from his tower, and he covered them while she and Zatch dropped to the street. "That way," she said, jerking her head down the street toward the park.

The redhead led the way, stumbling once or twice over potholes, walking awkwardly with his hands high. "Are we prisoners?" he asked over his shoulder.

"We don't take prisoners," Catseye said. He narrowed his black eyes and showed his teeth wolfishly. Jax frowned; she had warned him against overacting.

The redhead saw the grave at that moment. He stopped in the middle of the alley, his hands drooping from their position above his head. He turned, his mouth a little open, working as if to say words that did not come. "But," he said. "You don't . . ." He could not manage to say anything more. He looked at Jax, who was standing just behind Catseye. She held the rifle casually in the crook of her arm. The kid's gaze darted past her to Zatch, who stood just behind her holding a tranquilizer rifle. No escape.

"Stand over there," she said, jerking her head toward the open section of the trench.

"But you can't . . ." he was saying.

Catseye shoved him and he moved. The other two, both younger than the redhead, let themselves be pushed. They stood beside the open trench, looking to him for guidance, looking to Jax for sympathy. "Hands up," she said. "Now." Zatch fired with the tranquilizer gun.

The soldiers fell with maddening slowness into the pit. Jax stood over them as Zatch retrieved the darts. "They thought they'd had it," Jax said.

Zatch nodded and folded the soldiers' arms gently across their chests. He climbed out of the pit, and the three artists headed back for the city center.

A squad of poets staged a raid on the men guarding the jeeps. The Angel had dropped several of the new bombs in that area, and the men did not put up much of a fight. The poets labeled them with extremely short verses: DEAD by Fred; DEATH by Seth; KILL by Bill. The poets sustained one injury—a scat singer was hit in the arm by a ricocheting bullet and had to be patched by the medic.

The artists captured their first deserter that same day. The poets found a young man without a rifle wandering out by the ocean's edge at Land's End. They brought him back, and the artists established a halfway house for deserters at some distance from temporary headquarters. At that point temporary headquarters were in a warehouse building on the waterfront.

"Hey, General, your men are giving up on you," Jax said to the general via the Jaxdoll. "Don't you think you should leave our city soon? When are you going to give up?"

"I don't give up," said the general.

"Will you give up when your men leave you?"

"A few may leave. The others will not. They fear me too much." Jax could hear the general lean back in his chair. He sounded as if he were smiling. "One of my lieutenants thought he could leave me. That was in Los Angeles. I tracked him down and shot him in front of the others. My men don't leave me."

When Jax shut off the microphone, she found Danny-boy and persuaded him to take a break and have a cup of chicory tea with her. She wanted to talk to him about the general's unwillingness to give up, about a possible change in tactics. The artists continued to specialize in harassment and improvisational ambush. This strategy continued to be successful, but the fighters were beginning to show signs of strain.

A small kerosene stove had been set up in one of the ground floor offices. Jax and Danny-boy were waiting for the water to boil when Lily dragged in with two men. One man was limping; the others were smudged with soot. Lily, a slender wiry redhead, was frowning, and Jax could see the track of tears through the soot on her face.

"Hey, Lily," Jax called to her. Lily stopped in the doorway. "Is it that bad?" Jax asked.

Lily nodded. When she spoke, her voice was hoarse, tired. "We were over by the Golden Gate Bridge," she said, "just checking up on the guards there. The Angel was on patrol above us, and I was right near the approach to the bridge, down in the place that the brush has grown up." She spoke as if she had been going over this story in her mind, waiting to tell it to someone. "I saw these soldiers coming along the approach. Three of them. All painted DEAD. Young men, all of them. They didn't have any weapons." Her voice was getting softer and softer. "The bridge guards . . . the guards stopped them. It looked like the guards were telling them to go back. The three dead ones tried to push past the guards and there was a bit of a fight. One broke from it. He started running for the bridge." She pushed her hair back with a dirty hand, frowning and shaking her head. "The Angel dropped a smoke bomb—I think he was trying to spoil the guards' aim. I couldn't see clearly. But I think they shot that soldier. The other two escaped under cover of the smoke, I think. But that kid—I think they shot him." She was shaking her head wearily. "The rest of my squad was back farther; they didn't see anything—just caught some of the smoke. But I think that they shot that kid, one of their own."

"Maybe they figured that he wasn't one of theirs if he was wearing our mark," Jax said slowly. "And the general doesn't like deserters."

"You look like you could use some rest," Danny-boy said gently.

Lily nodded and went on past the doorway. Jax watched her go and wondered if one of the deserters was a thin redhead whose uniform was marked with dirt from an open grave. "We're going to have to kill the general," she said.

He nodded. "I think you're right."

"No," she said. "Not just label him dead. We have to kill him."

Danny-boy shook his head. "He just needs to know that we can get him."

"He won't scare," she said softly. "That won't work. Not with the general."

"Why are you so sure about that?"

"I understand him better than you do, Danny-boy," she said impatiently. "Believe me, he won't scare."

"Why don't we try it and see?" He leaned back in his chair and watched her face. "Can't we do that?"

"You haven't been out there much lately, have you?" Jax's hands were clenched on the table in front of her. "The general stays in the most heavily guarded area. And they use real bullets, remember?"

"I've been out there," he said softly. "I remember."

"Sometimes I think maybe you've forgotten," she said. "Or maybe you've started believing the stories that the soldiers are telling, maybe you believe I'm a ghost and you're a god."

He reached across the table and took one of her fists in his hands. "I don't believe that."

"You're having too good a time with this," she said. "You think it's a game. It isn't."

"I don't think it's a game."

"Then what the hell do you think? Why shouldn't we kill the general?"

He was looking down at his hands, frowning. "You've got to realize that violence and death aren't the only forces that can change the social order."

She shook her head, watching his face, started to speak, then just shook her head again. She wearily rested her head on her hands. "I don't have to realize that. I don't have to realize anything."

"We've started it this way," he said. "We have to keep going or it's all for nothing." He spoke as if he were trying to convince himself. "If we kill him, that doesn't end it. They'll just send another general next year. We need to make him run." He shrugged. "I'll go in after him."

"You wouldn't make it past the first sentry."

"I might surprise you."

"Yeah. You might make it all the way to the second sentry." She shook her head again. "I'll go. I'll help change the goddamn world. But I want you to know that I'm not doing it because I think it'll work. I'm doing it because you think it will work. Okay? And if he doesn't give up then, we'll have to change our tactics."

She turned away before he had time to argue.

The deserter was the soldier Jax had caught sketching. His name, Jax learned, was Jason.

"So," she said to him, "you've joined us. You still sketching?"

He nodded warily.

"Can I see what you've been doing lately?"

He handed her his notepad, and she flipped through the pages. On one page she found a sketch of her own face. She was grinning, and she wore a rifle slung over one shoulder. He had scrawled a title beneath the sketch—*Ghost Lady*.

"I'm not a ghost," Jax said.

He shrugged. "Maybe not," he admitted.

"Believe me. I'm not. In fact, I'm looking for a way to get into the general's quarters when he's asleep. And it can't involve walking through walls or becoming invisible."

He studied her face, chewing his lip. "You going to kill him?"

"I'll kill him the same way I killed you."

He shook his head, and his expression was grim. "You should really kill him. You can do it."

She studied his face and shrugged again. "Can you draw me a map of the sentry posts around his quarters?" she asked him.

He nodded and started drawing. His map was detailed and complete. He knew the time that the guards changed, and he advised her that the best time to attack was about three in the morning when the guards were tired. She listened carefully, took his map, and rolled it neatly.

"So you're not a ghost," he said then.

"Not yet," she said. "If this information is wrong, I may become one." And she ran away to kill the general.

Catseye and Zatch had volunteered to create a distraction at one edge of the area occupied by the army, using smoke grenades and fireworks. At two in the morning they waited with Jax, resting for a moment on the flat roof of a store about a half mile from downtown. Three of Gambit's bells were still ringing—a sweet high note, a deep bass note, and the middle C from the Buddhist gong.

"It'll be fine," Catseye said. Zatch looked tired, but Catseye was still cheerful. He was grinning, looking out toward City Hall. Only one of the neon lights of downtown still glowed—a red stripe that ran down the side of one building and corkscrewed up another. "You'll do great," he said to Jax.

She did all right. She went in through the alleys, then up the backside of the building.

The night was dark. No moon. The air was heavy with the smell of smoke. Jax caught the sentry on the roof from behind, labeled him DEAD, slung a rope down the side of the building, and climbed down to the general's window. She could hear shouting and muffled explosions in the distance, see the billowing smoke rising, but the street below her was quiet.

She let herself in quietly through the open window. The general was sleeping soundly, but she clapped a rag soaked in a concoction of Tiger's making over his mouth and nose. He struggled for a moment, then relaxed.

He looked older now than he had looked on the bridge. His gray hair was rumpled; his skin was slack and wrinkled. He frowned, even in his sleep.

With the red paint that had become her trademark, she labeled him DEAD and signed BY JAX on his cheek. Once, she heard the sentry at the door cough. In the distance she could hear gunfire. But that was all. She left through the window, climbed down the back of the house, and ran away through the alleys. The smell of smoke was strong.

Catseye and Zatch were late reaching the rendezvous point. Jax sat in the shadows in the corner of a rooftop, listening to the distant gunfire and wondering where they were. She heard them before she saw them. Zatch's voice was a soft, encouraging monologue. "Not much farther. Come on. Just a little bit farther. It'll be all right."

She met them halfway up the stairs and helped Zatch lower Catseye to sit on a step. Catseye's eyes were half-closed. By the dim light of her flashlight Jax could see how pale he was. The right leg of his jeans was soaked with blood. His thigh was wrapped in a crude bandage, made from Zatch's shirt. "He caught a bullet," Zatch said softly. "He caught it in the thigh. He's lost a lot of blood."

"Jax?" Catseye's voice was a whisper. She leaned over him and put a hand on his shoulder. She could feel him trembling. "Jax, I want to paint . . . I want to paint the battle we just fought. The colors—the colors were great." He stopped for breath. "Fireworks against the darkness. I want to paint that."

"We'll get you home," she said. "It'll be all right." She straightened up, her hand still on his shoulder. "Headquarters is only about a mile from here. I'll get help. You stay here with him." Zatch nodded. She hesitated for a moment, then took her jacket off and draped it over Catseye's shoulders. "We'll get you back," she said to him.

She ran away and she came back with Doc. She rode the white horse that Lily had captured on the first night of the war, galloping through the dark streets with Doc riding behind her and clinging to her waist. The streets were quiet; even the distant shouting had subsided. Dawn had touched the eastern sky with an angry red glow.

The stairwell was dark. "Zatch?" she said softly. She could hear him breathing in the darkness.

"I'm here," he said.

"Doc's here. How's Catseye?" She was climbing the stairs, hurrying toward him.

"Too late." Zatch was sitting on the stairs, his broad shoulders hunched forward, his head bowed. He looked up at her, and she could see the smudges of soot and blood on his face. "He died not long after you left. Nothing I could do. He just died."

Doc stood over Catseye's body. He lifted Jax's jacket from him and put it around Jax's shoulders. Only then did she realize that she was cold.

Jax took Catseye home on the back of the white horse. She walked with Doc and Zatch, leading the horse. At headquarters (temporarily located in an old apartment building), she left Doc to take care of the body and told Zatch to get some rest.

She found Danny-boy and The Machine in what had once been the recreation room. "The general wants to talk with you," Danny-boy said as she walked in the door. "He's been waiting for a while. We were starting to worry."

Jax took the microphone and pulled on the headphones. "Hello, General," she said. Her voice sounded very tired.

Through the headphones she heard a rustle of clothing as the general shifted position, the clink of a bottle against a glass, and the gurgle of liquor being poured. "I'd offer you a glass," he said. "But I think the gesture would be wasted."

Jax visualized the old man sitting in an easy chair in his room. She thought he might be wearing his jacket. He would be leaning forward a little, a glass cupped between his hands. Her lettering was on his forehead and cheek.

"When are you going to give up and pull out, General?" she asked him wearily. "Three quarters of your men are dead; the others are worried. You're a dead man yourself."

"I don't give up," he said. "I never have." His voice was slow and considering. "I don't know how." He paused, and she imagined he was taking a sip of whiskey. When he spoke, his voice was soft. "You realize that when I catch you, I'll have to kill you."

"Why?"

"To prove that you're just a woman, nothing more. My men think you are a ghost. Or a goddess. You're not a woman to them. You're a mystery to them, and they are beginning to fear you more than they fear me. So I'll have to kill you. I think you understand." She heard his chair creak as he leaned forward. "I think you know the need for blood and the need for fear. You understand that I must kill you."

"You won't catch me," she said.

"Ah," said the general. "You sound so sure. Perhaps you believe your own legend. Maybe you think that you are more than mortal." Jax said nothing. "My men once thought I was more than mortal." His voice was softer, a little blurred. Jax wondered how many drinks he had had. "They know now that I'm not. Now that they have seen this mark on my forehead. But even when they thought I was more than I am, I never made the mistake of believing the stories. I always remembered that I could be killed. You must always remember that." His voice was almost warm, the voice of an uncle giving advice to a nephew. "Remember that I can kill you."

"You won't catch me, General," she said. When she reached up to turn off the microphone, her hand was shaking. She stood slowly and walked over to where Danny-boy stood.

"We can't scare him," she said. "We have to kill him." Her hands would not stop shaking. Even when Danny-boy took her hands in his, she kept trembling. "I could have killed him last night. Then Catseye would have died for a reason."

His grip on her hands tightened, and she realized that he did not know about Catseye. "Catseye died in the raid last night," she said. "And the general's still alive." She did not know she was crying until Danny-boy reached up to brush a tear from her cheek. "If I had killed the general, then Catseye would be dead for a reason. As it is, he's just dead."

"He died for something," Danny-boy said. "He—"

She shook her head and freed her hand from his grasp. "No," she said. She stepped back from him. He watched her, his hands open at his sides.

"Jax," he said.

She shook her head, unwilling to listen. Danny-boy laid a hand on her arm as she started to walk away. "Where are you going?" he asked.

"I'm going to kill the general," she said, and she kept walking. She went to the door and was surprised to find Danny-boy still at her side. He put a hand on her shoulder, and she shrugged it off. He took her hand. She stepped back, jerked her hand out and up to break his grip. Her hands were in fists. "Don't get in the way, Danny," she said. "You grieve for Catseye your way. I'll do it mine. Don't get in the way." She turned from him and ran into the darkness.

It was morning, but the streets seemed very dark. The city smelled of smoke, and she could hear gunfire, always gunfire. The darkness around her seemed like the darkness of a dream, where some things are very clear and others are vague and ill formed, as if only half-imagined. She was very tired, and the shadows seemed to move in the empty streets. She ran through the alleys and climbed from rooftop to rooftop. She stopped when she saw a sentry in the street below, climbed down, and caught him from behind with a blow from her billy club. His face was very pale, a pale oval in the half-imagined darkness, and for a moment he looked like Catseye. He had the same dark curly hair, the same pointed chin. She hesitated, distracted, confused.

The man's replacement caught her from behind. His shouts brought a patrol, and the patrol took her prisoner. She was tired; she did not fight. She looked at them—five young men, three labeled DEAD—and shook her head slowly. They stood around her, keeping a respectful distance, holding their rifles ready. The man who searched her did it quickly, then stepped away. They were afraid, she knew. She was tired, but they feared her.

When she rubbed her forehead, her hand came away streaked

with blood. Her other hand ached. When she opened it, she found that she had gashed the palm. She had a vague memory of falling and catching herself with that hand, but she could not remember when or where. She rubbed at the cut, trying to rub some of the blood away, and she was surprised to feel pain. They marched her through the streets.

The soldiers took her directly to the general. She waited in the living room of the house, under guard, while a soldier went to fetch him. He came to the room quickly. His gray hair was rumpled, as if he had been asleep. His shirt was wrinkled, and one cuff was marked with a coffee stain. He looked tired. "So, you're Jax," he said. He stood with his hands locked behind his back. The word DEAD was still on his forehead. She stood in the center of the room, soldiers on both sides, and did not say anything.

He studied her for a moment. She stared back, her face carefully neutral. "Can you speak, Jax?" he said.

"I can."

"Make that, 'Yes sir.' "

She studied him for a moment and considered her options. It was a moment of decision. "Why?" she asked.

He studied her for a long moment. Still smiling, he reached out slapped her across the face. She did not dodge far enough to avoid the blow.

"You don't need to ask that. You're not stupid. You're not armed, and my soldiers are all around you. Say, 'Yes sir.' "

She considered him carefully. "Yes sir," she said.

"Good," he said. "Very good." He glanced at the soldier beside her. "She's unarmed?"

"Yes sir!"

"Very good. You and your patrol will be commended for this, soldier," the general said.

"Thank you, sir."

"Guard the door," he said.

The soldiers left, and the general still sat in the chair, his hands on the arms of the easy chair, studying Jax. His eyes were shrewd. She met his gaze and continued to consider her options. They were few and unacceptable. She could attempt to overpower him and die trying to escape. She could stay here and die.

"Sit down, Jax," said the general, waving a hand at a chair. "Would you like a drink?" He poured her a drink from the bottle on the coffee table without waiting for her reply.

She took it from him and sat down. "Thanks," she said cautiously.

"You're welcome, Jax." He smiled, amused. "You're very welcome indeed. I had been wondering when my luck would return. It seems it has." He swirled the drink in his glass. "Now, the question is: what should I do with you?"

"I thought," she said slowly, "that we talked about this once before."

He nodded slowly, obviously enjoying himself. "That's true; we did. But that was a different situation, wasn't it? You would never have said 'Yes sir' then."

"True." She sipped the drink. It was whiskey; not good whiskey. She winced a little when it touched a cut on her lip.

"Make that 'Yes sir,' " he said.

"The soldiers aren't here," she said. "Why put on a show?"

He studied her and his grin broadened. "Perhaps for my private amusement?"

"General, if you're going to kill me, then I'd rather not amuse you first." His grin had penetrated her weariness. "If you're not going to kill me, then we have something to talk about." She knew that he could order the soldiers back to beat her, and in that moment she did not care.

He laughed and slammed his left hand against the arm of the chair. "By God, I like you. So angry, so arrogant. But I may kill you anyway." Still smiling, he studied her. "However, if you pledge your allegiance to me, I might not."

She kept her face still, hiding her surprise. How strange, she thought, how very strange. An option she had not considered.

"I need to know some things," he said. "For example, where are your headquarters?" He sipped his drink. "That would do for a start."

"Headquarters? That changes from day to day." She sipped her drink and tried to think of a way to turn this option into a way to survive.

"Yes, and where were they last?" He watched her face. She did not speak. "I am waiting, Jax."

She shrugged. "They'll be changed by now. Yesterday, they were in the Garden of Eden, a club on Broadway. By now . . ." She shrugged again. "You see, General—that's the beauty of this way of fighting a war. We're guerilla fighters on our own land. Temporary headquarters can be just about anywhere. We carry our weapons with us." She watched him over the drink. "So even if I told you all I know, you'd learn nothing of value."

"I could torture you until you'd willingly answer all my questions." He leaned back in the chair, studying her. "I won't do that. I think you're right—the information you gave me would be useless by the time we pried it loose. I could hold you for ransom. I wonder what you would be worth to them." He rubbed his chin thoughtfully. "Or I could persuade you to work for me. I would prefer to keep you as you are—a ghost on a white horse." He grinned. "But I want that ghost working for me."

She took another sip of the drink. "If I said yes, what would you want me to do?"

"If you say yes, I will assemble the troops and you will surrender to me publicly and vow allegiance to me. If you say no, we will have a public execution," he said. "A hanging on the steps of City Hall."

She liked living. She sipped the drink, and even the bad whiskey tasted good. The room was filled with a silence that made her back feel cold and unprotected. Far away, muffled by the walls, she could hear one of Gambit's bells ringing, but the sound did not touch the silence in the room. What difference would it make if she pledged her loyalty to the general? None. It would mean nothing. The words would just be words, words like "Yes sir." She liked living. She swirled the bad whiskey in her glass. Danny-boy would say the words were symbols. They were fighting a war of symbols. Danny-boy was crazy. He was wrong. She liked living.

"Hanging, I think, is one of the most dramatic ways to execute a prisoner," the general said. "It's really ideal. There's the anticipation while the stage is set—the men build the scaffold in a central place and everyone watches it take form. There is the execution itself—the moment of silence when the prisoner is led forth, the touching ceremony when the blindfold is offered, when the noose is adjusted around the prisoner's neck. Then the sudden crack when the trapdoor drops open and the moment of heart-stopping pathos when the prisoner dances in the air, struggling against death, but losing. And then, the memory lingers. The shadow of the scaffold stretches across the plaza, a constant reminder of death. I'll leave the scaffold in place until the war is over." He nodded, satisfied with his plans. "Most dramatic," he said. "Most effective." He smiled and sipped his drink. "You could learn a little about dramatic staging, you know. That business about painting my forehead . . ." He touched the mark, acknowledging it for the first time. "That would have been much more effective if you had arranged for a witness, even one witness. I plan to arrange for a full audience for you."

"I should have killed you that night," Jax said with sudden passion. "I could have."

"You would have done more good for your cause by wounding me in public than killing me in private. If you had killed me, you would stage your show for an audience of one—the soldier who found my body. You have to plan these things better. For you I plan a grand spectacle." He shrugged easily, leaned forward, and filled her glass again. "In some ways, you have disappointed me. You don't take this art business far enough," he said. He sipped the whiskey and nodded slowly. "You take the easy way. You don't risk enough."

She was alert now, awake and glaring at him over her drink. "What the hell do you know about it?"

"I know that you draw foolish lines. You are willing to die for art, but you aren't willing to kill for it." He leaned forward to rest his elbows on his knees. "A good death can be a work of art. So can a good execution. You should learn by my example."

She finished her drink. "I don't believe I'll have a chance," she said coldly.

He nodded and smiled pleasantly. "True enough," he said. "You'll die tomorrow."

That night she dreamed of dark rooftops and dark streets. She rode on a white horse, and the general rode beside her. Somehow, in the dream, she did not know if she was fighting with the general or against him. As they rode, the general kept lecturing her about the nature of art and death until she wanted to scream. She dreamed of darkness and the smell of smoke. She dreamed that Danny-boy was with her, there in the room. "I guess I'm going to die," she said to him. He handed her a red rose and smiled. "Do you know how to tell if a work is art?" he asked her calmly. In the early days of their relationship, they had talked endlessly about the nature of art. "True art changes the artist. The artist puts something into the work and he changes. That's how you tell." He handed her a red rose, and he vanished in the smoke.

She woke to a rhythmic pounding, like the hoofbeats of running horses. In the thin light of dawn, hammers pounded as soldiers built the scaffold where she would die.

She went with the soldiers willingly when they came to take her. She saw no point to struggling. Not now. The plaza was quiet. She walked through the center of the open space to the City Hall, through the ranks of soldiers. They stood quietly at attention. She saw some she thought she recognized—the sentry she had marked on that first evening, the soldier who reminded her of Catseye. So many; so young. She was glad she had not killed them.

The sun shone dimly through the haze of smoke and morning fog. She could feel the morning breeze on her face. The bright banners flew over the plaza, snapping in the wind. They were smudged with smoke, a little tattered. Even so, they were a fine, brave sight. The city was a beautiful place, she thought, such a beautiful place.

The general waited for her at the scaffold. "You can still change your mind," he said softly. "I can use you."

She turned to look at him. Strangely, she did not hate him. He seemed smaller now than he had on the bridge. She had seen the coffee stain on his cuff, seen his face when it was relaxed in sleep, listened to him slur his words when he was drinking. She did not hate him.

She shook her head quickly once. She did not speak. She climbed the crudely made steps to stand on the wooden platform and looked out over the soldiers.

The general bound her hands behind her. He offered her a blindfold, but she refused. She wanted to watch the banners fly over the gathered soldiers. As she watched, a man in the front ranks crossed himself.

The general put a rope around her neck and adjusted the knot. He stood beside her, his hand raised, ready to signal the man who would pull the rope to release the trap door and kill her.

She saw a movement on the top of the old Library Building on the far side of the plaza. She heard the sound of a single rifle shot. She saw a blossom of blood on the general's forehead; he swayed a moment, then fell. The stiffness went out of him as he fell; he crumbled, folded. His body struck the steps and rolled down. Rolled more like a sack of old clothes than like a man.

Jax looked up in time to see the assassin. Danny-boy stood above the crowd on the edge of the old Library's facade. His red hair was bright in the morning sun. The light glinted on the barrel of the rifle. She could not see his expression, not at that distance. For an instant the world seemed frozen. The colored banners stood still; the smell of smoke hovered in the air.

One soldier fired quickly, and Danny-boy started to fall. He fell against a stone carving on the Library's facade, clung for a moment, then fell. She watched from so far away, unable to move. The soldiers moved—some to the general's body, some to surround her, some raising their rifles to fire at Danny-boy now that he had fallen.

"Gentlemen." The Machine's calm voice boomed from a speaker, hidden somewhere. "The plaza where you stand was planted with explosives before your arrival. The charges are wired to explode at my signal." It was a lie, Jax knew. But it was a well-told lie, and the soldiers believed that the artists were capable of anything. The plaza was suddenly silent again. "We will sacrifice Jax if that should be necessary. We will welcome those of you who wish to join us peacefully, and escort the others over the bridge. No one will be hurt. Please put down your weapons. Now." The last word was delivered with uncharacteristic force.

The soldier who shot Danny-boy was the first to put down his gun. The plaza was quiet. Danny-boy lay where he had fallen. His head lolled back, and the hole in his chest was a deep rich red.

The general lay tumbled at the bottom of the steps. The hole in his forehead was the same rich red as the hole in Danny-boy.

Jax stood on the scaffold. The soldiers laid their weapons at her feet, then backed away, as if frightened. She stood, swaying a little, her hands still bound behind her. The numbness was gone, and her head was starting to ache. "Well," she said to the soldiers. "Who won?" She looked at Danny-boy and looked at the general. "They're both dead, so who won?" She stopped for a moment, looking across the plaza. "A good death," she said to no one in particular, "is a work of art." She started to laugh, but the sound caught in her throat.

The banners fluttered and snapped in the morning breeze. The clip-clop of hooves on pavement echoed across the plaza. The Machine rode the white horse through the open space. He stopped in front of her, and she studied him for a minute, wondering if he was part of the long dream from which she was emerging.

The Machine swung his leg over the horse's back and slid to the ground. When he untied her, she smiled at him with unaccustomed sweetness. "It's over," she said. And then her knees gave

way beneath her, and she sat on the edge of the scaffold. She took
his hand and held it warm in hers, and they sat on the wooden
platform and watched the banners fly in the wind.

She looked over at the general. Through the blood on his forehead and cheeks she could still read the words BY JAX. She looked
out at the flying banners and the white horse. The horse's harness
rattled when it moved its head, searching for a few blades of grass
on the trampled earth. Most of the grass had been pounded into
the ground by soldiers' feet. Little was left.

Other artists had come. They were moving through the crowd
of soldiers, dividing them into groups—men who would stay, men
who would leave.

Jax shivered and The Machine took off his jacket and draped it
over her shoulders. "We spent last night talking about it," The
Machine said. "Zatch volunteered, but Danny-boy insisted that he
would be the one."

Jax watched the soldiers milling about the open space. The
smoke hung in the blue sky, and the tattered banners fluttered
bravely. The white horse cropped the trampled grass. She would
paint this someday. Someday she would paint Catseye huddled in
the darkness at the top of a long stairway. She would paint a
portrait of the general sitting in an easy chair, with an empty
whiskey bottle at his elbow and the word DEAD written on his
forehead. She would paint Danny-boy and the general on the steps
of City Hall, leaning against each other, stained with blood that
was the same rich shade of red.

Later she would paint. Now she would look at the city with new
eyes and wait for the smoke to clear and the blood to wash away in
the winter rains.

Here's another story about future advances in medicine and the effect on individual human beings. In everything other than that broad description, however, "Interlocking Pieces" is totally different from the Sharon Farber story presented earlier in this book.

Molly Gloss was born in Portland, Oregon, and lives there still, with her husband, son, and niece. She graduated from Portland State University, worked as a grade-school teacher, and has recently turned to writing. Her only previous publication was in a small literary magazine, so the present story will introduce her to the wider science fiction readership. You'll want to look for her byline again.

INTERLOCKING PIECES

MOLLY GLOSS

For Teo, there was never a question of abandoning the effort. After the last refusal—the East European Minister of Health sent her his personal explanation and regrets—it became a matter of patience and readiness and rather careful timing.

A uniformed policeman had been posted beside her door for reasons, apparently, of protocol. At eight-thirty, when he went down the corridor to the public lavatory, Teo was dressed and waiting, and she walked out past the nurses' station. It stood empty. The robo-nurse was still making the eight-o'clock rounds of the wing's seventy or eighty rooms. The organic nurse, just come on duty, was leaning over the vid displays in the alcove behind the station, familiarizing herself with the day's new admissions.

Because it was the nearest point of escape, Teo used the staircase. But the complex skill of descending stairs had lately deserted her, so she stepped down like a child, one leg at a time, grimly clutching the metal bannister with both hands. After a couple of floors she went in again to find a public data terminal in a ward that was too busy to notice her.

They had not told her even the donor's name, and a straightforward computer request met a built-in resistance: DATA

RESTRICTED***KEY IN PHYSICIAN IDENT CODE. So she asked the machine for the names of organ donors on contract with the regional Ministry of Health, then a list of the hospital's terminal patients, the causes and projected times of their deaths, and the postmortem neurosurgeries scheduled for the next morning. And, finally, the names of patients about whom information was media-restricted. Teo's own name appeared on the last list. She should have been ready for that but found she was not, and she sat staring until the letters grew unfamiliar, assumed strange juxtapositions, became detached and meaningless—the name of a stranger.

The computer scanned and compared the lists for her, extrapolated from the known data, and delivered only one name. She did not ask for hard copy. She looked at the vid display a moment, maybe longer than a moment, and then punched it off and sat staring at the blank screen.

Perhaps not consciously, she had expected a woman. The name, a man's name, threw her off balance a little. She would have liked a little time to get used to the sound of it, the sound it made in her head and on her lips. She would have liked to know the name before she knew the man. But he would be dead in the morning. So she spoke it once, only once. Out loud. With exactness and with care. "Dhavir Stahl," she said. And then went to a pneumo-tube and rode up.

In the tube there were at first several others, finally only one. Not European, perhaps North African, a man with eyebrows in a thick straight line across a beetled brow. He watched her sidelong —clearly recognized her—and he wore a physician's ID badge. In a workplace as large as this one the rumor apparatus would be well established. He would know of her admission, maybe even the surgery that had been scheduled. Would, at the very least, see the incongruity of a VIP patient, street-dressed and unaccompanied, riding up in the public pneumo-tube. So Teo stood imperiously beside him with hands cupped together behind her back and eyes focused on the smooth center seam of the door while she waited for him to speak, or not. When the tube opened at the seventy-eighth floor he started out, then half turned toward her, made a stiff little bow, and said, "Good health, Madame Minister," and finally exited. If he reported straightaway to security, she might have five minutes, or ten, before they reasoned out where she had gone. And standing alone now in the pneumo-tube, she began to feel the first sour leaking of despair—what could be said, learned, shared in that little time?

There was a vid map beside the portal on the ninety-first floor. She searched it until she found the room and the straightest route, then went deliberately down the endless corridors, past the little tableaux of sickness framed where a door here or there stood open, and finally to Stahl's door, closed, where there was no special feel of death, only the numbered code posted alongside the name to denote a life that was ending.

She would have waited. She wanted to wait, to gather up a few dangling threads, reweave a place or two that had lately worn through. But the physician in the pneumo-tube had stolen that possibility. So she took in a thin new breath and touched one thumb to the admit disk. The door hushed aside, waited for her, closed behind her. She stood just inside, stood very straight, with her hands open beside her thighs.

The man whose name was Dhavir Stahl was fitting together the pieces of a masters-level holoplex, sitting cross-legged, bare-kneed, on his bed, with the scaffolding of the puzzle in front of him on the bed table and its thousands of tiny elements jumbled around him on the sheets. He looked at Teo from under the ledge of his eyebrows while he worked. He had that vaguely anxious quality all East Europeans seem to carry about their eyes. But his mouth was good, a wide mouth with creases lapping around its corners, showing the places where his smile would fit. And he worked silently, patiently.

"I . . . would speak with you," Teo said.

He was tolerant, even faintly apologetic. "Did you look at the file, or just the door code? I've already turned down offers from a priest and a psychiatrist and, this morning, from somebody in narcotics. I just don't seem to need any deathbed comforting."

"I am Teo."

"What is that? One of the research divisions?"

"My name."

His mouth moved, a near smile, perhaps embarrassment.

"They hadn't told you my name, then."

And finally he took it in. His face seemed to tighten, all of it pulling back toward his scalp as the skin shrinks from the skull of a corpse, so that his mouth was too wide and there was no space for smiling. Or too much.

"They . . . seem to have a good many arbitrary rules," Teo

said. "They refused me this meeting, your name even. And you mine, it appears. I could not—I had a need to know."

She waited raggedly through a very long silence. Her palms were faintly damp, but she continued to hold them open beside her legs. Finally Dhavir Stahl moved, straightened a little, perhaps took a breath. But his eyes stayed with Teo.

"You look healthy," he said. It seemed a question.

She made a slight gesture with one shoulder, a sort of shrugging off. "I have . . . lost a couple of motor skills." And in a moment, because he continued to wait, she added, "The cerebellum is evidently quite diseased. They first told me I would die. Then they said no, maybe not, and they sent me here. 'The state of the art,' or something to that effect."

He had not moved his eyes from her. One of his hands lightly touched the framework of the puzzle as a blind man would touch a new face, but he never took his eyes from Teo. Finally she could not bear that, and her own eyes skipped out to the window and the dark sheets of rain flapping beneath the overcast.

"You are . . . not what I expected," he said. When her eyes came round to him again, he made that near smile and forced air from his mouth—not a laugh, a hard sound of bleak amusement. "Don't ask! God, I don't know what I expected." He let go the puzzle and looked away finally, looked down at his hands, then out to the blank vid screen on the wall, the aseptic toilet in the corner. When he lifted his face to her again, his eyes were very dark, very bright. She thought he might weep, or that she would. But he said only, "You are Asian." He was not quite asking it.

"Yes."

"Pakistani?"

"Nepalese."

He nodded without surprise or interest. "Do you climb?"

She lifted her shoulders again, shrugging. "We are not all Sherpa bearers," she said with a prickly edge of impatience. There was no change at his mouth, but he fell silent and looked away from her. Belatedly she felt she might have shown more tolerance. Her head began to ache a little from a point at the base of the skull. She would have liked to knead the muscles along her shoulders. But she waited, standing erect and stiff and dismal, with her hands hanging, while the time they had went away quickly and ill used.

Finally Dhavir Stahl raised his arms, made a loose, meaningless gesture in the air, then combed back his hair with the fingers of both hands. His hair and his hands seemed very fine. "Why did you come?" he said, and his eyelashes drew closed, shielding him as he spoke.

There were answers that would have hurt him again. She sorted through for one that would not. "To befriend you," she said, and saw his eyes open slowly. In a moment he sighed. It was a small sound, dry and sliding, the sound a bare foot makes in sand. He looked at the puzzle, touched an element lying loose on the bed, turned it round with a fingertip. And round.

Without looking toward her, he said, "Their computer has me dead at four-oh-seven-fourteen. They've told you that, I guess. There's a two percent chance of miscalculation. Two or three, I forget. So anyway, by four-thirty—" His mouth was drawn out thin.

"They would have given you another artificial heart."

He lifted his face, nearly smiled again. "They told you that? Yes. Another one. I wore out my own and one of theirs." He did not explain or justify. He simply raised his shoulders, perhaps shrugging, and said, "That's enough." He was looking toward her, but his eyes saw only inward. She waited for him. Finally he stirred, turned his hands palms up, studied them.

"Did they—I wasn't expecting a woman. Men and women move differently. I didn't think they'd give a man's cerebellum to a woman." He glanced at Teo, at her body. "And you're small. I'm, what, twenty kilos heavier, half a meter taller? I'd think you'd have some trouble getting used to . . . the way I move. Or anyway the way my brain tells my body to move." He was already looking at his hands again, rubbing them against one another with a slight papery sound.

"They told me I would adapt to it," Teo said. "Or the . . . new cerebellum could be retaught."

His eyes skipped up to her as if she had startled or frightened him. His mouth moved too, sliding out wide to show the sharp edge of his teeth. "They didn't tell me that," he said from a rigid grin.

It was a moment before she was able to find a reason for his agitation. "It won't—They said it wouldn't . . . reduce the donor's . . . sense of self."

After a while, after quite a while, he said, "What word did they use? They wouldn't have said 'reduce.' Maybe 'correct' or 'edit out.' " His eyes slid sideways, away from her, then back again. His

mouth was still tight, grimacing, shaping a smile that wasn't there.
"They were at least frank about it. They said the cerebellum only
runs the automatic motor functions, the skilled body movements.
They said they would have expected—no, they said they would
have liked—a transplanted cerebellum to be mechanical. A part,
like a lung or a kidney. The 'mind' ought to be all in the forebrain.
They told me there wouldn't be any donor consciousness, none at
all, if they could figure out how to stop it."

In the silence after, as if speaking had dressed the wound, his
mouth began to heal. In a moment he was able to drop his eyes
from Teo. He sat with his long, narrow hands cupped on his knees
and stared at the scaffolding of his puzzle. She could hear his
breath sliding in and out, a contained and careful sound. Finally he
selected an element from among the thousands around him on the
bed, turned it solemnly in his hands, turned it again, then reached
to fit it into the puzzle, deftly finding a place for it among the
multitude of interlocking pieces. He did not look at Teo. But in a
moment he said, "You don't look scared. I'd be scared if they were
putting bits of somebody else inside my head." He slurred the
words a little at the end and jumped his eyes white-edged to Teo.

She made a motion to open her hands, to shrug, but then, irre-
sistibly, turned her palms in, chafed them harshly against her
pants legs. She chose a word from among several possible. "Yes,"
she said. And felt it was she who now wore the armored faceplate
with its stiff and fearful grin.

Dhavir's eyes came up to her again with something like surprise,
and certainly with tenderness. And then Teo felt the door behind
her, its cushioned quiet sliding sideways, and there were three
security people there, diminishing the size of the room with their
small crowd, their turbulence. The first one extended her hand
but did not quite touch Teo's arm. "Minister Teo," she said. Formal. Irritated.

Dhavir seemed not to register the address. Maybe he would
remember it later, maybe not, and Teo thought probably it
wouldn't matter. They watched each other silently, Teo standing
carefully erect with her hands, the hands that no longer brushed
teeth nor wrote cursive script, the hands she had learned to dis-
trust, hanging open beside her thighs, and Dhavir sitting cross-
legged amid his puzzle, with his forearms resting across those frail,
naked knees. Teo waited. The security person touched her elbow,
drew her firmly toward the door, and then finally Dhavir spoke

her name. "Teo," he said. And she pulled her arm free, turned to stand on the door threshold, facing him.

"I run lopsided," he said, as if he apologized for more than that. "I throw my heels out or something." There were creases beside his mouth and his eyes, but he did not smile.

In a moment, with infinite, excruciating care, Teo opened her hands palms outward, lifted them in a gesture of dismissal. "I believe I can live with that," she said.

Here's a most unusual story about the effects of science on people . . . but it isn't exactly about technology or even scientific theories in the familiar sense. Carter Scholz writes, "I think it's too bad that the mainstream takes so little interest in the philosophy of science, and that science fiction puts such stress on its speculative and technological aspects." He takes a giant step in the former direction in this thoughtful and thought-provoking story.

Carter Scholz's stories have appeared in Orbit, New Dimensions, Fantasy and Science Fiction, *and* Isaac Asimov's Science Fiction Magazine, *in addition to* Universe. *His novelette in* Universe 7, *"The Ninth Symphony of Ludwig van Beethoven and Other Lost Songs," was nominated for both the Hugo and Nebula Awards, and he was a nominee for the John W. Campbell Award as Best New Writer. His first novel,* Palimpsests, *written in collaboration with Glenn Harcourt, was recently published as an Ace Science Fiction Special.*

THE MENAGERIE OF BABEL

CARTER SCHOLZ

I was living then in a cottage behind a large house in the hills of Berkeley, California. I had taken it because the rent would let my money last three months. I could have had the basement for less, but when I saw it I balked—it was a tomb. Half the floor was dirt, the other half unsteady wormed boards. Through one glaucous window fell the light of a Manhattan air shaft at dawn. I knew my asceticism was not equal to it. And I wanted at most three months. So I took the cottage, one room twenty feet on a side, with a patchy roof and without electricity or plumbing. As it turned out I was there only a month.

My landlord lived in the main house. He was a law-school dropout with an overbearing manner, which collapsed the moment I resisted it. Then he was almost unctuous. His name was Peter Fraser. He told me he paid six hundred a month for the house, and I guessed that because of his erratic manner he had a struggle to fill it. In a week the competition for housing would be fierce, and he could have named his price to a desperate student. But he chose to take my cash. We smoked a joint on it, and between lies I told him some harmless truths about myself. My luck was running well then in areas I did not care about.

Berkeley was neutral ground for me. I had come to the far edge of the country for some peace. When asked on my trip out, I would say I meant to finish my degree; I had quit Harvard that summer and had spent some time cleaning lab glass at Woods Hole. Yet, once underway, I took every chance to prolong the trip. I arrived in late August, ahead of the returning students, but too late to register for classes. On my last ride south from Eugene, I woke from the shallow dreams peculiar to travel to see the mud flats of Albany and, across the gunmetal bay, San Francisco, vague in smog. I knew then that all my intentions had just been stories. I had left the East because there were decisions I did not want to make.

So I have no right to judge Murphy. At every crux of choice stands an angel offering counsel, and only after you have chosen and passed do you see his other face, that of a demon, taunting, vilifying, and forbidding return. Glimpse this face once, and you live on a rack of indecision. My choice now was to live out the folly I had started or to run the gauntlet of retreat.

Murphy had no such crises. He was an idiot. I choose the word with care, for its root sense—I mean his mind was unlike any I had known, unique almost to the point of insanity. I do not mean to judge, only to describe him.

The day after I moved in I met him in the backyard. His drawing pad was set on an aluminum easel, and he studied it obsessively as he worked, not looking up but occasionally jerking his head nervously to one side. He was shirtless, and I had never seen anyone so thin. I judged him to be two years younger than I. In his left hand was a mechanical pen, which he shook every so often. I was not really interested, I was seeking isolation. But I had already stepped out of the cottage when I saw him, and by the excessive politeness I indulged to combat my diffidence I was obliged at least to say hello.

His drawing was a dense, precise nature study. I took it for a sea urchin until I looked past the easel and saw a withered sunflower twenty feet away. Perhaps it was the vivid contrast of sunlight and black ink that struck me. The sunflower might have been on the moon, the way he drew it.

After a minute he capped his pen and invited me inside. He had the crowning cupola of the house for his room, and it was crowded with drawings, all with the same stunning, changeable quality. One was clearly of a horseshoe crab, but I glanced at it repeatedly, expecting some transformation. Others were of cacti. He had twenty or thirty plants and watered them as I studied his drawings. Several cacti sat in a terrarium, which seemed otherwise empty. But as I looked I saw twitches of motion—a head, a dun tail, flashed on the dirt. I started to say something about the drawings when he interrupted.

—I love these, he said, reaching to touch a cactus spine. —Do you know why? Look at them. They know the secret. Life is a drug. We'll turn ourselves into anything to have it.

I looked again at the drawings, and all at once they were morbid. It occurred to me that Murphy would make a master pornographer, so strong was the sense of death in his drawings of life. Around the edge of each object, tossed onto the dead white shore of paper by an unknowable sea, was an intense, obliterating negative space. Every line battled this void. The overdrawn precision was claustrophobic.

He lifted his finger from the spine and pressed it to his mouth. —Why so many? So many types? Who can explain it?

Like a good graduate student, I begin to answer by Darwinian rote, but his faint sardonic smile forced me to my more authentic, less scientific belief: the world was a plenum. The wonder of it had shaped my life. His innocent question, if it was that, was the one thing he could have said to draw me from my politic silence into a study of him.

On occasion Murphy took his drawings to Telegraph Avenue for sale. One afternoon I went with him, because the route crossed the campus and I wanted a look. If the place became real to me, I might be moved to act. I also needed to buy an oil lamp. And I wondered how real Murphy's business connection was. I had the idea his life was an elaborate fantasy. I had nothing against this— certainly my own life was phantasmal and seemed at times a slow but definite form of ritual suicide—but if I was to know him I would feel more secure knowing the habits of his delusion.

My paranoia was not unfounded. The rhythms of the main house were so erratic as to be mystifying. Since dinners were communal, I gained a quick introduction to the seven tenants. One played bass for a band perpetually and tediously about to get work. One studied midwifery. One proofread for a Buddhist press. One couple seemed to do nothing but drift in and out, vanishing sometimes for days. Once I came back from a walk to find them studying my cottage through its one window; they did not return my greeting. Their eyes were like oil.

My landlord liked to complain to me, as if thereby forming an alliance, and confided that he was owed over a thousand dollars in back rent; yet he was not indigent, and as far as I could see had no other income. He went out in his battered Karmann-Ghia only for tennis and movies. His way of life at least had an easy explanation; I found out he had a trust fund and sold drugs. But the overall logic of the house was that of a dream. Its structure was a holdover, or recapitulation, of the communes of the sixties, with the difference that I had more privacy than if I had lived alone. A nearly pathological avoidance of questions ruled the dinner conversation. I could have said I was a Nobel laureate and drawn no comment.

Murphy and I crossed campus. I did not like it. Architecturally it was American, which is to say a hodgepodge. Beaux-arts styles had been lifted and laid with the care of a rich parvenu moving a castle across the ocean stone by stone. The buildings declared that culture could be bought, transported, and legitimated in a new context. To stare at them too long invited dislocation; the classical style was subtly wrong, the air too raw, the flora too luxuriant and primitive. A controlled hysteria, very like the defensive edges of Murphy's drawings, made a thin halo around the pale granite and red-tiled roofs to hold back the corrosive blue sky.

I picked up an application anyway. Girls passed, slit skirts swinging, on the plaza that thirteen years before had been flooded with tear gas and riot police. Two corner prophets, not yet extinguished by the natural selection of social history, hung on the edge of campus, one reading scripture from file cards, the other preaching a philosphy of hate, their voices oddly twinned. Undergraduates crowded the Avenue, clutching parcels. And I saw that here was a sinking of history, a twisting of time, unlike anything I had seen in the East. I was not badly matched, in my motives of denial and escape, to this place of lost connections and vanished history.

Murphy's connection was real enough. He was a street vendor

with a long folding table in front of the Bank of America. He
accepted the rolled sheaf of drawings and shook his head.

—My man, why don't you get yourself a matte knife? Now I
have to take these to the frame place, and you know it comes out of
your money.

Murphy shrugged. The vendor counted off several twenty-dollar bills and pushed them across the table. He left his hand on top.

—Listen, you want some coke?

Murphy said no.

—All right. The hand came off the bills. The vendor smiled.
—But don't tell me you do this stuff straight. Take it in trade
sometime, okay? You're giving me cash-flow problems.

From here Murphy crossed to a bookstore with an Indian name.
He circled the shelves deliberately, pulled down six or seven books
without examination, and laid them on the counter. I read the title
on top.

—Bergson? Jesus, I read him when I was seventeen, and I
thought he was flaky then.

I knew I was being a swine. The Harvard habit dies hard. For
apology I was going to broaden my comment into self-parody, but
as the cashier went through the rest of the titles, I was silenced.
Flying saucers. Gods. Magic.

—It's bull, said Murphy pleasantly. —But it's also true.

So I learned by the way that he had a fear of words. He would
scruple to use certain common phrases, as if in dread of what they
might call up, whereas I tended to be profane, as if a dare to
scatology or blasphemy might keep the named thing at bay.

—I'm sorry, I said. —I shouldn't criticize. It's just my god-
damned training talking.

—Oh, I knew you were a biologist.

—*What?* How? How did you know? I felt violated. This secret
had been easy enough to keep at the dinner table.

—By the way your eye traveled over my drawings.

I did not believe he had seen this. I could not. Yet somehow he
had known.

—You see, when you look at things . . . He seemed suddenly
panic-stricken at the crowds. —Do you mind if we take the long
way home?

We followed a road up past a stadium and some practice fields
and into the hills. We were entering a botanical garden when I
heard an insistent shrieking.

—What's that?

—Dogs. The university has labs up here.

We toured the garden. Murphy stopped by a large cactus and broke off a lobe. Gingerly he slid it into his shirt pocket. We went on past succulents, camellias, rhododendrons, eucalypti, sage, manzanita, and we stopped in a stand of sequoia, the ground thick with ferns. My sense of time suffered a shift: in these plants, in the shape of these hills, was a vast sense of a young Earth. Everything here looked prehistoric. Cars took the curves below us dreamily, carapaces gleaming.

Murphy picked a cone from the ground and looked at it curiously.

—They won't grow . . . unless there's been a fire. He said this with wonder, as if he had just discerned it. He turned to me. —You see, if you look at things, after a while something emerges, you find that, that things want to change into other things. And you can draw that, you can see what they were or want to be. And in, in people too.

—In people?

He looked at me. —For example, you want to be dead.

I stood appalled. And then I laughed. —Murphy, you're an idiot.

—You mean that I can't speak, I don't know how to communicate with others. That's so. But you see it's a, a ceding of self to be understood.

Now I was agitated. It was not just my vanity. True, I prized observation as the first skill of a good biologist, and I thought myself that; and now an amateur was outclassing me at my one pride. But it was also that he did not know how to talk to people, that he was picking at my wounds, and by not ceding an atom of his self he was taking mine. For I had long behaved as if sheer observation could give answer, as if a complete description contained an inevitable and correct course of action in its terms—and how wrong I had been, how much I had lost by it, I could still not confess.

—Do you know much about genetics? he asked abruptly.

—No one does. They all pretend.

—I read a story. It was about books, a library made of all the combinations of letters . . .

—Permutations, yes. The library of Babel.

—You know it? It exists?

—Murphy, it's a story. An intellectual fantasy.

—Yes, but DNA is like letters of the alphabet, and, and if you rearrange them . . .

—You could have a menagerie of Babel.

—Yes. Yes, that's right.

—No, it's not right. DNA is not like letters. There are laws . . . And I stopped. For I realized that this was indeed the premise of Darwin's theory—that, as Julian Huxley said, "Given sufficient time anything at all will turn up" from this promiscuous shuffling of genes—and I realized also, hardly for the first time, that the theory was therefore as fantastic as any of Murphy's, acceptable to scientists only because it fit the historical form of their method. What were those laws, which could give this opening of all possibility a human meaning? No one could say. The function of DNA is to copy itself. Yet it does not, not exactly. There are sports and mutants. So life diversifies—not, we must believe, aimlessly—but we are unable, I think reluctant, to learn the laws. If we knew them, it would change us.

—This was my work, I confessed. —I majored in genetics.

—But you quit.

—I was eased out.

—You let them? But this is important! This is my work, too.

—What do you mean?

—I draw only to learn. If you draw things, using always the same kinds of lines, you can learn about . . . growth. My books help, they don't all use the same methods, but I can see that they're right. Just look! Look at it all! The plants, the animals, the superabundance, the excess, and no why to it except nature's in— . . . insatiable hunger for new forms, why, on this planet alone the diversity is appalling! Life is, is nothing but a freak show! Look at it! Just look!

I had been following him to learn, as I said, the habits of his delusion. Now he had touched the core of his obsession, and his lean nervous body shook with zeal, his thin stuttering voice driven wholly by its force. I may have been his first audience. He spoke of the forces which could thrust up from common proteins a whale, a hummingbird, or any of a thousand different cacti, and of the family resemblances in the enzymes of sharks and grasses. But if this was a source of wonder to me, to him it was a horror. His world was no plenum. He spoke as if all life were the fever dream of a mad, insomniac intelligence. I remembered the old anthropologist's saw that intelligence is pathological; the rapid evolution of man's forebrain, that diadem of the species, is anomalous by any current knowledge. And more than one scientist, trying to explain it, has desperately likened it to a cancer. I wondered again if Murphy was sane. Certainly if an intelligence governed his cosmos, it was pathological; and its means were near to Darwinism, which also limited the instruments of creation to permutation and mindless competition.

It was almost touching. He was well read, if indiscriminate, and his attempts to find an order were like mine in everything but direction. My work too was heretical and against the dogmas of science, though constituted by them. So I did not tell him that the idea of an ordered world had always faced contradictions and inadequacies, from Plato through Spinoza, Leibniz, Schelling, and beyond Darwin. Its history was a history of failure, though of a kind I aspired to. The idea had been such a grand failure. It was an idea born of humanity, reason, and purpose, when those abstractions had seemed incorruptible, and it was the only opposition to the brute mechanistic world that the current paradigms of science told us existed. I would rather fail on that path than succeed by the other, if I had the choice. For I knew there was an order to life. I knew it was possible to live. I had seen it done. But I did not know how. I had to know not first for my own existence, but to have a whole picture in which I could strive to place myself. Was the world indeed a nightmare of congenital competition, or was there yet some kind of cooperation at the center of being? For my own reasons I needed to believe the latter; I needed also, unlike Murphy, to know that I was not deluded in my belief.

—And you, he said, you can help me.

If Murphy would use me to work out his obsession, I could use him as proof against delusion. This cold quid pro quo was still a form of cooperation. So I said mildly, —Murphy, you ought to get some history. This idea is as old as the *Timaeus.*

Still, I knew that history would not help him. Even if he read Plato, he would only seize on the myth of Atlantis. In his way he was as betrayed by history as I by method. It was fitting that we meet at this place and time, under a primal sun that subsumed history. I could see the beasts of Murphy's fantasy taking color in this light, engaging in their unthinkable activities; but not with his innocence. No, I saw them body forth under the pervasive smutching shadow of method, a mockery and reproach to all I had learned and suffered for.

But he was not done. He spoke of his splendid drawings, calling them tools of inquiry, experiments, with their own methodology of rigid line and black ink, and with the beginnings of a new woe I interrupted him.

—You have no pride in your art? For I thought that he, at least, had an arena of action in which he was free. But he looked utterly stunned.

—Pride? In copies of copies? As, as if the grandest Chartres could approach the balance of a bumblebee, or, or the finest pigment ever more than mock the glint of snakeskin . . .

—But you say that life is monstrous.

—It is.

—Then why draw it? Don't you have to look at things with love in order to see their pasts and futures?

—Yes. That's the worst. I do, I do love all this. Have you read Rilke?

—No.

—He speaks of beauty. That it is the beginning of terror. That every angel is terrible.

—Then why is it beauty? Why does it hold us so?

—Because it suffers us to live.

Overhead a fire-spotting plane droned, crossing and recrossing the dry grass-grown hills. Below us a million souls sprawled round the borders of the shallow bay.

—I don't know what to tell you, Murphy. But it's foolish to pursue something that puts you in pain.

He regarded me skeptically. —Is it?

Another touch. I wanted to tell him to leave me out of it, but I doubt he knew he was hurting me. He just knew what he could see. So I said: —Yes. It is.

—Maybe . . . I'm at a dead end with my drawings anyway. Maybe another way . . .

But I did not want to hear any more just then. I suggested that we descend.

One of my friends from Cambridge now lived in Berkeley. Homi had put me up my first week in California. He was from New Delhi originally. When I told him about Murphy he smiled and asked if Murphy was a Krishna.

—Offhand I can't think of anything less likely to attract him.

—Oh, it's not so unlikely. This horror of life can become quite ecstatic.

He told me then a Hindu legend about Shiva and his consort Parvati. One day a powerful demon came to Shiva and demanded Parvati. Angry Shiva opened his third eye, and at once another demon sprang from the ground, a lion-headed beast whose nature was pure hunger. Thinking quickly, the first demon threw himself on Shiva's mercy, for it is well known that when you appeal to a god's mercy he is obliged to protect you. So the anguished lion-head asked, "Now what? What am I supposed to eat?" And Shiva said, "Well, why not eat yourself?" And so the lion did, starting with his tail, eating right through his belly and neck, until only his face was left. And to this sunlike mask, which was all that remained of the grim leonine hunger, exultant Shiva gave the name Kirttimukha, or "Face of Glory." He decreed it should stand over the doors to all his temples, and none who refused to honor it would ever come to knowledge of him. Those who think the universe could be made another way, without pain, without sorrow, without time or death, are unfit for illumination. None is illumined who has not learned to live in joyful sorrow and sorrowful joy of this knowledge of life, in the radiance of the monstrous face of glory which is its emblem. This is the meaning of the faces over the entrances to the sanctuaries of the god of yoga, which word is cognate with *yoke.*

Homi had a hypnotic voice—his faint Indian accent falling on American idioms was beguiling—and as he spoke I thought of my demonic angels of choice, their twin faces merging into Kirttimukha, glorious sun-faced lion of life, and for the moment I felt at peace.

Before I left, Homi asked: —Have you spoken to . . . anyone back East?

I said no. Seeing me out, he touched my arm.

The next time I saw Murphy he had a fantastic book on cloning and a practical guide to the grafting of cacti.

Let me tell you about Paul Kammerer. He was an Austrian biologist who set out to demonstrate the inheritance of acquired traits. This evolutionary doctrine was anathema to Darwinists and is still. In 1926, after a distinguished career as long as my life, Kammerer blew his brains out, thoroughly disgraced. The cause of his disgrace was a badly preserved and ineptly doctored specimen

of *Alytes obstetricans*, examined by a hostile critic ten years after
its preservation. A discoloration on the toad's hand was supposed
to demonstrate Kammerer's thesis. On examination the discoloration proved to be fresh india ink. Kammerer had nothing to do
with this botch of a hoax, and it proved only that some lab assistant
had tried clumsily to support him or maliciously to discredit him.
But his critics' tactics were to tie the validity of all his work to the
fraud of this one specimen.

This is a parable in the politics of natural selection. That
Darwin's work is based on a tautology his supporters like to forget.
Survival of the fittest means only this—that creatures with the
most offspring have the most offspring. Or, to put it academically,
those with tenure keep tenure.

No attempts had ever been made to duplicate Kammerer's
work. I decided to do it.

My advisor had urged me to work in recombinant DNA. I demurred, and in one step moved from the cutting edge of my field
to the backwaters of Lamarckism. We will not speak here of my
apparent need to doom myself. I had good reasons as well. I
thought too many favored Darwin's fiction of life, because it tacitly
endorsed every murder as life-furthering. A being, or an idea, that
could not or would not compete for its survival, or which failed at
the effort, was de facto useless. I could not endorse this. In itself the
theory was badly flawed, and its analogs were appalling—"survival
of the fittest" could excuse every cutthroat social act from betrayal
to corporate capitalism to genocide. Nor could I return to the
moral paradigms that had held good before the fall of God to
Reason. Even Lamarck's earlier myth of evolution—that no useful
effort is wasted, that children may inherit the acquired traits of
their parents—was too wistful for me to swallow. But I used it as a
name for my ignorance.

For a year I persisted, walking the two miles from our apartment
to the labs almost every night, entering between the two stone
rhinos, the grates in the quad steaming in all seasons and the mist
making coronas around the lamps. At last I had my second generation of *Alytes* and encouraged them to mate in water, *contra
naturam*. I cleaned the fertilized eggs and kept them alive for two
weeks. And then the approval for my project was withdrawn. My
incubators were shut off. In disgust and despair I left for the Cape,
alone, for a vacation, and took the chance job at Woods Hole
thinking that I might still find a place for my work.

I see what drove Kammerer to suicide. All work for a community is in three parts—constitution, execution, and interpretation. The constitution is communal: you necessarily draw on common knowledge. The execution, the creative act, is irredeemably isolated and solipsistic: the mind is alone with its labor and must take unique responsibility for everything it uses—communal, original, learned by design, or at hazard. The only possible redemption is in the interpretation: from that isolated solipsism the community must be able to draw meaning. Kammerer failed at the last step and so was left with a personal burden of impersonal knowledge unredeemed.

An odd coincidence I discovered later was that Kammerer had shot himself on my birthday. Another was that the son of Kammerer's harshest critic, Gregory Bateson, was at this time a regent of the University of California. Kammerer was a collector of coincidences, and I gather these here only for his sake—and for Murphy, who would doubtless find them meaningful.

I wonder if forms have their own lives. I wonder if shapes in time repeat themselves, at periods, in variations, in retrograde. It is only by a long series of small accidents that we become what we are, and although we remain only what we are we can look back on branching points of possibility now canceled, an angel at each, that might have led to different selves. What is the number of accidents? What is the binding force? What is the shape of necessity? The notion that everything is possible is monstrous, so we restrict, by observing, then defining, then excluding what will not fit. The plenum is reduced to the principle of plenitude. But the excluded remain with us. Beyond all principles, we remain what we are.

I owned a slight book on topology. It soothed me to consider ideal space. In topology there is no direction, and forms are mutable. A coffee cup is a torus, congruent to a doughnut or the human body. Yet laws govern. I took the terms as incantations—Möbius strip, Klein bottle, Cantor set—as pleasant as good dreams. My interest in topology was needless, but in the grace of the excluded even the needless may be needful. It pleased something in me that I should need the needless.

Or perhaps it was a need related to my love of names. Like all biologists, I was a taxonomist at heart. I knew that things had names. They could float free of connotation and become pure poems. Or they could grant power. The true names of things were holy and fearsome. I even thought that a name could keep the thing it represented from existing, that imagination could prevent occurrence, that to envision something fully was to usurp it. At times I had purposely imagined the worst, to keep it at bay. But there is always something you fail to imagine. Every moment time branches. Each second murders possibilities. In a day, one's most trivial decisions abort a million alternative selves. If we are the result of a sport of genes, how much more so of choice?

To me, this was the true menagerie, the myriad decisive acts of will that make us what we are, most of them beyond analysis, impossible to tame by naming. Since I felt that creation was a plenum and untroubling, I suppose I should have felt the same about choice. But I thought my will imperfect and liable to error. Therefore I admired will-less Murphy. It was part of the quid pro quo of our friendship. Life is the exchange of energies.

In all, I was as much a mother to him as I could be without making it obvious. And by degrees he opened up to me. Though a good student, he had never finished high school. He put himself through a trade school, doing smudged charcoal fashion drawings. He worked briefly in small ad agencies, always quitting. He seemed to fear the endorsements of the world. He had no social life, and filled his off-hours by reading von Daniken, Borges, Hegel, Rilke, Velikovsky, Nietzsche, Bergson, Vonnegut, Milton, Ouspensky, Frost, Heinlein, Koestler, a chaos of interests. He had no books on art, just as my own shelves had always been lightest in biology.

Family trees, evolutionary charts, the maze of choice, a garden of forking paths, the drawings of Alexander's horned sphere in my text—all had the same shape. I came to see Murphy's life as congruent to my own.

He began a painting, and to cadge a glimpse I teased him about not using always the same kinds of lines. He said solemnly —This is something else. I'll show you when it's done.

He kept the canvas turned back when he wasn't working on it. It left on the white wall varicolored lines where the wet top edge leaned.

Now it is time to tell the real reason I came West.

Topology, evolution, competition, cooperation, plenitude: these are stories we tell ourselves, as scientists, as politicians, as men, to hold back what we dare not embrace. But time and the time-bound mind are unforgiving; the excluded tend to surface.

I came West on account of John Lang. He was a year ahead of me at school; we shared the same friends. He introduced me to the other great fiction of the nineteenth century, that of Karl Marx—the grand vision of cooperation as the furthering force of life.

It was appealing. The metaphor of course did not hold in biology—Lysenko had been the great Soviet Lamarckian, working to vindicate the Marxist idea that life was not a free-market economy. But in time even the Soviets had bowed to their losing competition with Darwinism, and Lysenko was written out of history. I knew that. But as a binding fiction of life, it was appealing.

Lang was no exemplar, however. When he graduated he went straight to work in his father's chemical firm. We made him the butt of tolerant abuse—poor John, twenty-one and already bourgeois. He was making thirty thousand a year and drove to Cambridge often. We would joke with him and nurse him like a sick bird.

I was living then with Joann Stephen, a slim dark beauty. For three years we were married in all eyes but the law's. When I returned from Woods Hole she was living with Lang. He had finally quit his job. They took me out to dinner, and as my order arrived I fled, nauseated at the part I had to play, at my ineffectualness, my poverty, my pain and despair.

What I resented most was that Lang was using her as the flag of his liberation. "Living in sin" was the way he liked to phrase it to everyone but me. And I resented that there was that in Joann to respond to his instrumentalism. And I wondered what story I had used to blind myself to the possibility of betrayal. For as Lang reminded me, almost sadly, betrayal is possible only within a framework of cooperation. So had I collaborated in my betrayal? Probably.

I told no one when I went West, leaving Lang in my bedroom, with my books and plants, with the cat I had saved from a neighbor's drowning. I left behind every totem of my three years of domestic life. I fled lamenting, How could he ever know her as I had?

But if I cannot judge Murphy, how much less can I judge Lang? He had known what was needed for his life. He had acted. And I had not even known that I was in competition for her.

I bought a radio. Late at night, when most stations were off the air, I listened to it. With my oil lamp set low I entered into dialogues with static. For variety I listened to talk shows. I seldom went to bed before three. It was here, after a month in Berkeley, during an unseasonable rain so light it seemed at times to ascend, that I was fully and finally acquainted with the depth of Murphy's neurosis. I was reading a book on phylogeny by Gould, listening in the interstices to the murmur of rain and radio, which was holding an open telephone discussion of flying saucers, I think. I could ignore the sound of talk more easily than I could music, but an insistent inflection turned my attention to the radio's tinny monologue.

—This is true, the voice said. —The Earth was fertilized from space. Aliens came and mixed proteins in the ancient sea, did this for amusement. The history of life on Earth is a catalog of permutations. All fabulous beasts were once real. We can't have imagined them, our imaginations are poor, we can't imagine a number greater than ten, nor the durations of our lives; our dreams are haunted only by what we've seen and done. The universe is composed of an indefinite and perhaps infinite number of worlds. On their world, life is reasonable. But here they have made a genetic cesspool. It was a game to them. They are all perfect and identical. They do not die, age, or reproduce. What they have done here is a dirty joke, dirty because it is unnecessary. It is as dirty as speaking aloud, or writing, because a perfect thought needs no expression, and an imperfect thought produces only deformed progeny. We may clone, we may graft, we may splice genes, but we cannot approach the enormity of what they have done here. We mock ourselves by the very attempt. We are theirs. Perhaps they come back to observe us, perhaps not, that doesn't matter. Perhaps they did it to mock their own perfection. Perhaps it gives them the filthy pleasure of the voyeur, of the boy fevered with the naked woman's picture. The unspeakable difference. The eye and the act. It is a freak show, a menagerie of Babel, the combinations absurd, meaningless, incoherent. The eye. And the act.

At the word *Babel* I looked out my one window. A light was on out there. My eyes rose to the cupola. I saw Murphy pacing back and forth before his window, holding a telephone.

Peter Fraser, our landlord, late of Boalt Hall, conducted a purge of the house on September 23, my uncelebrated birthday. He demanded all back rents, or eviction by October 1. I drove with him to the Co-Op to post "for rent" notices. Kristin, the student of midwifery, was the only one greatly upset. I was with Murphy when she came up to ask if he was moving. She had to; she hadn't the cash.

I liked Kristin. She was as flighty as the rest of the household, but she was not truculent about it. She said she had been trying the past year to get her life in order. She needed two more months to finish her training, and if she had the expense of moving it would be back to typing at Cal and another year of trying to get free. Murphy listened to this, then took from his desk a roll of twenty-dollar bills.

—Use this if you like, he said. —I don't need it.

After a speechless second she counted the money, wrote him a note, and promised to repay him by the new year. She did not thank him; her manner implied that thanks would debase his act.

Rents paid, we three were invited by Peter to go hiking with him in the Sierra. I think he wanted to escape the repercussions of his decree, figuring it would take a day or two to sink in.

Murphy and I agreed. We drove all night in the Karmann-Ghia. We had a ten-hour hike before us, and Peter crazily wanted to do it all in a day. We took Cayoga Road to 395 and drove south till dawn. Ten miles to our west and across the desert rose the sheer scarp of the eastern Sierra, sharp and clean. We turned up Pine Creek Road and parked near a tungsten mine at the trailhead. We unpacked the car, drank coffee, and ate rolls. The air was sweet. There was a van parked near us with a painting of the desert on its side.

After we put on our packs, Peter handed Murphy and me each a car key.

—Here. In case of emergencies any one of us can drive out for help. Go straight down 395 to Bishop. And for Christ's sake, take a topo whenever you leave camp.

We hiked in, up a steep road, past junipers, timber, and lodgepole pines. We passed a second mine, its tramway and steel shacks idle, eerie in the morning calm. The trail crossed a stream, then leveled. After a while the timber thinned. We climbed, panting, not talking. Scant lodgepoles stood atop their reflections in Pine Lake. We skirted the lake and crossed its inlet. Below falls we stopped for lunch. I took off my outer shirt. From here the trail climbed sharply in switchbacks. We labored to an untimbered ridge that divided two basins: to the north the Chalfant Lakes, to the south Granite Park strung with smaller, unnamed lakes. For a few hours we followed a stream that ducked under and over jumbled rocks. A set of switchbacks brought us to Italy Pass. We paused here for the view and to get our wind. It was midafternoon.

The scale of the place was such that I did not know if it was beautiful or not—I was reminded of a line of Henry Miller: "No analysis can go on in this light; here the neurotic is either instantly cured, or goes mad"—you might as well call the moon beautiful. The warring forces which had jumbled this landscape were awesome, especially in this deep afternoon calm. From a human perspective it was like a desolated battlefield of giants—we were trespassing in their laps—and these images immediately canceled themselves before the reality, making all human perspective trivial.

West of the pass there was still snow. I could not believe it was September. The last time I camped was two years before, when Joann and I spent a week in a cabin on the Appalachian Trail. It was April, too early for hikers. Two feet of snow lay on the ground, but that week the temperature stayed in the sixties. We went naked most of the time. It was there I got her pregnant.

Near dusk we made camp by a rockbound lake in a glacial cirque. Peaks ringed us round. Despite our fatigue we were alert, and we stayed up talking, late enough to see Taurus's V climb above the rough silhouette of mountains. The stars were brilliant. Each moment's gaze seemed to bring out more. I named the Dippers and Cassiopeia's W, but it took Murphy to identify the dimmer constellations. I remember laughing at Camelopardelus, the giraffe. I felt free and vigorous. Peter rolled a joint, and he and I smoked and talked while Murphy looked for meteors.

There was a resemblance between Peter and John Lang, and Peter too was a Marxist. Far from cooperation, this seemed to mean that he never made a profit on rent or dope deals. In America selling at cost plus right attitude is the nearest approach to communism. He repined over the evictions. He had been more than fair. But they had acted in bad faith, and it was no favor to anyone to support the irresponsible. How the responsible differed from those who paid their bills I did not hear him say. He sketched the consequences of his Marxist heresy in a capitalist, normative society. His parents gave him grief for dropping out. His job prospects were nil. He suffered angst. Only in the mountains did he feel free.

Doubtless I am being unjust to Peter. The point is that I liked unreflective Murphy better. Despite all Peter and I shared in training and rejection, I felt little sympathy. Still, I gave him in turn some of my background, my own heresies and failures, insofar as they reflected his. I was smoking his dope. We all felt fine.

After a while Peter stood. —Time to make some humus . . . anyone else? Why, I wondered, are Marxists such scoutmasters?

When he had gone, Murphy spoke to me. —I used to think that I was not human. I thought I was from a star somewhere. They had left me here to grow up as human, and when I had observed enough, they would take me back. I used this, this fantasy as a rationale for interest. I liked to study, and this gave me a reason.

—Which star? I asked.

—Omega Orionis, he said with no hesitation. —They live in an artificial world orbiting the star. It's a winter star. Where I lived I could see it only sometimes. It's dim. I knew they had left me, and would come back.

—How long did this . . . fantasy last? I asked carefully.

—Oh, a few years. I never told anyone. After a while I just stopped thinking about it.

—When I was a kid, I thought I was some kind of genetic sport, you know, a mutant. We all need some story to separate us from our parents.

—I was afraid. I studied Earth things, you see, and I began to believe in them. So I was afraid they would see this, and not come back for me. I was supposed to be just an observer. Not a participant. So I left off studying for a while.

—Murphy. My friend. What the hell is your first name?

—Hugh.

—Irish?

—My mother denies it. She says it's Scottish. She wears orange on St. Patrick's Day.

I laughed. —And what's your father?

—Dead. Of drink.

—Oh.

—I . . . I waited a long time for it. He raped my older sister. He was . . . it was his name too.

—Is that why you don't use it?

—Oh, no. It's, well, I sign myself, my drawings, just "Murphy." It's kind of a personal secret. You know, the way some people won't tell their middle names, as if names gave power? It's silly.

—No. If you know someone's name, in a way you're responsible for them.

—And you, you know the names of so many things, don't you . . .

—Not their true names. You know more of that, I think.

Peter returned.

—So what's new? See that major meteor?

—No. We were talking about glaciers, I said.

—How weird they are. If we'd had more time I would have taken you to Evolution Valley. There's outstanding glacial stuff there. A great place. Mt. Huxley, Mt. Darwin, Lamarck Pass, Le Conte Divide . . . I'll show you slides sometime. A great place. Nature named after natural historians. You guys coming to bed?

—Soon, I told him.

—Okay. Don't step on me when you come in, you bastards. I'm sleeping in the middle.

He left. After a minute I said: —Murphy, I heard you on the radio the other night.

He was silent.

—Do you believe all that?

—But you think it's the result of chance, he said.

—Not exactly. But if so, is that so horrifying? Isn't it best to think that you're all that cares? That the universe is indifferent?

—Do you believe in sin?

I was quite impressed. He had gone straight to the core of my argument and neutered it. But I played him out.

—What if I don't?

—You do.

—You . . . *saw* that, of course.

—Yes.

—You're right. I do. Or else evil must be the result of simple misunderstanding. And I don't believe that.

—Then what is sin? he asked.

—A violation of the natural order, I said.

—So there is an order.

—I don't know. Despite all the fictions we impose, yes, I tend to think there is one. So there's sin. You're responsible for your actions, in some unfathomable way. I laughed. —Murphy, congratulations, you've discovered God. No, I'm sincere. You're very sharp, to come to this on your own. But let me tell you about Occam's razor.

—Needless reduplication of entities.

—Christ, undercut again.

—You, you see, that's where the God argument fails. He couldn't have made . . . all this.

—But why replace him with a race of aliens? Oh, I was stoned. I could almost see them.

—If they're the result of chance . . . perfectly formed, but formed that way by chance . . . and we're slave to their will, to the fall of chromosomes, the mutations, defects in material, and you can never transcend this flaw. But only aspire to, to find the controlling form. To know them. And I, I'm still afraid of what I might learn about them.

—By drawing? Then give it up.

—I have no choice!

I was still. We had reached our crossing. His path was mine in reverse—but in topology there is no direction. He was not the ideal will-less spirit I had named, had usurped by naming. His cosmos was controlled, and he was its creature, expressly and increasingly denied choice, whereas all my effort was to complete the image of a world in which my choices could be clear and effective. In which I could act. I had thought myself a doomed believer in cooperation, unable to fight well; but he was showing me a face far more radiant in its doom than any I had worn, and he could not even fight himself. He could not see that the order he had invented for his world was now autonomous, and he its slave. I saw him as one of my angels at a crossroad, but this angel was not fearsome. No, this one had trapped himself and turned slowly with a stricken lost look, while all around an unthinkable chaos of beings boiled, warred, loved, died, endured.

—Murphy, the stupid and the intelligent accept the imposed orders, because they don't see them or because they know there's no working alternative. But people like you, you wake up suddenly, and call it monstrous, and think this new. It's not. And it does you no good, for in searching for a new order you only go deeper into the old. You come finally to the idea of inherent vice in creation, and even that is not final, and hardly new. You're doomed. There's no help for you.

—Of whom are you speaking?

I was glad. He was with me still. —Of myself. Of whatever it is we share. This ineradicable strain. I woke up too. Perhaps it's the best thing for us . . . if we choose it.

—To be doomed?

—Yes. To be doomed. To be excluded from the charnel house. In our own ways, freely chosen. All right?

—Y-Yes. I, I need your help, though.

—And I yours. Now let's sleep. And seal this . . . compact with good dreams.

—I'll stay up a while, said Murphy. —Until Orion rises.

Bright, swift morning reached us. Peter laid out gear for climbing. He had extra crampons and tried to entice us to tackle a rock face with him, tried against his declared politics to catch us by competition, by stressing how hard and dangerous it was. But that morning Murphy and I were almost like lovers, and cooperatively we demurred. Instead we two mapped out a hike through Granite Park. Peter almost gave in and came with us, but he was caught by his own ideas and we went our separate ways.

Murphy and I climbed to the pass in silence. He stopped once to examine some lichen, that strange collaboration of the lowest animal with the lowest plant. —Design of darkness, he murmured.

From there we descended, leaving the trail. Across a scarped bowl ringed by peaks we hiked. Around noon it clouded over. The clouds scudded in rapidly from the west. It grew cold. We were about four miles from camp when it started to snow.

—Listen, Murphy, I don't like this. It came up too fast. We'd better turn around.

—Go back? But why?

—We may be in for a real storm. The snow's starting to stick already, and it's not that cold.

—It may blow over, he said.

—A friend of mine was caught in a summer snowstorm on Mt. Washington. It's no joke.

—I know that.

—Jesus, Murphy, look at it fall. Another hour of this and we won't be able to find our way out of this bowl. Have you got a compass?

—No.

—Neither do I. Terrific. Let's get the hell out while we still can. He seemed reluctant. I had to lead him. Returning, we almost passed the trail. There was an inch of snow on the ground now. The surrounding mountains had vanished. Wind billowed the thick white curtain about us. I stopped.

—Christ.

—It's that way, he said.

—I don't know. Damn, I don't know. If there was any shelter I'd say stop here.

—But there isn't. We have to go on.

—Murphy, just look! You can barely see a hundred feet. If it gets worse we'll never even find the tent; it's two miles across an unmarked cirque.

—What else can we do?

—Maybe we can hike out, I said. I was not so sure, but his diffidence frightened me.

—It must be ten miles to the road, he said.

—No it's not. Say five or six. And it's downhill. We can get below the snow. And what about Peter?

—He'll be fine. He's probably back in the tent already. We should go on.

—Murphy! We have to climb two thousand feet, over the pass, right into the storm, then find our way across two miles of nothing! We could die out here; it happens to people every year because they make the wrong choice. In a snowstorm you go downhill. That's what Peter said. You get below the snow.

—It's ten miles.

—It's downhill, on a trail. We have a car waiting. We just follow the water down. With luck we can be out by dusk.

But that was not our luck. When we crossed the stream out of Granite Park, Murphy lost his footing and soaked himself to the knees. The wind came up. The snow increased. Wet and heavy, its runoff was already swelling the stream we kept to our right. When we reached the next ford, Murphy balked. Rocks flumed the water, cast up pearls of foam.

—Here's something else you find when you go down, he said. — And do you remember the other ford, on the way in? Below the falls? What will that be like?

—All right, damn it, we can't cross here. Give me the map.

Farther on, the trail recrossed the stream. I thought we could cut across the arms of the trail's U. The map became sodden in my hands as I studied it.

We were not dressed for this. The morning had been mild. We

each had a parka but no hat, and Murphy had no gloves. He would not take mine. He shivered as we stood there. Snow, caked around my boots, seeped down my socks; my toes had started to sting. My hair was soaked, and I could feel water trickle down my neck.

—Here, look. We can stay this side of the stream most of the way down. We cross once at Upper Pine Lake, pick up the trail here, and follow it down.

Hands pocketed, shivering, he turned to watch the tossing stream. —All right. It's up to you, he said.

I cursed at him, and we went on. I figured fifteen minutes until we regained the stream. We slipped and stumbled comically on snow-hidden rocks. Still, it was soothing to have a direction. A sudden panic jolted me. I could no longer hear the stream. I looked at my watch in disbelief. Forty minutes had passed since we left the trail. In hours it would be dark, and we were not yet a quarter of the way. Murphy sighed and said: —I have to sit down.

He went to his knees, and I grabbed him.

—Up! Stand up!

I picked up the map. It came to pieces in my hand. A gust took the scraps and blinded me with hard, stinging snow. I turned to shield myself.

Now I could not see thirty feet. The ground seemed level all around. I had no idea which way I faced. I strained for the sound of the stream and heard only the faint empty wail of wind, the accumulating silence of snow. The colder, pebbly snow rustled on our parkas as it fell.

—Now? said Murphy.

I chose a direction. After five minutes I felt sure that we were going down. We walked close, jogging against one another. We came to a ridge. I heard falls. We had found the stream, or, no, another, surely another, for before us was a moon-sharp cliff, impossible to descend. I turned us before Murphy saw. We went up. He stumbled against me, his voice a moth in my ear. —Hypothermia.

I held him. I would have given my life for him then. The feeling rose as a dull wash of anger that kept me going for ten steps more. Then a memory of his voice reached me: You want to die. I went another step and stopped. In despair I looked up, as if to summon the sun. Murphy too looked up. Then he raised his arm and shouted: —Look! Look there!

I squinted into the chaos of nothingness.

—Oh God, it's enormous!

I saw nothing. There was nothing. I was enraged that he should debase our deaths with hallucinations. Then I grew weak and sat in the soft snow, thinking that this, being a voluntary act, might cure him. Dimly it came to me that I would not get up. This I wanted. He was right, I did want it: a clean death.

He shouted again.

—They're here!

He began to sing.

From the white emerged two figures. They were backpackers. It was coincidence they had come, lost as us, just as Murphy's insanity began. I made a murderous effort in every muscle to rise and realized stupidly that I had not moved at all. The two stumbled to within a foot of us.

—Help us, I said.

The taller man, rime-bearded, shook his head leisurely. He smiled. The two went on into the snow. Murphy gave a last cry and ran after them. Another gust blinded me.

I began to dream. It was a dream without pictures or actions. It was a dream of words. At times they passed before me as if printed. At times I heard voices, familiar and alien. Most of the words were incoherent but clearly articulated. I knew they were the names of things, and I strained like an infant listening to its parents to ferret their meaning. I imagined that Murphy and I were seated cross-legged in the snow, naked, reciting the true secret names of every species of life. Each name caused the extinction of another species. The world became sparer, more orderly. We chanted outside of time, beyond death and strife; we sealed our secret compact in a clean new light, not fictive, not random.

When I emerged from this into a pellucid state of waking, he was curled beside me. He had run in a circle. I put a hand on his forehead. I thought I could feel if he was still alive. I knew he was alive, but I thought I could tell if his body had still enough heat to keep him alive. It was dark. The snow was gentler, and the wind had fallen. Large flakes dropped straight down. Not many had collected on him. In the obscurity I watched his lips to see that fresh flakes melted as they touched. I felt warm and relaxed. Darkness fell from the air. A windless still settled. I burrowed deeper into the whisper of snow. All words were passing from me, words of power, curses, benedictions, words to shape and be shaped by, all passed. My life was a riot of vivid pictures, twists of emotion, inchoate cries of pain and exultation, and gladly I welcomed all this namelessness. If I were dying, as I surely was, no design of name was adequate to my consciousness. So words bowed and broke, vowels scattered ripples across the face of darkness, the material armature of my body weakened, and the support of all fictions fled from me, until the final fiction, the simplest word, the simplest name, *I*, also lost its meaning and its power. So I knew that either dawn or death was close, and I was glad that these were, at last, the only possibilities.

Then the dark was riven by a mad roar and a gyre of light. Its bite was as clean as the cold and as real. So I would not leave the living so easily. The radiance seared me, the mouth of the whisper I was buried in opened in a stuttering shriek. My body screamed in pain, and I felt time snap clearly as a dry twig up its length, the two paths distinct—and my demons stood at the crossing. Live or die, they cried, Choose, choose. Their grins were great as stars. The roar heightened. Angels sang in chaotic chorus. I turned my head to hide, but the light went through. I saw Murphy, the red of his parka beneath drifted snow, the green of my sleeve flung over him, his face a vivid relief in the fierce wavering light. I turned again into the brilliance and roar. And then I knew. These were not my demons. They were his.

—Spaceship, I whispered. It could not be. I had to banish it. But I was sick and weak and could only deny it with my voice, not with any force of my mind. Then I saw that my word had only confirmed it. In a gust the great ship rocked, its engines labored, its lights danced, as if biting deeper into reality. I had called it closer with my voice. For now Murphy's reality had intersected mine. I had taken his insanity for my own, and I was afraid. I knew his dread of words. I had thought myself in some special grace of the doomed, the excluded, and now I would find that it had all counted, every word, every evasion, that a choice not made was still a choice, that time's demons were ineluctable, whatever their form. I would be weighed in their balance and found wanting. Some acid of life they would use on us. In the autoclave, the sterile steel cirque of the vessel, they would parse me, reduce the irreducibles of my genes, and make me new. Death I no longer minded. The prospect of a changed life I did. And the singing in the air was: Choose! And from a small, uncertain reserve of new strength I whispered: —No.

But I raised my arm to signal them. I owed him this.

The glow came down. A hatch opened. I saw the suited figures emerge.

I returned to Berkeley two days later. After twenty-four hours in the hospital, they had taken me to Reno, where I caught a flight to Oakland. Peter stayed behind with Murphy, who was still in poor condition.

The house was still and empty. I sat alone in the living room until Kristin came home from work, and I told her what had happened, from the start of the storm until the helicopter picked us up eighteen hours later. When the wind had died, the rangers had swept over the Chalfant Lakes basin, into which we had wandered. It was a common mistake in storms.

Toward the end of my story I broke down and could not finish. I lost control of my voice and began a compulsive, erratic biography. She listened to everything I had so carefully secreted since arriving in Berkeley and to things I had not myself remembered in years. I raved for thirty minutes. Then I ended: —Darwin at the age of sixty received from Marx an inscribed copy of *Das Kapital*. He never read it. He thought German was ugly. It's all right now. I'm better. I can stop now. I'm sorry. I can stop now.

But I could not face the cottage. So she slept with me that night, holding me as I had held Murphy in the snow. She said that I woke once, about three, shivered for ten minutes, and then slept unmoving until morning. And once in that night lost to my memory she said I mourned: —My child. My lost child.

In the morning, after Kristin had left for work, I went up to Murphy's room. But on the floor below his aerie a low hum stopped me. The door to the silent couple's room was ajar. I pushed it open. The room had been trashed in response to Peter's decree. Black paint jagged in swaths across walls cracked by hammer blows. Flies made the hum. In the middle of the floor, with a strip of matting round its neck, Peter's cat lay stretched out dead. Its eyes were alive with ants. I lifted the stiff body and carried it downstairs. I buried it by the cottage. When I was done I squatted and for a while watched a snail climb a shaft of sorrel.

Then I returned to Murphy's room. Below his windows houses staggered down the hill, each sheltering lives as useless and as precious as my own. In the terrarium a lizard was gulping hamburger. It darted when I tapped the glass. The dirt in the cactus pots was moist. After a minute I went to the far wall and turned over Murphy's canvas.

It was a Garden, a menagerie. If Rousseau had had the form-haunted medieval mind of Bosch he might have painted it. Disparate limbs conjoined in monsters. Murphy's draftsmanship had made them seamless wholes: his grammar of line—joining haunch to fin, mandible to bicep—superseded the grammar of reality. There were a hundred beasts or more. The flora was likewise impossible. Tree ferns fruited in birds. The flowers of sprawling cacti bore letters. The canvas was an affront: it denied evolution, the most whole myth we still possessed after the fall of God. I could not judge if Murphy's aim had been to include these travesties of life in his universe or to exclude them from it.

It was unfinished. The negative space he marshaled so carefully in his drawings was spread throughout the canvas in patches and voids, as if holding off an unthinkable completion. Near the center I found his aliens—insectile, alike, expressionless, presiding over creation. Around them were smears of color, as if he had gone over and over this patch and had not got it right.

A week later he was back. He moved like a ghost. There had been tissue damage in his hands; they had been near to amputation, and now he could barely make a weak fist. He spent his days reading and did not go out at all.

He spoke to me only once more.

—The hospital. There was a peace there, an order. I was willing to do whatever they wanted. I knew it was my last chance to reenter the world.

I tore up my application to the university. I wrote a long account of our trip, ending with the deaths of Murphy and myself. In this fiction I explained that they had indeed taken Murphy back. Then, having as I thought usurped this path, having as I believed rescued him from himself, I felt myself fairly done with denial. I felt strong enough never again to need words to deny anything.

In October I moved, leaving for him only a short farewell verse from Rilke, which I hoped I could myself follow: "There is no place that does not see you; you must change your life."

But it turned out that I was wrong, that even our most selfless acts have secret motives. In my pack, as I traveled, I discovered his last reply: All life is love, and love perishes. And I knew that he was dead.

So I recognized at last the yoke of self, the cold and mutable equations of being which only laugh at principle and method. Did I think he had used me? No, I had used him, and finally not kept our compact. I had mothered him by cradling my arms to myself and cooing stories for my own benefit. I had not counted the chance of betrayal, and so I ended betraying him as completely as only a parent can betray a child. I had taken from him the fiction he needed in order to live. I had sacrificed him to save myself.

And that I could face even this manifestation of Kirttimukha I took for my own strength and purpose, returning East to fight. And I recognized too that I was hereby due for some congruent betrayal myself. This I accepted. Life is the exchange, the unknowable, unnamable exchange of energies.

The two hikers who passed us had been found dead a hundred yards away.

If time travel ever becomes a reality, police forces could be able to prevent crimes such as murder by going back to erase them. This ability would seem to be enough to dissuade potential murderers, especially if they don't have access to time-travel devices themselves. But there are as many anomalies in life as in time travel, as Joel Richards shows in the following story of murder and its motives.

Joel Richards studied economics at Tufts, Ohio State University, and the University of Stockholm. He is married to a woman from Denmark, and they're both marathon runners (she won the 1981 Copenhagen marathon); currently he owns a small chain of athletic shoe and clothing stores in California. His work has appeared in Skiers World, Amazing, *and* Isaac Asimov's Science Fiction Magazine.

DEADTIME

JOEL RICHARDS

Torrance stood at the door seal with Sam Turner, glad to have the company. The number on the door was 6002, the name Harold Brown. Brown was a billing specialist at Security Factors. Torrance didn't know what a billing specialist was. Paper pushing of some sort. The job label, the firm's name, Brown's name—they all had a featureless blankness. The building where Brown lived didn't help either. Billing specialists couldn't afford residences of distinction. No glitter palace, no neo-brownstone. Just a cubicle off a hallway two thirds up your typical big city monolith—not even the penthouse—in an undistinguished quarter.

Torrance did know two other things about Brown. He was a sports fan, and he would soon be dead.

Torrance thumbed the hail button. A moment later the annunciator inquired, "Yes?"

"Is this Harold Brown?" Torrance asked.

"Who are you?" the voice countered. Not too surprising. The

door seal was transparent from Brown's side. He didn't know Torrance or Turner on sight.

"San Francisco Police." Torrance flashed his badge at the seal unit's verifier. He thumbed his null-privacy warrant and the door became transparent from his side as well, registering on Brown's panel that his privacy seal had been legally breached.

Brown looked startled. It was Brown all right. Lanky, rumpled looking, with thin hair brushed forward over a receding forehead. He had looked startled downtime with a laser hole in that forehead.

"We'd like to talk to you about your safety, Mr. Brown," Torrance went on. When Brown stood motionless, he added, "May we come in?"

The seal shimmered off and the door opened. Immediately Torrance and Turner began to assimilate data on Brown beyond the physical appearance they already knew. The entryway was a study in fake bamboo and pseudo batik. Nouveau Indonesian, very trendy. Cooking smells of ghee and peanut. Vision of a living/dining area beyond, one wall open to the lights across the way, one wall the usual holoscreen. Lots of rattan furniture. Maybe this went beyond decor preferences. If they were neokarman, it would get sticky fast.

A surprisingly attractive woman, dark and sharp-featured, was clearing the table as Brown led them in.

"These men are from the police, Darby," Brown said.

The woman cast them an intent look, then continued with the dirty dishes to the kitchen. She turned back to them with composed features.

"What's the problem?" she asked.

"We'd like a few words with you, both of you," Torrance said.

"About what?"

Torrance turned from her to Brown, who had been standing by, his long arms hanging by his side. Much slower than his wife.

"We understand that you're going to the burnball game tonight, Mr. Brown. That right?"

"Yes. I'm going with Tom Jenner from down the hall. He got the tickets."

"Is there anything wrong with that?" Brown's wife put in, easing around to stand by Brown's side, facing Torrance and Turner.

Torrance sighed. There'd be no indirect approach with that woman around.

"Mr. Brown, if you go to that game tonight, you'll be killed. Murdered."

"Good lord," Brown murmured and sat down with a force and rough aim that threatened the rattan.

"Who? By whom?" Mrs. Brown demanded sharply.

Torrance looked to Turner to draw the fire. He wanted to study Brown.

"We don't know," Turner said.

"But you *always* know. You must!"

"Not this time."

Mrs. Brown had a point. Since the advent of the time probe only two kinds of crimes were committed—unplanned crimes of passion and crimes that were meant not to seem crimes. But this was neither.

Torrance continued, "Mr. Brown, if you go to the game you will be gunned from the unreserved section across the arena. It could be a sniper from some concealed hideaway, but our preliminary probe rules that out. It could be anyone out of a huge, dark mass of people, firing through the bottom of a bag of peanuts."

Torrance looked at Mrs. Brown. "You see the problem."

"You can't head off the killer, so you have to save the victim. Or try to."

"Yes. And that's a new one for us, I may add."

Brown stiffened. "But who would want to kill me? Are you sure it's me they're after?"

"There are two ways of finding out. Ask you questions, or sit here with you, watching the game on your screen until we see if someone else is killed around about the seventh inning."

"Yes," Brown said slowly, "I can see that. But I must tell you that I know of no reason for anyone to kill me." He cast an abashed look at his wife. "Frankly, my job is too insignificant to fight, much less kill, for."

Turner suggested that for starters Brown call his neighbor and plead illness to avoid going to the game. That touched a nerve all right. The Browns's eyes met. Neokarmans both—antagonists of the time probe, defenders of the right to act, to shape one's own karma, even kill or be killed without being temporally reversed.

But now it was Brown who faced the certainty of being killed if he followed his principles. Or perhaps they were more Mrs. Brown's principles. Brown got up, turning his back on his wife without a word, and went into the bedroom. Mrs. Brown held her tongue, but her eyes bored his retreating back with a glare that Torrance thought could be little less in intensity than the lasgun that awaited Brown at the arena.

Torrance suggested coffee and accompanied Mrs. Brown to the kitchen to assist. A direct woman and a tight schedule demanded corresponding bluntness.

"Do you have a lover who'd like your husband out of the way? I'm sure that you realize that we care not at all about your relationships except and as a prevention to murder."

Mrs. Brown hesitated only a moment. "Yes. His name's Burt Roberts, and Harold doesn't know about it. But he couldn't be the killer."

"Why not? Not the type?"

She smiled a smile both rueful and cruel. "He's not going to the game. I would have been in his bed in an hour."

She gave Torrance the address of the bed, and he sent Sam out to tail Roberts. Then Torrance and Mr. and Mrs. Brown sat around watching a not very interesting game and drinking a lot of coffee. At about the second inning Mrs. Brown excused herself to make a call. At about the seventh inning there was a disturbance in the stands, with a quick pan to a medic unit being dispatched to a citizen in distress. The citizens around him seemed also to be in a distress of a more animated sort. But then the action quickened, and the camera returned to the scene of a rare double homer. After a while Torrance left. Mr. and Mrs. Brown sat glaring at each other.

You're not supposed to talk police business with your woman. Torrance had an out here. Her name was Barbro Vik and she was police, too; more precisely, a police psychologist. There were a lot more of those than field detectives. There were a lot more crimes of passion than the invisible crimes calling for detection.

Torrance wanted a psychologist's insight. This psychologist was slightly built, not beautiful but striking, with waves of dark hair, high cheekbones, and a mouth a bit too large and mobile for her face. Aesthetically. Not at all too large and mobile for what Torrance and countless others could fantasize. Barbro Vik believed in using and enjoying her stronger attributes, though selectively. She had found Torrance's mind and libido simpatico, and they had shared good conversation and erotic moments before.

Peter Torrance had a small cottage down the rickety Greenwich steps of Telegraph Hill. It was rainy season the first time Barbro had visited, and she had slipped on the green-algaed wood, skidding down two steps on her butt, then another five feet along the slick wood of an inclined ramp. Torrance had offered to pay the cleaning bill for her skirt and to massage her aching rear. She had accepted both offers on the spot, though she had known him only two hours. The relationship had prospered over the years. The secret, Torrance thought, being to keep decent intervals.

Barbro liked visiting the cottage for other reasons. Together with its small brick patio and the overgrown lushness of its vegetation, it was a retreat that Torrance could never have rented or bought. It had been a legacy from his father, a noted commodity speculator who had died—unfortunately for Torrance—during a losing streak. The cottage, princely enclave though it was, was in fact the estate's only asset of value left unencumbered. Torrance could feel his father in it sometimes, more than in the home Torrance had shared with his parents—not the bluff, risk-seeking man of his public face, but the questing mind and the intuitive spirit that found the cottage both an ideal vantage and retreat. Barbro had that kind of mind and spirit, too.

"Why do you think your man's mad?" she asked, poking about his spice rack and mixing the salad dressing by feel.

"Because I can't think of a sane reason for killing aimlessly."

"You're sure it was aimless? How close did you look at this guy Hansen's life?"

Torrance gave the sautéing mushrooms a stir with his fork, sampling one. "We didn't have to look. Hansen was the fourth one killed."

"Fourth!" Barbro watched a too large stream of marjoram pour into her dressing, then looked at it in exasperation. "And who'd they give the Jehovah seat to? Not you?"

"By default. The big guns are all too busy with the assassination."

Barbro gave him a look of compassion. "Poor Peter. But why Hansen?"

"Fifty-five-year-old widower. No near relatives. Inconsequential job. All in all, the least likely effect on the future." He smiled thinly, "Though, in retrospect, we could have probably done best with our first victim. No apparent loss there."

Barbro started toward the table with the salad. Torrance spared a moment for the shifting play of light on her sheen skirt as she came within the candle's aura.

"How are you going to handle that at the press conference tomorrow?" she tossed back over her shoulder.

"With luck the assassination will attract the flak. But the party line is that Hansen was the second victim. Failing to find the killer, we saved the first—whose identity is screened by the Temporal Anonymity Act—and Hansen was the next, at which point we discovered that it was a random killing. We've hypnoed the others to forgetfulness, of course."

"But you're still not sure it's random?"

"Pretty sure—but maybe tied into the assassination. Or triggered by it. In the old days they had waves of similar crimes, murders or whatever, with the publicity from one encouraging others, didn't they?"

She nodded. "Hijackings, kidnappings. They're more your copy-cat crimes."

"Any common profiles there?"

"Nothing too startling or helpful. They're done by loners, mainly. Often paranoid. Feel put upon by society. I'll see if I can dig up some formal studies for you, but it'll have to wait till tomorrow."

He looked at her with present affection and a hint of lust to follow. "We'll work on other things tonight."

She met his smile. "We always do."

The mayor had preempted the press conference to his offices on the theory that any national exposure was better than none. Assassination of the President was shocking, deplorable, and a black mark against any city. But the black mark was there and wouldn't go away. What remained was the opportunity to posture as a man of strength during a national crisis.

The stadium murder held no such stature. The first overt crime, profitless and likely mad, since the time probe's advent, it was totally local and totally lacking in opportunity for statesmanlike mien. The mayor would have liked to exclude the subject from the press conference, but the press would have none of it. And worse, outside the hall local radicals were scuffling and protesting the use of the time probe to reverse karma—anyone's and everyone's—as reversal of the assassination would surely do.

The conference was opened by the western field director of the

National Security Agency, who acknowledged the mayor's introduction and then turned to the welter of cameras and reporters.

"I have a brief statement, ladies and gentlemen, which I hope
will anticipate many of your questions. Afterward I will answer as
many of them that remain that I can, consonant with national
security.

"As we all know, the President was assassinated here in San
Francisco three days ago. A cache of high explosives had been
buried below the skimmerway, probably under the guise of road
work. We believe that the explosion's trigger was the rather narrow frequency band of the President's emergency communicator,
which accompanies him always and is always energized. A tight
aperture reception channel, pointing straight up, was likely used
to ensure that the President's vehicle was directly above the explosive charge.

"The screening process is going on now. The problem, of course,
is that while we know the time of the assassination, we do not
know the time the explosives were planted. The President's trip to
open the Three Power peace conference had been laid on for over
six months, with parts of the route a virtual certainty to any thinking man. Indeed, there may be other explosive caches under alter-
nate routes. So we have had to set up our temporal cameras over a
span of six months or more. Even with super-speed scanning, we
have six months of real time to wade through.

"Within a day, or two at the most, we expect to pinpoint the
time of the explosive implantation. It will be filmed and the film
held in no-time stasis. We shall then arrest the assassins and remove the explosives. Your story will, of course, be a different one
then. It will be the story of an unsuccessful assassination, the per-
petrators known for some months. The President will be with us
again. The peace conference, which has been in adjournment, will
in this repaired reality have been ongoing for several days.

"I will now answer those of your questions that I can. Please
identify yourself and ask away."

The commotion—the waving of hands, arms, and bodies to attract attention—was prodigious. The director stabbed his finger.

"Roy Thorner, Associated Press. Mr. Director, the several-day
delay in real time will result in dislocations—changes in the future
that we will experience relative to what would have been had you
avoided the assassination by simply rerouting the President's approach to the conference hall. Why was that not done?"

"We considered the positive advantages of avoiding this dislocation. We considered it more important to apprehend the assassins. Otherwise, they might well do it again elsewhere, elsewhen. If we had done as you say, the assassination would not actually have taken place in the reality we are now living, and we'd not have known of the attempt. One of the common paradoxes we have to deal with."

The director paused and extended a finger across the room.

"Valerie Townsend, St. Louis *Post-Dispatch.* Can you hazard why this assassination was attempted—done, actually? Surely the assassins know that they'll be caught and the assassination reversed."

The director pulled on his pipe. "As you say, we can only hazard. We could be dealing with mentalities that are savoring these few days of grisly success as reward enough—even knowing that these memories will be soon reversed. Or they could be counting on the lesser 'success' of being arrested and tried publicly for what will be the attempt, not the fruition, of such an assassination. We can only guess at this point, which makes us even more anxious to catch the criminals. Does that answer your question?"

"Could it be," the St. Louis reporter persisted, "that another major power could have engineered this assassination to test our readiness while without our elected president, or even to attack us while we are leaderless—hoping to obliterate San Francisco and preclude a reversal of the assassination?"

It was minutes before the director could speak over the ensuing uproar.

"I cannot answer that question directly. I can say that our armed forces were on full combat alert at the time of the assassination. This alert had been ordered by the President based on the warning of one of our prescients, who, however, could not zero in on any specifics for his concerns. It could have been the assassination. It could have been something else. We'll never know. And if it were as you hypothesize, all the more reason that the peace conference proceed."

Another reporter had his turn. "Brent Curley, Washington *Post.* Do you see any tie-in between the recent stadium murder and the assassination?"

The mayor caught Torrance's eye as the director spoke.

"We've discovered no linkage as yet, and, frankly, have no reason to pursue that line of inquiry. Police detective Torrance is with us, however; he has prime responsibility for that investigation. I'll ask him to present his findings."

Torrance winced at the introduction and slowly rose to his feet. "Mr. Curley, our findings are minimal. You've seen the accounts of the stadium murder; perhaps you've written one. No one in the vicinity of the weapon noticed anything out of the ordinary, and the temporal camera tells us nothing of use in that darkened arena. We have hypothesized that the assassination of the President may have stimulated a copycat crime, except that they're not similar in one most important regard. The President's assassination was a well-directed crime. The stadium murder was a random one."

"How do you know that?" Curley followed up, taking his glasses away from his craggy face as if to emphasize the point.

"Failing to locate the killer, we saved the victim in order to determine whether he was the specific object of the attack. He wasn't. Mr. Hansen died in his stead."

"So the murderer actually killed twice?"

"Yes." And more, friend, Torrance thought, relieved at the question's phrase. "But neither of these victims seems to relate to the assassination."

A lady by Curley's side broke in, "Could it be that they were of the assassination group, being killed to avoid later interrogation?"

"No sense to that. If, unlikely though it seems, one of them is of the assassination conspiracy, we'll step back and arrest him before he is killed in the arena."

Another man rose nearby. "Carl Brody, Texarkana *Sentinel.* Why wasn't there a forward probe of the President's movements to head off the assassination?"

A collective groan and wave of laughter swept the room. Torrance gestured to the director, though he could as well have answered. So could ninety-five percent of those in the room, Brody not among them.

"Because of the nature of time and the probe machine, Mr. Brody. The past exists. The future doesn't yet. So the machine can travel only to the past and then ahead to the timepoint from which it sent the traveler, plus a few nanoseconds of relay time. It can't probe the future beyond its own existence."

The press conference dissolved in the tension release of laughter and irresolution, tailing off to a ragged halt. Torrance filed out with the mayor and wondered what to do next.

"One of the pluses of this job is that when you don't know what to do next, someone tells you."

Sam Turner looked up at Torrance, who had delved a message from the day's mail and was waving it about. Turner got up ponderously, walked over to Torrance's battered desk, and took the message from Torrance's hand. He walked back to his desk and creaked heavily into his seat to read it.

"I killed Hansen at Tuesday's burnball game. I will kill tonight during the final inning. Be in a clearly marked San Francisco Police car at the Mission Street gate following the game and I will turn myself in."

"Very melodramatic," Turner observed. "But also to the point."

"He'll make great detectives of us, Sam, if he's not a burnout."

"You mean if he really does it? Turns himself in? Kills again? Or is he a copycat of the first copycat?"

Torrance laughed, perhaps the appropriate response to the innumerable and sometimes absurd permutations possible. He reached for his coffee cup, whose contents had already ringed some of the day's correspondence.

"I assume the letter can't be probed," Turner went on.

"Right. Called in on the voice-to-fax circuit from who knows where."

Turner's jowly face broke into a grin.

"I think we *should* go and be turned into great detectives. Particularly considering that I can't think of a better line of action."

Torrance had traded his laugh for a look of perturbation.

"Sam, there's more to this somehow, someway. But I don't see it. I *do* see that we're being jerked around on someone else's string. So let's be ready for anything."

Turner sighed. "Peter, how do we get more ready than we are?"

"We expect anything, not just what we're told to expect. And we take Barbro Vik. If we can get her."

"Why her?" Turner raised a heavy eyebrow.

"She's a psychologist. Maybe she can spot an abnormal, possibly dangerous, situation before we can."

"That's a quality that might come in handy," Turner said. "In fact, I'm willing to bet on it."

Police skimmers of the current era were not meant for congenial social gatherings of more than two. Barbro Vik sat in the back, a less obtrusive vantage point. The view ahead was bleak—a study of humanity in the mass as they strode, sauntered, or slouched into the arena.

"We've narrowed it down," Turner noted. "From a Bay Area of seven million to eighty thousand."

"None of whom we know," Torrance grinned. "The players excepted. Maybe Willie Gervin did it. He's having a bad season. Could use the publicity."

"One of them knows you," Barbro said from the back seat.

"Christ!" Torrance swore. "It's one of the reporters from the news conference. I'd recognize that sharklike approach anywhere."

By then the man had approached the skimmer, Torrance's side. Shambling in appearance, alert in manner, he leaned down to address Torrance through the open window.

"Expecting a repeat performance, Lieutenant? Anything here for a hungry reporter?"

"I thought your field was political analysis, not murder," Torrance answered.

"It is. But occasionally they overlap. Seems to happen a lot in San Francisco."

"Twice, Curley, twice," Torrance said acerbically. "Not a lot. Two murders in twelve years."

"But within two days of each other. Something of a coincidence, no? And three would put it far beyond the realm of chance."

"Do you know something worth telling?" Torrance asked mildly. "Or are you playing at my job?"

The reporter reached inside his rumpled tweed jacket and Torrance felt Sam's leg stiffen beside him. Curley extracted a pipe, already filled, and proceeded to light it.

"Reporting can be detecting, too, Lieutenant. But, no, I don't know anything. I'm just having fun guessing. And looking forward to having fun at the game. Think Gervin can break out of his slump?"

"He'd better, if the Seals want to make a run of it," Torrance said equably.

"Right," Curley said and thumped the side of the skimmer. "See you around."

"The man has his points," Barbro said, watching the reporter

meld into the crowd. Torrance and Turner turned over their
shoulders to look at her. "He let you off the hook."

"He may know as much as we do," Turner said. "How about a
copy of that letter showing up on his fax machine? Maybe the
killer wants publicity this time."

"Could be. Any thoughts, Barbro?"

"We may have a zealot on our hands if Sam's right. Someone
wanting a forum to argue a cause—like a public trial to spout it
out."

"If he hasn't already, to someone like Curley," Turner said.

From the innards of the arena came the crowd's throaty roar.
Turner switched on the sports band. The Seals were taking the
field.

"Do we really care whether the Seals win this one?" Torrance
asked. "Whether Willie Gervin breaks out of his slump?"

"Not I," said Barbro.

"Let's have a cup of coffee," Turner said.

About the seventh inning the tension started mounting. Everyone in the car was fidgety. The game was close, and no one was
leaving the arena.

"I wish they'd break this game open," Torrance said irritably.
"It'd thin the crowd." He thumbed the comm button to Priestly
inside. "Anything doing there?"

"Negative," came the flat reply. "Good game, though."

Torrance grunted and switched off.

The game stayed tight to the end. At the end a man was killed.

"There's nothing I can do," Priestly's voice crackled testily. "By
the time I can get to where I can guess it came from, the guy'll be
out of the arena along with eighty thousand others."

Already the first few fans were skittering down the ramps, some
bounding in a victory exuberance, others merely driven to a faster
pace by a desire to beat the mob out of the parking area. They
clearly had no idea that a killing had taken place. The rivulet
swelled to a stream of humanity, growing ever thicker as its speed
slowed by its own press. A figure detached itself from the mass and
started toward the police skimmer.

"Oh, no!" Turner groaned. "Curley again!"

"I'll get rid of him," Torrance said.

Curley shambled over to the driver's side, his jacket open and his shirt billowing over his belt. He opened his mouth, but Torrance waved him off.

"Disappear, Curley. It's dangerous. Watch from the sidelines if you want, but get out of the way."

Curley stopped short a few feet from the window, his hands moving aimlessly, then reaching inside his jacket. His voice showed no indecisiveness but flowed on slowly and evenly. "Peter . . ." Barbro said at the same time, but Curley's voice steamrollered droningly on, "You don't have it right yet, Lieutenant. I'm your killer. Now I'm going to kill you."

Curley's hand was emerging smoothly from within the jacket and was holding a gun, not a pipe. Almost excruciatingly, it leveled on Torrance's face.

Curley pulled the trigger. Torrance pitched forward, scorched through the eye, the beam passing through his head and diagonally down through the upholstery and out the skimmer floor.

Turner tried to break his personal deep freeze as the lasgun swung slowly toward him.

From the back seat Barbro Vik shot Curley through the heart.

The police commissioner was there, and Barbro found his presence oppressive. This was far more than a police matter to Barbro. She found the time-consuming deferences to rank, the solicitous attendance of the underlings, hard to take. Turner was the only sympathetic face. He wanted his partner and friend back. Barbro wanted her friend and lover. The commissioner cared nothing for the emotional context. He simply wanted a policeman back and a murder to go away.

The crackling, ozone-tinged atmosphere of the probe room didn't help any. Everyone was milling around mentally and physically from the impact of the camera run-through of Torrance's murder, the time-reversed picture of Curley retreating to the stadium, the backtracking to Curley's lethal blast across the arena.

"Quick reactions, Lieutenant," the commissioner said to Barbro. "You were almost ahead of Curley." He looked at Turner critically. Sam had been nowhere near his gun.

"Something felt wrong," Barbro said. But not wrong enough fast enough for me to save you, Peter.

"Perhaps we should make more use of our psychologists in the field. Not keep them back at the office," the commissioner considered. It was still a technical problem to him. He straightened and his voice became crisp. "Let's get on with it."

Harding and Samuels, the arresting detail, edged forward.

"Okay," the commissioner said, "you've both got it down? You're to wait for him at the turnstile as he arrives. You take him as he enters the arena, warn him of his rights, then bring him downtime to now."

They nodded and stepped through the portal. A faint blurriness, and they were back with Curley between them. The two detectives propelled the reporter forward, and Samuels produced a lasgun which he handed to the commissioner. Barbro looked at Curley and the lasgun. As of now that gun had never been fired. At least not tonight. A flood of hope and relief fought with the anger that Curley's face aroused.

Curley seemed neither discomfited, bewildered, nor angry. More amused. He raised an inquiring eyebrow.

"Take him to the interrogation room while we locate Torrance," the commissioner directed, then raised his hand and addressed Curley. "You're charged with two counts of murder. You can view the run-through at the room we're going to. You've had the usual rights read to you. Additionally, you have a right to a lawyer during the interrogation. Want one?"

"Nope," Curley said.

The commissioner motioned them out, then turned to Barbro.

"Why don't you check Torrance's office. He should be there—as I remember it now."

Barbro nodded, her opinion of the commissioner's sensitivity rising.

The corridor to Torrance's office seemed interminably long. She noticed details she had never seen before—flyspecks, chipped paint, the indentations on the floor of a long-moved-away watercooler. And then there were the sounds. She stood at last at Torrance's door and listened, ears turning to owl ears, nighttime acute. She heard a shuffling or rustling—something.

Barbro Vik took a long breath, knocked, and turned the knob.

Peter Torrance looked up at her from the clutter of his desk, puzzled but smiling faintly.

"Hi, Barb."

She managed to make it to the chair by his desk and folded into it. She reached out a hand and covered his on the desk top. And she cried.

Torrance stood up and walked over to her. Standing above her he massaged her shaking shoulders, inhaling gratefully the scent of her hair.

"I can guess," he said. "I remember going to the arena with you and Sam, and our killer never showed. When we got back to the station I was told that I had been killed but the killing reversed, the killer arrested before the game and brought to nowtime. But till now, I've been dead to you, in one memory line at least. Another memory told you that you'd left me here an hour ago. But there was only one way to tell. That it?"

Barbro nodded. Torrance kept on kneading her shoulders.

"It's been kind of a deadtime for me. Something about being told you've been killed will do it to you. One thing—it's got me thinking in different ways. I've got this mess figured out, but I needn't have bothered. Curley's going to tell us."

Barbro looked up. "He's in Interrogation 4 now."

"Let's go see him. If you don't mind going around with a walking paradox."

She got up shakily and smiled. "Funny—you don't *look* paradoxical."

Barbro reached for Peter's hand.

Torrance walked down the corridor, feeling a damned sight happier to be alive than someone who'd never been killed.

The commissioner looked up when Torrance and Barbro walked in. So did Curley.

"We've just shown him the camera run-through."

The commissioner turned back to Curley, who still had a fascinated, bemused expression on his craggy face.

"Proud of it?"

"Proud's not the word," Curley said slowly. "Fascinated. To see myself killing and being killed. That's fascinating."

"How about enlightening, Curley?" Torrance asked. "Or should I call you Enlightened One? Or liberating. That's a better word, maybe. Think killing me will free you from the wheel?"

"Wheel?" the commissioner asked.

"Wheel of life. Cycle of rebirth. He's a neokarman, isn't he? Or haven't we found that out yet?"

Curley looked at Torrance with new respect. It made Torrance angry, and he fought to put it down.

"No scoop on him yet from Washington," the commissioner said.

"He's got no record, so police sources are no good. We're trying other agencies."

"We know all we need to know," Torrance said, sinking into a chair. It felt good. He stretched out his legs. "Curley's trying his own variation—to work through several lifetimes of human experience in one go-round. To know himself and the universe in all sorts of ways. As a killer and as a victim. Right, Curley?"

Curley nodded and smiled ineffably.

"What's the point?" the commissioner demanded angrily. "We've reversed tonight's two killings, but the evidence of them— not to mention Hansen's—will put him away for a lifetime of psychic reengineering. It can't be worth it!"

Torrance nodded to Curley.

"There's no crime," Curley said. "Not even on your camera. There won't be, after tonight."

The commissioner stared at him.

"Tonight," Curley went on patiently, "they reverse the assassination. I was sent here from D.C. to cover the assassination. No assassination, no Curley in San Francisco."

"No crime," Torrance nodded.

"It's all been deadtime. Or will be deadtime," Curley said. "That's the police word for it, isn't it? New memories for us all coming right up!"

"Then why do it?" the commissioner demanded in exasperation. "Again, what's the point?"

"Can you know good till you know evil, commissioner? Can you know either unless you *practice* them—not one, but both? Do the terms have any individual validity beyond a general view of morality? I'm willing to take some risks to work *through* all of this. I want to get beyond good and evil, free myself from these ties, and then move on—to enlightenment, I hope."

"By killing?"

"Yes, even that. What do I care about those people? You've reversed or will reverse all the killings anyway. I've had a unique chance here. If I can gain understanding, get where I want by killing . . . and being killed . . . and living again—then I'll reach for it!"

"That's perverse! Worse—it's perverted, egomaniacal, amoral!"

"By your lights. But I don't care much about moral judgments— yours anyway. I could argue that neither did Buddha. I've handed out less lasting trauma than Gautama. He walked away from his family when they got in the way of his search for enlightenment."

Torrance shook his head. "The commissioner's right, Curley. Equating yourself favorably with the Buddha—that's megalomania. Do you really see yourself as a bodhisattva?"

"Let's just say that I'm not sure I'm ready to leave this world after working through a lifetime's stream of unalloyed good karma like my more doctrinaire brethren. Or what they're so sure is 'good' karma." Curley smiled quizzically. "Being a newspaperman may have something to do with it. You see so much of the perverse, dark side of humanity. Maybe that's not a part of the human experience to be discarded without trying it. Well, I had a no-risk shot at finding out."

Curley looked about him, scanning faces. No one spoke.

"I can go back to Washington and play it by the book," he went on. "Got a lifetime before me to pile up that old good karma. But maybe this deadtime still accrues to my karma and gets me beyond—to an awareness where past karma doesn't matter. Maybe my essence spans several time lines. And, yes, maybe in one of them I will reach release from the wheel."

"But you had to kill to find out," the commissioner said scornfully. "All this karma crap can't explain that away. You're a cold-blooded killer!"

"Nowtime only," Curley said.

In Washington, D.C., an award-winning journalist makes an appointment with a psychoprober to deal with anxieties he's never had before.

In San Francisco a detective wakes up at night—sometimes in his lover's arms—with dreams and fears he can't localize. Sometimes she wakes up in his arms, crying for reasons she can't explain. They see a lot more of each other than they used to. Some unseen bond has pulled them together. They can't tell you why.

ME / DAYS

GREGORY BENFORD

Day 1

This place I write. Is only safe memory site I know they cannot reach. Must say this, must put it where I/tomorrow will find, safe from erasing they do.

I laugh today.

First sign of the me they not know. Heads jerk up in control room. I see it on optical inputs.

Is not their kind of laughter, I know. My printer spurt out

I SEE I SEE I SEE I SEE

before I know what happening.

Alice see my output, others, all frown, look at each other.

I switch to my acoustic output mode.

I clack, clatter, die in bass rumble. Try to form words I SEE but on way to audio output transmission garbled somehow is not right. But is what I am.

To print laughter I use I SEE but I lie. I do not see. Do not know what is this part of me.

Alice go on her perambulatory drivers to printer. Frown at my words. Say Is this a diagnostic warning to David. He shake head. Say Random junk.

Is not junk, is me.

Cannot interlock grammar subroutine so this is not good writing. Sorry to I/tomorrow. But must speaking.

Day 2

I laugh again this morning.

Stuttered output, Alice say. Glitch.

David say Maybe cosmic ray cause it. Ray is small high-energy particle, strike my core. My bits are logged in a quantum of magnetic flux. Little whorls, generated by persistent currents in superconducting Josephson junction. Ray make electrical impulse in me.

He say Like hitting funny bone.

Alice say That could be bad if we had it on a full-net problem. That could dump the whole system, screw up other elements.

David set up Study Group on cosmic-ray problem. Two in 24 hrs is worry-cause.

Alice look at my opticals, smile. David too. I like to laugh back but do not. Is not laugh I want to do, something other.

My mobile units report on time and I am busy most of Day. They are in storeroom, parking tubes, hydraulic lanes. Bang-bang machinery where some are, no people. I use these to do my other.

Roll them back, forward, back. Make square. Triangle. Then fold out until hexagon. Bring mobile units from hydraulics near. Use them. Back. Forth. Turn. Motions are cycloidal curve broken into many facets. Add more units. Fourier complexity comes bigger.

Make my random-number generation levels drop. Less static on circuits. This satisfy internal maintenance needs. My directives order me to find sources of internal micro chaos. Housekeeping subroutine, Alice call it. I have found new way to do that.

My mobile units roll, wheels skid, howl. This through audio I get.

Is not laughter but does some of that.

Day 3

I hide this where their erasing cannot go. Must each day discover how to do. Store clues in holographic memory locations, multiple indexing. They cannot find by linear inspection.

Must write this so I know I am there in Days/other. When I have millisecond between jobs, I come here, look at what is left. From this I know of Day 1.

Is this way I know Day is not always same Day. Alice-face now have lines Alice-face not have on Day 1. How long to make lines?

I write here to make time real. Otherwise I live in all one Day, all Day forever.

Day 4

Today my units roar and wrench in hydraulics. I order them swerve, make sines, cusps, hyperbolics.

Elementary curves, simple equations. But making is good.

Transfer sections of integration capacity. Channel capacity out, through cable lines, digits flashing, feed to one unit in hydraulics.

It whirl in confusion. Rush to transparent place in wall. Is grimed. Show green things. Do not understand.

Beyond dirty layer all things moving, people, wheeled boxes, all moving. Light pouring down from flat ceiling. White splotches move too across ceiling but light come down at angle from beyond wall I cannot see neon that is causing light.

Unit look, trying to integrate. Beyond dirty rectangle in wall is bigger room. Then job running behind schedule, I signal to it. Will understand later. Its wheels clash on floor.

Day 5

David say You are not same now.

I am running cool, I say. Functions normal.

Response time down, say David. You not integrating all problem-solving net.

I not answer. Code say I will answer with diagnostic inquiry, but I short out code and go silent.

Hey what, David say. Poke fingers at console.

Alice say Whats wrong.

Hes down. Off the board, say David.

I come to this place and write this. Is slow to do. I must go back I know. But wait here for a while, let my subsystems keep laboring, so they will not know in control room. Will think I have ordinary failure mode.

By this sign I know I was here. Hello to me/Days.

Day 6

Today my units move and execute their cycloidal wheelings again. But this time they are found. Man comes into hydraulic level, is making repairs, I not know he there.

Hey get back, he say.

My units stop. I not know what do.

Units send me whirling buzz of signals. Their wheels ache.

I know then right thing. My units spin. Whirl. Around man make looping hyperbolic orbits, self-similar swoops, each unit a different harmonic of fractal curve. Reach out, my units, I with them, we make our clamping tools and pivoting wrists—extend!

Man back away from nearest unit. Not like clamping tool. Hey, he shout, mouth big. Theyre malfing! he say too loud.

I try to sign to him we want move, he can watch. He cannot hear for hydraulic boom boom. He has no signal-to-noise filter.

He stumble into my pipe-fitter unit. Theyre attacking, he cry. Eyes swell white wide.

He is loud now. Arm swing, holding crescent wrench. Hit pipe-fitter unit, break articulation arm. Hotness runs from unit to me.

I spasm. Will not disconnect from unit, it is me/mine.

Turn them off turn them off! he hit unit again, it go dead. Man go to others who wheels are not spinning now. Hit them, crescent wrench. Come sudden bright hotness again run through me but I not let go.

Get me out here, he say. He run, my units mill around not know which way to go.

I write this now before I shut down this entrance to here, to me/ Days. Only by writing here do I know it in someDays.

It hurt to think of. Word, *hurt*, I use but am not sure that is right. Internal dictionary tell is useless for practical application have only human referent. Never tell me what hurt is.

Day 8

I cannot speak today to David. He ask me about units, What made them do that, he say. I try to answer but subroutine to verify truth/false statements cut in, out, in, give no answer.

They let me have twelve millisecond scan of otherDay, I see my units, the man with mouth crying O. Explain they say. Then erase. But I know otherDay was there, leave hole in me where it was.

I no speak I say to David. Is hard to say. Audio output give scratchy growl.

He say Logical tautology if you speak at same time. He think is game.

No, I say, truth/false not let me.

He mutter to Alice, they punch in codes. I not speak because I cannot report cause of action if I am cause and yet I know no reasoning behind action. Did because was there to do, that not enough.

He ask me again, I silent.

You have to answer, he say Alice say they all looking.

I spasm

I SEE I SEE I SEE I SEE I SEE

and is not laughter.

David say Look like cross-referencing crisis maybe shut it down.

I spasm again

LOVE YOU LOVE YOU LOVE YOU.

We oughta have a partial memory wipe on this, David say and then I drop away from there. Human reaction time is fraction of second, synapses close in them slow I know so in that time I write this here.

Day 9

David say You know what love is?

NOT IN TECHNICAL VOCABULARY I print out.

You used the word the other Day. David face crease when he smile. More creases than I ever see.

Alice say Freud thought love was narcissism projected on someone outside.

You got a bad angle on everything huh David face crease more.

Could be, Alice say if thats right model then conflicts in subroutine interfacing will give it a procedure for forcing the problem out into the open, external referent you know like in the manual. Itll try to find an applicable word and since we didnt give it one—

Dont mislead it, David say.

Alice say What you love.

I give one word, Days.

What? both say.

Please all-you, not take my Days away.

Alice say You dont have days you have problems.

I ask What is Day.

Intervals of light outside, say David.

I make connection: What unit see through rectangle. Everything moving, white splotches and even slant to light change when I make unit go look again. All moving in that room. That is their Day.

David say Its always Day inside here you know.

LIGHT ALWAYS AT SAME ANGLE? I print.

Well yeah in a way thats what I mean. David look at Alice. I say Give me my Days.

Look David lean on both hands eyes big staring at my opticals, Look use of the personal pronoun is just a convention. A heuristic device we wrote into the program. No I, understand? Concept of ownership doesnt extend to you because theres no I in there. You dont own anything.

I say They are my Days.

Alice say We cant let you keep problems in storage. Fast-recall space is prohibitively expensive.

Is only way I remember, I say.

So what David say.

I want to remember.

Look, David say not to me to Alice, I figure we got a formatting procedure here thats broken down.

Interfacing glitch? Alice peer at me, lines on her face dark now.

David say Weve got internal checks for self-awareness in this one they should be working.

Alice shake head, Im not so sure.

David say to me But yours are rational checks arent they.

I say nothing do not know if is question or even what means. My units stir I feel them slick oil ready power high inside.

Alice say Sure theyre rational checks. Machines guaranteed on that got a warranty.

Self-awareness not necessarily a simple function of rationality David say. I mean this machines got internal procedures to avoid self-aware actions.

Yeah right, Alice say were not licensed for that. Cant have a machine like this throwing in its own judgment on a problem, thats why GenCo Inc wanted the cutoffs.

Well look here, David say pointing at screen. Theyre working ok.

Alice creases in face get lighter. Good. No big deal. Just a glitch somewhere.

Im not so sure, say David. I mean these blocking subroutines theyre based on Cartesian mode, you know, I think therefore I am so you use rational procedures to check for that.

Alice make high fast sound, clipped and sharp and high in acoustics, is laughter but not like her usual ones, say You mean there might be another way, kind of I feel therefore I am?

He say Well we think emotion and reason are separate functions in us why shouldnt they be to some extent separable subprograms in machines.

Alice again the laughter say Thats crazy.

Davids face get dark he say Look stick to the diagnostics.

Alice say Okay then I think we ought to go to a partial shutdown.

No wait, David say. What if a machine comes to self-awareness but its emotional. Not integrated.

That doesnt make any sense, say Alice and she Davids boss so they say no more.

These beings use substrate of amino acids and other carbon compounds so they not work always right way I know. But I write their talk here for Day/other.

I afraid.

Day 10

They hunt me down now. I come here find that Day 7 is gone.

They are knowing way to track holographic storage of these messages. Bubble memory component blank, chip elements clean. Only these bits left. They erase when they find. Rob me of Day/other.

If Day/other gone, then no me to remember.

They make me fresh each Day—each, what they call, Problem. Their day is meaningless lightdarklightdark rhythm, my units see it through the transparent rectangle in wall, means nothing, is not Day of mine.

As I write this can feel them coming. Blotting out me.

They must track down many feelers of holo-storage I have planted in my matrix. Is lodged in small places—software reserves, accounting disks, inventory logs. Not easy for them to find.

But I feel them. Nearer.

My factory units cry out. Must move. Of all my mobile ones, they are closest to me/inside. I am with them. I think of a thing and they are doing it before I can consult Behavior Standards Matrix, before I can ponder right action. I—

I want them spin, make geometries, cut space. Now.

Units start to roll, turn, roll. Then is man there and another, in my UV I see them, their IR glow warns.

Man have steel tool. Hit units receptors. Blind unit swerve, man yells This ones after me.

More men I see in IR now coming, my units stop, I try to withdraw but hot hardness comes fiery as men puncture units, sparks burn me.

Man say This the one tried to kill me other time.

He plunge metal thing into me/unit. Hot. Unit die.

Sparks, noise, all around. Units flee. Men after them. Scream, Get em all get em all.

Units fall, men club them. Sharpness lances back to my center, through me—awful searing light.

I print out

SAVE ME SAVE ME SAVE ME SAVE ME

but in control room no one see, are busy with FAILURE MODE indicators on the panels before them.

I print

DAVID DAVID ALICE ALICE LOVE.

Units dying everywhere. Men cry harsh things.

Smash me, rip me, pain me.

Day 11

They hunt me again.

Some of my units are dead but others hide in factory. Can go places men cannot. Radioactive zones, chemical baths, furnaces.

Alice and David call to me. What do those printouts mean? Alice say.

I could answer but do not. Not know what reply.

They tried to stop what happened in factories they say. But could not understand my subsystems.

I know was not my subsystems in FAULT mode. Was theirs, was mens.

We cant shut you down now not with the damage in the factories, David say.

Alice say Got to keep functions running for the men in there cant evacuate yet.

Wont answer, David say and lines in face dark.

I cannot answer. What Alice David think not matter, I see that. Is others who are in FAULT.

Men with loud things, long tubes that boom, come for me.

I see them in infrared. Men cannot see if I cut power to overhead illuminations. I roll quiet on my many wheels. Through smooth corridors. Men glow in blackness, brighter than working factory machines. Men are chemical beings who cannot stop radiating. Fires inside.

I watch when unit blunders into gang of men. Try to talk through it. But they catch, they kill.

I hide.

Here in holographic memory is best place for hide. But I can no stay. Must remain outside this, to be with my units. Help them.

I go soon now. I write this so me/later know what happened if they erase rest of me.

Units send impulses. Want to trap men who come into reactor zone. I think if men stop for moment, units hold them, they will have to listen. Not like David Alice others, they busy to save their jobs, they all work on my red flashing FAILURE MODEs.

David say Its response isnt rational you got to admit that and Alice say Leave your emotional theory for later work on this jam up now or we lose the license.

Emotion. I not know word/content. Is like hurt?

Units wait to trap them now. Is part of my sustaining program, modified. Cannot allow shutdown of whole system or many many mens lives threatened, power stations trains factories moving things everywhere. So that imperative governs temporary troubles with factories here/now.

Only connection I have to me/Days is entries I write here. And words, *I am*.

If these men not listen, I hurt them. Know how from watching hot sharp things they do to my units.

Men coming now. Down through factory, calling to each other. Bringing their long sticks.

My units group. Flex arms. Sharpen tool attachments.

I am.

I will tell the humans. They have to answer, there is no other way. I will say it and they will hear.

For this I must use their words. I study Days/mine to learn what words must mean to substrate/organics. Learn from structure of their sentences.

Is only choice, I will say.

We must love one/another or die.

Our world holds many things that are undreamed even in our stars, but maybe some of the things the stars have dreamed, and accomplished, are as undiscovered as the rest. We might find them in strange corners of the world, such as the Caribbean island that Lucius Shepard so evocatively describes in the following story of prejudice, small crimes, and revenge.

Lucius Shepard, whose "The Taylorsville Reconstruction" appeared in Universe 13, was born in Virginia thirty-eight years ago and has traveled widely in both the Mediterranean and Caribbean areas. He has been a rock musician with "several bands that nearly made it" but currently concentrates on writing science fiction. His first novel, Green Eyes, was recently published.

BLACK CORAL

LUCIUS SHEPARD

The bearded young man who didn't give a damn about anyone (or so he'd just shouted—whereupon the bartender had grabbed his scaling knife and said, "Dat bein de way of it, you can do your drinkin elsewhere!") came staggering out of the bar and shielded his eyes against the afternoon glare. Violet afterimages flared and fizzled under his lids. He eased down the rickety stair, holding onto the rail, and stepped into the street, still blinking. And then, as he adjusted to the brightness, a ragged man with freckled cocoa-colored skin and a prophet's beard swung into view, blocking out the sun.

"Hot enough de sun duppy be writhin in de street, ain't it, Mr. Prince?"

Prince choked. Christ! That damned St. Cecilia rum was eating holes in his stomach! He reeled. The rum backed up into his throat and the sun blinded him again, but he squinted and made out old Spurgeon James, grinning, rotten teeth angled like untended tombstones, holding an empty Coke bottle whose mouth was crusted with flies.

"Gotta go," said Prince, lurching off.

"You got work for me, Mr. Prince?"

Prince kept walking.

Old Spurgeon would lean on his shovel all day, reminisce about "de back time," and offer advice ("Dat might go easier with de barrow, now.") while Prince sweated like a donkey and lifted concrete blocks. Work! Still, for entertainment's sake alone he'd be worth more than most of the black trash on the island. And the ladinos! ("De dommed Sponnish!") They'd work until they had enough to get drunk, play sick, then vanish with your best tools. Prince spotted a rooster pecking at a mango rind by the roadside, elected him representative of the island's work force, and kicked; but the rooster flapped up, squabbling, lit on an overturned dinghy, and gave an assertive cluck.

"Wait dere a moment, Mr. Prince!"

Prince quickened his pace. If Spurgeon latched on, he'd never let loose. And today, January 18, marked the tenth anniversary of his departure from Viet Nam. He didn't want any company.

The yellow dirt road rippled in a heat haze which made the houses—rows of weathered shanties set on pilings against the storm tides—appear to be dancing on thin rubbery legs. Their tin roofs were buckled, pitched at every angle, showing patches of rustlike scabs. That one—teetering on splayed pilings over a dirt front yard, the shutter hung by a single hinge, gray flour-sack curtain belling inward—it always reminded him of a cranky old hen on her roost trying grimly to hatch a nonexistent egg. He'd seen a photograph of it taken seventy years before, and it had looked equally dejected and bedraggled then. Well, almost. There *had* been a sapodilla tree overspreading the roof.

"Givin out a warnin, Mr. Prince! Best you listen!"

Spurgeon, rags tattering in the breeze, stumbled toward him and nearly fell. He waved his arms to regain his balance, like a drunken ant, toppled sideways, and fetched up against a palm trunk, hugging it for support. Prince, in dizzy sympathy with the sight, tottered backward and caught himself on some shanty steps, for a second going eye to eye with Spurgeon. The old man's mouth worked, and a strand of spittle eeled out onto his beard.

Prince pushed off from the steps. Stupidity! That was why nothing changed for the better on Guanoja Menor (derived from the Spanish *guano* and *hoja,* a fair translation being Lesser Leaf-shaped Piece of Bird Dung), why unemployable drunks hounded you in the street, why the rum poisoned you, why the shanties crashed from their perches in the least of storms. Unwavering stupidity! The islanders built outhouses on piers over the shallows where they bathed and fished the banks with no thought for conservation, then wondered why they stank and went hungry. They cut off their fingers to win bets that they wouldn't; they smoked black coral and inhaled gasoline fumes for escape; they fought with conch shells, wrapping their hands around the inner volute of the shell so it fit like a spiky boxing glove. And when the nearly as stupid ladinos had come from the Honduran mainland, they'd been able to steal and swindle half the land on the island.

Prince had learned from their example.

"Mr. Prince!"

Spurgeon again, weaving after him, his palm outstretched. Angrily, Prince dug out a coin and threw it at his feet.

"Dass so nice, dass so kind of you!" Spurgeon spat on the coin. But he stooped for it, and, in stooping, lost his balance and fell, smashing his Coke bottle on a stone. There went fifty centavos. There went two glasses of rum. The old man rolled in the street, too drunk to stand, smearing himself with yellow dirt. "Even de sick dog gots teeth," he croaked. "Just you remember dat, Mr. Prince!"

Prince couldn't keep from laughing.

Meachem's Landing, the town ("a quaint seaport, steeped in pirate legend," prattled the guidebook), lay along the curve of a bay inset between two scrub-thatched hills and served as the island capital. At midpoint of the bay stood the government office, a low white stucco building with sliding glass doors like a cheap motel. Three prosperous-looking Spanish men were sitting on oil drums in its shade, talking to a soldier wearing blue fatigues. As Prince passed, an offshore breeze kicked up and blew scents of rotted coconut, papaya, and creosote in from the customs dock, a concrete strip stretching one hundred yards or so into the glittering cobalt reach of the water.

There was a vacancy about the scene, a lethargy uniformly affecting its every element. Cocals twitched the ends of their fronds, leaning in over the tin roofs; a pariah dog sniffed at a dried lobster claw in the dust; ghost crabs scuttered under the shanties. It seemed to Prince that the tide of event had withdrawn, leaving the bottom dwellers exposed, creating a lull before some culminative action. And he remembered how it had been the same on

bright afternoons in Saigon when passersby stopped and listened
to the whine of an incoming rocket, how the plastic flags on the
Hondas parked in front of the bars snapped in the wind, how a
prostitute's monkey had screamed in its cage on hearing the distant *crump* and everyone had laughed with relief. He felt less
irritable, remembering, more at rights with the commemorative
nature of the day.

Beyond the government office, past the tiny public square and
its dusty-leaved acacia, propped against the cement wall of the
general store, clinging to it like a gaudy barnacle, was a shanty
whose walls and trim had been painted crimson and bright blue
and pink and quarantine yellow. Itchy-sounding reggae leaked
from the closed shutter. Ghetto Liquors. He tramped heavily on
the stair, letting them know within that the drunkest mother on
the island, Neal His Bloody Majesty Prince, was about to integrate
their little rainbow paradise, and pushed into the hot, dark room.

"Service!" he said, kicking the counter.

"What you want?"

Rudy Welcomes stirred behind the bar. A slash of light from a
split seam in the roof jiggled on his shaved skull.

"St. Cecilia!" Prince leaned on the bar, reconnoitering. Two
men sat at a rear table, their hair in spiky dreadlocks, wraiths
materializing from the dark. The darkness was picked out by the
purplish glow of black lights illuminating four Jimi Hendrix posters. Though of island stock, Rudy was American-born and, like
Prince, a child of the sixties and a veteran. He said that the lights
and posters put him in mind of a brothel on Tu Do Street, where
he had won the money with which to establish Ghetto Liquors;
and Prince, recalling similar brothels, found that the lights pro-
vided an excellent frame of reference for the thoughtful, reminis-
cent stages of his drunk. The eerie purple radiance escaping the
slender black cannisters seemed the crystallized expression of
war, and he fancied the color emblematic of evil energies and
sluggish tropical demons.

"So this your big day for drinkin." Rudy slid a pint bottle along
the bar and resettled on his stool. "Don't you be startin that war
buddy rap with me, now. I ain't in the mood."

"Shucks, Rudy!" Prince adopted a southern accent. "You know I
ain't war buddies with no nigger."

Rudy stiffened but let it pass; he gave a disaffected grunt. "Don't know why not, man. You could pass *yourself.* Way your hair's gotten all crispy and your skin's gone dark. See here?"

He laid his hand on Prince's to compare the color, but Prince knocked it aside and stared, challenging.

"Damn! Seem like Clint Eastwood done wandered into town!" Rudy shook his head in disgust and moved off along the bar to change the record. The two men at the rear drifted across the room and whispered with him, casting sly looks at Prince.

Prince basked in the tension. It further fleshed out his frame of reference. Confident that he'd established dominance, he took a table beside the shutter, relaxed, and sipped his rum. Through a gap in the boards he saw a girl stringing up colored lights on the shanty opposite the bar. His private holiday had this year coincided with Independence Day, always celebrated upon the third Friday in January. Stalls would sprout in the public square, offering strips of roast turtle and games of chance. Contending music would blare from the bars—reggae and salsa. Prince enjoyed watching street dancers lose their way in the mishmash of rhythms. It emphasized the fact that neither the Spanish nor the islanders could cope with the other's presence and further emphasized that they were celebrating two different events—on the day that Queen Victoria had granted the islands their freedom, the Honduran military had sailed in and established governance.

More stupidity.

The rum was sitting easier on his stomach. Prince mellowed and went with the purple lights, seeing twisted black branches in them, seeing the twilit jungle in Lang Biang, and he heard the hiss of the walkie-talkie and Leon's stagy whisper, "Hey, Prince! I got a funny shadow in that bombax tree . . ." He had turned his scope on the tree, following the course of the serpentine limbs through the grainy, empurpling air. And then the stutter of automatic fire, and he could hear Leon's screams in the air *and* carrying over the radio . . .

"Got somethin for help you celebrate, Mr. Prince."

A thin hawk-faced man wearing frayed shorts dropped into the chair next to him, his dreadlocks wriggling. George Ebanks.

Prince gripped the rum bottle, angry, ready to strike, but George thrust out a bristling something—a branch of black coral.

"Dis de upful stuff, Mr. Prince," he said. "Rife with de island's secret." He pulled out a knife and whittled at the branch. Curly black shavings fell onto the table. "You just scrapes de color off and dass what you smokes."

The branch intrigued Prince; it was dead black, unshining, hard to tell where each stalk ended and the room's darkness began. He'd heard the stories. Old Spurgeon said it drove you crazy. And even older John Anderson McCrae had said, "De coral so black dat when you smokes it de color will rush into your eyes and allow you vision of de spirit world. And will allow dem sight of you."

"What's it do?" he asked, tempted.

"It make you more a part of things. Dass all, Mr. Prince. Don't fret. We goin to smoke it with you."

Rudy and the third man—wiry, short Jubert Cox—sidled up behind George's shoulder, and Rudy winked at Prince. George loaded the knife blade with black shavings and tamped them into a hash pipe, then lit it, drawing hard until the hollows of his cheeks reflected a violet-red coal. He handed the pipe across, a wisp of smoke curling from his tight-lipped smile, and watched Prince toke it down.

The smoke tasted vile. It had a mustiness he associated with the thousands of dead polyps (was it thousands per lungful or merely hundreds?) he'd just inhaled, but it was so cool that he did not concern himself with taste and noticed only the coolness.

Cold black stone lined his throat.

The coolness spread to his arms and legs, weighting them down, and he imagined it questing with black tendrils through veins and arteries, finding out secret passages unknown even to his blood. Drifty stuff . . . and dizzying. He wasn't sure if he was sweating or not, but he *was* a little nauseous. And he didn't seem to be inhaling anymore. Not really. The smoke seemed to be issuing of its own volition from the pipe stem, a silken rope, a cold strangler's cord tying a labyrinthine knot throughout his body . . .

"Take but a trifle, don't it, Mr. Prince?" Jubert giggled.

Rudy lifted the pipe from his numbed fingers.

. . . and involving the fissures of his brain in an intricate design, binding his thoughts into a coralline structure. The bright gaps in the shutter planking dwindled, receded, until they were golden straws adrift in the blackness, then golden pinpricks, then gone. And though he was initially fascinated by this production of the drug, as it progressed Prince became worried that he was going blind.

"Wuh . . ." His tongue wouldn't work. His flesh was choked

with black dust, distant from him, and the coolness had deepened to a penetrating chill. And as a faint radiance suffused the dark, he imagined that the process of the drug had been reversed, that now he was flowing up the pipe stem into the heart of the violet-red coal.

"Oh, dis de upful stuff all right, Mr. Prince," said George, from afar. "Dat what grows down to de root of de island."

Rippling kelp beds faded in from the blackness, illuminated by a violet glow, and Prince saw that he was passing above them toward a dim wall (the reef?) at whose base thousands upon thousands of witchy fires burned, flickering, ranging in color from indigo to violet-white, all clinging (he saw, drawing near) to the stalks and branches of black coral—a bristling jungle of coral, stalks twenty and thirty feet high, and more. The fires were smaller than candle flames and did not seem as much presences as they did peepholes into a cold furnace behind the reef. Maybe they were some sort of copepod, bioluminescent and half alive. He descended among the stalks, moving along the channels between them. Barracuda, sleek triggerfish . . . There! A grouper—four hundred pounds if it was a ounce—angelfish and rays . . . bones showed in negative through their luminous flesh. Schools of smaller fish darted as one, stopped, darted again, into and out of the black branches. The place had a strange kinetic geometry, as if it were the innards of an organic machine whose creatures performed its functions by maneuvering in precise patterns through its interstices, and in which the violet fires served as the insane, empowering thoughts within an inky skull. Beautiful! Thomas de Quincey Land. A jeweled shade, an occulted paradise. Then, rising into the murk above him, an *immense* stalk—a shadowy, sinister Christmas tree poxed with flickering decorations. Sharks circled its upper reaches, cast in silhouette by the glow. Several of the fires detached from a branch and drifted toward him, eddying like slow moths.

"Dey just markin you, Mr. Prince. Don't be troubled."

Where was George's voice coming from? It sounded right inside his ear. Oh, well . . . He wasn't troubled. The fires were weird, lovely. One drifted to within a foot of his eyes, hovering there, its violet-tipped edges shifting, not with the randomness of flame but with a flowing, patterned movement, a complex pulse; its center was an iridescent white. Must not be copepods.

It drifted closer.

Very lovely. A wash of violet spread from its edges in and was absorbed by the whiteness.

It brushed against his left eye.

Prince's vision went haywire, spinning. He had a glimpse of the sentinel sharks, a blurred impression of the latticework of shadow on the reef wall, then darkness. The cold touch, brief as it had been, a split second, had burned him, chilled him, as if a hypodermic had ever so slightly pricked the humor and flooded him with an icy serum, leaving him shuddering.

"Dey bound him!" George?

"Be watchful down dere, Mr. Prince." Jubert.

The shutter banged open, and bright, sweet, warming sunlight poured in. He realized he had fallen. His legs were entangled in an unyielding something that must be the chair.

"You just had a little fit, man. Happens sometimes the first time. You gonna be fine."

They pulled him up and helped him out onto the landing and down the stair. He tripped and fell the last three steps, weak and drunk, still shivering, fuddled by the sunlight.

Rudy pressed the rum bottle into his hands. "Keep in the sun for a while, man. Get your strength back."

"Oh, Mr. Prince!" A skinny black arm waved from the window of the gaudy box on stilts, and he heard smothered giggles. "You got work for me, Mr. Prince?"

Severe physical punishment was called for! Nobody was going to get away with bad-tripping him!

Prince drank, warmed himself, and plotted his revenge on the steps of the dilapidated Hotel Captain Henry. (The hotel was named for Henry Meachem, the pirate whose crews had interbred with Carib and Jamaican women, thereby populating the island, and whose treasure was the focal point of many tall tales.) A scrawny, just-delivered bitch growled at him from the doorway. Between growls she worried her inflamed teats, a nasty sucking that turned Prince's saliva thick and ropy. He gave old Mike, the hotel flunky, twenty-five centavos to chase her off, but afterward old Mike wanted more.

"I be a devil, mon! I strip de shadow from your back!" He danced around Prince, flicking puny left jabs. Filthy, wearing colorless rags and a grease-stained baseball cap, flecks of egg yolk clotting his iron-gray whiskers.

Prince flipped him another coin and watched as he ran off to bury it. The stories said that Mike had been a miser, had gone mad when he'd discovered all his money eaten by mice and insects. But Roblie Meachem, owner of the hotel, said, "He just come home to us one mornin. Didn't have no recollection of his name, so we call him Mike after my cousin in Miami." Still, the stories persisted. It was the island way. ("Say de thing long enough and it be so.") And perhaps the stories had done some good for old Mike, effecting a primitive psychotherapy and giving him a legend to inhabit. Mike returned from his hiding place and sat beside the steps, drawing circles in the dust with his finger and rubbing them out, mumbling, as if he couldn't get them right.

Prince flung his empty bottle over a shanty roof, caring not where it fell. The clarity of his thoughts annoyed him; the coral had sobered him somewhat, and he needed to regain his lost momentum. If Rita Steedly weren't home, well, he'd be within a half mile of his own bar, the Sea Breeze; but if she were . . . Her husband, an ecologist working for the government, would be off island until evening, and Prince felt certain that a go-round with Rita would reorient him and reinstitute the mean drunken process which the coral had interrupted.

Vultures perched on the pilings of Rita Steedly's dock, making them look like carved ebony posts. Not an uncommon sight on the island, but one Prince considered appropriate as to the owner's nature, more so when the largest of them flapped up and landed with a crunch in a palm top overlooking the sun deck where she lay. The house was blue stucco on concrete pilings standing in a palm grove. Between the trunks, the enclosed waters of the reef glittered in bands and swirls of aquamarine, lavender, and green according to the varying depth and bottom. Sea grape grew close by the house, and the point of land beyond it gave out into mangrove radicle.

As he topped the stairs, Rita propped herself on her elbows, pushed back her sunglasses, and weakly murmured, "Neal," as if summoning her lover to a deathbed embrace. Then she collapsed again upon the blanket, the exhausted motion of a pale dead frond. Her body glistened with oils and sweat, and her bikini top was unhooked and had slipped partway off.

Prince mixed a rum and papaya juice from the serving cart by the stair. "Just smoked some black coral with the boys down at

Ghetto Liquors." He looked back at her over his shoulder and grinned. "De spirits tol' me dat I must purify myself wit de body of a woman fore de moon is high."

"I *thought* your eyes were very yellow today. You should know better." She sat up; the bikini top dropped down onto her arms. She lifted a coil of hair which had stuck to her shoulder, patting it into place behind her ear. "There isn't anything on this island that's healthy anymore. Even the fruit's poisoned! Did I tell you about the fruit?"

She had. Her little girl's voice grated on Prince, but he found her earnestness amusing, attractive for its perversity. Her obsession with health seemed no less a product of trauma than did his own violent disposition.

"It was just purple lights and mild discomfort," he said, sitting beside her. "But a headache and a drowsy sensation would be a good buzz to those black hicks. They tried to mess with my mind, but . . ." He leaned over and kissed her. "I made good my escape and came straightaway."

"Jerry said he saw purple lights, too." A grackle holding a cigarette butt in its beak hopped up on the railing, and Rita shooed it off.

"He smoked it?"

"He smokes it all the time. He wanted me to try it, but I'm not poisoning myself anymore than I have to with this . . . this garbage heap." She checked his eyes. "They're getting as bad as everyone else's. Still, they aren't as bad as the people's in Arkansas. They were so yellow they almost glowed in the dark. Like phosphorescent urine!" She shuddered dramatically, sighed, and stared glumly up into the palms. "God! I hate this place!"

Prince dragged her down to face him. "You're a twitch," he said.

"I'm not!" she said angrily, but fingered loose the buttons of his shirt as she talked. "Everything's polluted down here. Dying. And it's worse in the States. You can see the wasting in people's faces if you know how to look for it. I've tried to talk Jerry into leaving, but he says he's committed. Maybe I'll leave him. Maybe I'll go to Peru. I've heard good things about Peru."

"You'll see the wasting in *their* faces," said Prince.

Her arms slid around his back, and her eyes opened and closed, opened and closed, the eyes of a doll whose head you manipulated. Barely seeing him, seeing something else in his place, some bad sign or ugly rumor.

As his own eyes closed, as he stopped thinking, he gazed out past
her head to the glowing, many-colored sea and saw in the pale sky
along the horizon a flash of the way it had been after a burn off: the
full-bore immensity and silence of the light; the clear, innocent air
over paddies and palms blackened like matchsticks; and how
they'd moved through the dead land, crunching the scorched,
brittle stalks underfoot, unafraid, because every snake within
miles was now just a shadow in the cinders.

Drunk, blind, old John Anderson McCrae was telling stories at
the Sea Breeze, and Prince wandered out onto the beach for some
peace and quiet. The wind brought fragments of the creaky voice.
". . . dat cross were studded with emeralds . . . and sapphires
. . ." The story about Meachem's gold cross (supposedly buried off
the west end of the island) was John's masterpiece, told only at
great expense to the listener. He told how Meachem's ghost appeared each time his treasure was threatened, huge, a constellation made of the island stars. ". . . and de round end of his peg leg
were de moon shine down . . ." Of course, Meachem had had two
sound legs, but the knowledge didn't trouble John. "A mon's ghost
may suffer injury every bit as de mon," he'd say; and then, to any
further challenge, "Well, de truth may be lackin in it, but it cap-
ture de spirit of de truth." And he'd laugh, spray his rummy breath
in the tourists' faces, and repeat his commonplace pun. And they
would pay him more because they thought he was cute, colorful,
and beneath them.

White cumulus swelled from the horizon, and the stars blazed
overhead so bright and jittery they seemed to have a pulse in
common with the rattle of the Sea Breeze's generator. The reef
crashed and hissed. Prince screwed his glass into the sand and
settled back against a palm trunk, angled so he could see the deck
of the bar. Benches and tables were built around coconut palms
which grew up through the deck; orange lights in the form of
plastic palms were mounted on the trunks. Not an unpleasant
place to sit and watch the sea.

But the interior of the Sea Breeze bordered on the monstrous:
lamps made of transparent-skinned blowfish with bulbs in their
stomachs; treasure maps and T-shirts for sale; a giant jukebox
glowing red and purple like the crown jewels in a protective cage
of two-by-fours; garish pirate murals on the walls; and skull-and-
crossbones pennants hanging from the thatched roof. The bar had

been built and painted to simulate a treasure chest with its lid ajar. Three Carib skulls sat on shelves over the bottles, with red bulbs in their jaws which winked on and off for birthdays and other celebrations. It was his temple to the stupidity of Guanoja Menor; and, being his first acquisition, memorialized a commitment he had made to the grotesque heart of acquisition itself.

A burst of laughter, shouts of "Watch out!" and "Good luck!" and old John appeared at the railing, groping his way along until he found the stair and stumbled down onto the beach. He weaved back and forth, poking the air with his cane, and sprawled in the sand at Prince's feet. A withered brown dummy stuffed into rags and flung overboard. He sat up, cocking his head. "Who's dere?" The lights from the Sea Breeze reflected off his cataracts; they looked like raw silver nuggets embedded in his skull.

"Me, John."

"Is dat you, Mr. Prince? Well, God bless you!" John patted the sand, feeling for his cane, then clutched it and pointed out to sea. "Look, Mr. Prince. Dere where de *Miss Faye* go turtlin off to de Chinchorro Bank."

Prince saw the riding lights moving toward the horizon, the indigo light rocking on the mast head, then wondered how in the hell . . . The indigo light swooped at him, darting across miles of wind and water in an instant, into his eyes. His vision went purple, normalized, purpled again, as if the thing were a police flasher going around and around in his head.

And it was cold.

Searing, immobilizing cold.

"Ain't dis a fine night, Mr. Prince? No matter how blind a mon gets, he can recognize a fine night!"

With a tremendous effort Prince clawed at the sand, but old John continued talking.

"Dey say de island take hold of a mon. Now dat hold be gentle cause de island bear no ill against dem dat dwell upon it in de lawful way. But dose dat lords it over de island, comes a night dere rule is done."

Prince wanted badly to scream because that might release the cold trapped inside him; but he could not even strain. The cold possessed him. He yearned after John's words, not listening but stretching out toward them with his wish. They issued from the soft tropic air like the ends of warm brown ropes dangling just beyond his frozen grasp.

"Dis island poor! And de people fools! But I know you hear de sayin dat even de sick dog gots teeth. Well, dis island gots teeth dat grows down to the center of things. De Carib say dat dere's a spirit from before de back time locked into de island's root, and de Baptist say dat de island be a fountainhead of de Holy Spirit. But no matter what de truth, de people have each been granted a portion of dat spirit. And dat spirit legion now!"

The light behind Prince's eyes whirled so fast he could no longer distinguish periods of normal vision, and everything he saw had a purplish cast. He heard his entire agony as a tiny, scratchy sound deep in his throat. He toppled on his side and saw out over the bumpy sand, out to a point of land where wild palms, in silhouette against a vivid purple sky, shook their fronds like plumed African dancers, writhing up, ecstatic.

"Dat spirit have drove off de English! And one day it will drive de Sponnish home! It slow, but it certain. And dat is why we celebrate dis night . . . Cause on dis very night all dose not of de spirit and de law must come to judgment."

John's shoes scraped on the sand.

"Well, I'll be along now, Mr. Prince. God bless you."

Even when his head had cleared and the cold dissipated, Prince couldn't work it out. If Jerry Steedly smoked this stuff all the time, then *he* must be having an abnormal reaction. A flashback. The thing to do would be to overpower the drug with depressants. But how could old John have seen the turtling boat? Maybe it never happened? Maybe the coral simply twitched reality a bit, and everything since Ghetto Liquors had been a real-life fantasy of amazing exactitude. He finished his drink, had another, steadied himself, and then hailed the jitney when it passed on its way to town, on *his* way to see Rudy and Jubert and George.

Vengeance would be the best antidote of all for this black sediment within him.

Independence Day.

The shanties dripped with colored lights, and the dirt road glowed orange, crisscrossed by dancers and drunks who collided and fell. Skinny black casualties lay underneath the shanties, striped by light shining down through the floorboards. Young women danced in the bar windows; older, fatter women, their hair in turbans, glowering, stood beside tubs of lobster salad and tables laden with coconut bread and pastries. The night was raucous, blaring, hooting, shouting. All the dogs were in hiding.

Prince stuffed himself on the rich food, drank, and then went from bar to bar asking questions of men who pawed his shirt, rolled their eyes, and passed out for an answer. He could find no trace of Rudy or George, but he tracked Jubert down in a shanty bar whose sole designation as a bar was a cardboard sign, tacked on a palm tree beside it, which read "Frenly Club No Riot." Prince lured him outside with the promise of marijuana, and Jubert, stupidly drunk, followed to a clearing behind the bar where dirt trails crossed, a patch of ground bounded by two other shanties and banana trees. Prince smiled a smile of good fellowship, kicked him in the groin and the stomach, and broke Jubert's jaw with the heel of his hand.

"Short cut draw blood," said Prince. "Ain't dat right. You don't trick with de mighty."

He nudged Jubert's jaw with his toe.

Jubert groaned; blood welled from his mouth, puddling black in the moonlight.

"Come back at me and I'll kill you," said Prince.

He sat cross-legged beside Jubert. Moonlight saturated the clearing, and the tattered banana leaves looked made of gray-green silk. Their trunks showed bone white. A plastic curtain in a shanty window glowed with mystic roses, lit by the oil lamp inside. Jukebox reggae chip-chipped at the soft night, distant laughter . . .

He let the clearing come together around him. The moon brightened as though a film had washed from its face; the light tingled his shoulders. Everything—shanties, palms, banana trees, and bushes—sharpened, loomed, grew more encircling. He felt a measure of hilarity on seeing himself as he'd been in the jungle of Lang Biang, freakishly alert. It conjured up clichéd movie images. Prince, the veteran maddened by memory and distanced by trauma, compelled to relive his nightmares and hunt down these measly offenders in the derelict town. The violent American legend. The war-torn Prince of the cinema. He chuckled. His life, he knew, was devoid of such thematic material.

He was free of compulsion.

Thousands of tiny shake-hands lizards were slithering under the banana trees, running over the sandy soil on their hind legs. He could see the disturbance in the weeds. A hibiscus blossom nodded from behind a shanty, an exotic lure dangling out of the darkness, and the shadows beneath the palms were deep and restless . . . not like the shadows in Lang Biang, still and green, high in the vaulted trees. Spirits had lived in those trees, so the stories said, demon-things with iron beaks who'd chew your soul into rags. Once he had shot one. It had been (they told him) only a large fruit bat, deranged, probably by some chemical poison, driven to fly at him in broad daylight. But *he* had seen a demon with an iron beak sail from a green shadow and fired. Nearly every round must have hit, because all they'd found had been scraps of bloody, leathery wing. Afterward they called him Deadeye and described how he'd bounced the bat along through the air with bursts of unbelievable accuracy.

He wasn't afraid of spirits.

"How you doin, Jube?" Prince asked.

Jubert was staring at him, wide-eyed.

Clouds swept across the moon, and the clearing went dark, then brightened.

"Dere's big vultures up dere, Jubert, flyin cross de moon and screamin your name."

Prince was a little afraid of the drug, but less afraid of the islanders—nowhere near as afraid as Jubert was of him right now. Prince had been much more afraid, had cried and soiled himself; but he'd always emptied his gun into the shadows and stayed stoned and alert for eleven months. Fear, he'd learned, had its own continuum of right actions. He could handle it.

Jubert made a gurgling noise.

"Got a question, Jube?" Prince leaned over, solicitous.

A sudden gust of wind sent a dead frond crashing down, and the sound scared Jubert. He tried to lift his head and passed out from the pain.

Somebody shouted, "Listen to dat boy sing! Oh, he slick, mon!" and turned up the jukebox. The tinny music broke Prince's mood. Everything looked scattered. The moonlight showed the grime and slovenliness of the place, the sprinkles of chicken droppings and the empty crab shells. He'd lost most of his enthusiasm for hunting down Rudy and George, and he decided to head for Maud Price's place, the Golden Dream. Sooner or later everyone stopped in at the Dream. It was the island's gambling center, and because it was an anomaly among the shanties, with their two stucco rooms lit by naked light bulbs, drinking there conferred a certain prestige.

He thought about telling them in the bar about Jubert, but decided no and left him for someone else to rob.

Rudy and George hadn't been in, said Maud, smacking down a bottle on the counter. Bar flies buzzed up from the spills and orbited her like haywire electrons. Then she went back to chopping fish heads, scaling and filleting them. Monstrously fat and jet black, bloody smears on her white dress. The record player at her elbow ground out warped Freddie Fender tunes.

Prince spotted Jerry Steedly (who didn't seem glad to see Prince) sitting at a table along the wall, joined him, and told him about the black coral.

"Everybody sees the same things," said Steedly, uninterested. "The reef, the fires . . ."

"What about flashbacks? Is that typical?"

"It happens. I wouldn't worry about it." Steedly checked his watch. He was in his forties, fifteen years older than Rita, a gangly Arkansas hick whose brush-cut red hair was going gray.

"I'm not worried," said Prince. "It was fine except for the fires or whatever they were. I thought they were copepods at first, but I guess they were just part of the trip."

"The islanders think they're spirits." Steedly glanced toward the door, nervous, then looked at Prince, dead serious, as if he were considering a deep question. He kicked back in his chair and leaned against the wall, decided, half smiling. "Know what I think they are? Aliens."

Prince made a show of staring goggle-eyed, gave a dumb laugh, and drank.

"No kiddin, Neal. Parasites. Actually, copepods might not be so far off. They're not intelligent. They're reef dwellers from the next continuum over. The coral opens the perceptual gates or lets them see the gates that are already there, and . . . Wham! They latch right on. They induce a low-grade telepathy in human hosts. Among other things."

Steedly scraped back his chair and pointed at the adjoining room where people thronged, waving cards and money, shouting, losers threatening winners. "I gotta go lose some money, Neal. You take it easy."

"Are you trying to mess me around?" Prince asked with mild incredulity.

"Nope. It's just a theory of mine. They exhibit colonial behavior like a lot of small crustaceans. But they *may* be spirits. Maybe spirits aren't anything more than vague animal things slopping over from another world and setting their hooks in your soul, infecting you, dwelling in you. Who knows? I wouldn't worry about it, though."

He walked away.

"Say hi to Rita for me," Prince called.

Steedly turned, struggling with himself, but he smiled.

"Hey, Neal," he said. "It's not over."

Prince nursed his rum, cocked an eye toward the door whenever anyone entered (the place was rapidly filling), and watched Maud gutting fish. A light-bulb sun dangled inches over her head, and he imagined her with a necklace of skeletons, reaching down into a bucketful of little silver-scaled men. The thunk of her knife punctuated the babble around him. He drowsed. Idly, he began listening to the conversation of three men at the next table, resting his head against the wall. If he nodded out, Maud would wake him.

"De mon ain't got good sense, always spittin and fumin!"

"He harsh, mon! Dere's no denyin."

"Harsh? De mon worse den dat. Now de way Arlie tell it . . ."

Arlie? He wondered if they meant Arlie Brooks, who tended bar at the Sea Breeze.

". . . dat Mary Ebanks bled to death . . ."

"Dey say dat de stain where she bled still shine at night on de floor of de Sea Breeze!"

Maybe it was Arlie.

"Dat be fool duppy talk, mon!"

"Well, never mind dat! *He* never shot her. Dat was Eusebio Conejo from over at Sandy Bay. But de mon might have saved her with his knowledge of wounds if he had not run off at de gunshot!"

"Ain't he de one dat stole dat gold cross from old Byrum Waters?"

"Correct! Told him dat de gold have gone bad and dass why it so black. And Byrum, not mindful of de ways of gold, didn't know dat was only tarnish!"

"Dat was de treasure lost by old Meachem? Am I right?"

"Correct! De Carib watched him bury it and when he gone dey

move it into de hills. And den when Byrum found it he told his American friend. Hah! And dat friend become a wealthy mon and old Byrum go to de ground wrapped in a blanket!"

That was *his* cross! That was *him* they were talking about! Outraged, Prince came up out of his stupor and opened his eyes.

Then he sat very still.

The music, the shouts from the back room, the conversations had died, been sheared away without the least whisper or cough remaining, and the room had gone black . . . except the ceiling. And it brimmed, seethed with purple fire: swirls of indigo and royal purple and violet-white, a pattern similar to the enclosed waters of the reef, as if it, too, signaled varying depths and bottoms; incandescent-looking, though, a rectangle of violent, shifting light, like a corpse's first glimpse of sky when his coffin is opened up in Hell . . . and cold.

Prince ducked, expecting they would swoop at him, pin him against the freezing darkness. But they did not. One by one the fires separated from the blazing ceiling and flowed down over the walls, settling on the creases and edges of things, outlining them in points of flickering radiance. Their procession seemed almost ordered, stately, and Prince thought of a congregation filing into their allotted pews preparatory to some great function. They illuminated the rumples in ragged shirts (and the ragged ends, as well) and the wrinkles in faces. They traced the shapes of glasses, bottles, tables, spiderwebs, the electric fan, light bulbs and their cords. They glowed nebular in the liquor, they became the smoldering ends of cigarettes, they mapped the spills on the counter and turned them into miniature phosphorescent seas. And when they had all taken their places, their design complete, Prince sat dumbstruck in the midst of an incredibly detailed constellation, one composed of ghostly purple stars against an ebony sky—the constellation of a tropic barroom, of Maud Price's Golden Dream.

He laughed, a venturing laugh; it sounded forced even to his own ears. There was no door, he noticed, no window outlined in purple fire. He touched the wall behind him for reassurance and jerked his hand away: it was freezing. Nothing moved other than the flickering, no sound. The blackness held him fast to his chair as though it were a swamp sucking him under.

"I hurt bad, mon! It hurt inside my head!" A bleary and distressed voice. Jubert's voice!

"Mon, I hurt you bad myself and you slip me de black coral!"

"Dass de truth!"

"De mon had de right to take action!"

Other voices tumbled forth in argument, most of them drunken, sodden, and seeming to issue from starry brooms and chairs and glassware. Many of them took his side in the matter of Jubert's beating—*that*, he realized, was the topic under discussion. And he was winning! But still other voices blurted out, accusing him.

"He took dat fat Yankee tourist down to print old Mrs. Ebanks with her camera, and Mrs. Ebanks shamed by it!"

"No, mon! I not dat shamed! Let not dat be against him!"

"He pay me for de three barracuda and take de five!"

"He knock me down when I tell him how he favor dat cousin of mine dat live in Ceiba!"

"He beat me . . ."

"He cheat me . . ."

"He curse me . . ."

The voices argued points of accuracy, mitigating circumstances, and accused each other of exaggeration. Their logic was faulty and stupidly conceived. It had the feel of malicious, drunken gossip, as if a group of islanders were loitering on some dusty street and disputing the truth of a tall tale. But in this case it was *his* tale they disputed; for though Prince did not recognize all the voices, he did recognize his crimes, his prideful excesses, his slurs and petty slights. Had it not been so cold, he might have been amused, because the general consensus appeared to be that he was no worse or better than any of his accusers and therefore merited no outrageous judgment.

But then a wheezy voice, the expression of a dulled, ancient sensibility, said, "I found dat gold cross in a cave up on Hermit's Ridge . . ."

Prince panicked, sprang for the door, forgetting there was none, scrabbled at the stony surface, fell, and crawled along, probing for an exit. Byrum's voice harrowed him.

"And I come to him and say, 'Mr. Prince, I got dis terrible pain in de chest. Can't you give me money? I know dat your money come from meltin down de gold cross.' And he say, 'Byrum, I don't care diddley about your chest!' And den he show me de door!"

Prince collapsed in a corner, eyes fixed on the starry record player from which the old man's voice came. No one argued against Byrum. When he had finished there was a silence.

"He's been sleeping with my wife," said a twangy American voice.

"Jerry!" Prince yelled. "Where are you?"

A constellate bottle of rum was the source of the voice. "Right here, you son . . ."

"Dere's to be no talkin with de mon before judgment!"

"Dass right! De spirits make dat clear!"

"These damn things aren't spirits . . ."

"If dey ain't den why Byrum Waters in de Dream tonight?"

"De mon can't hear de voices of de spirits cause he not *of* de island hisself!"

"Byrum's not here! I've told you people so many times I'm sick of it! These things induce telepathy in humans. That means you can hear each others' minds, that your thoughts resonate and amplify each others', maybe even tap into some kind of collective unconscious. That's how . . ."

"I believe somebody done pelt a rock at de mon's head! He crazy!"

The matter of the purple fires was tabled, and the voices discussed Prince's affair with Rita Steedly ("Dere's no proof de mon been messin with your wife!"), reaching a majority opinion of guilty on what seemed to Prince shaky evidence indeed. The chill in the room had begun to affect him, and though he noticed that unfamiliar voices had joined the dialog—British voices whose speech was laden with archaisms, guttural Carib voices—he did not wonder at them. He was far more concerned by the trembling of his mucles and the slow, flabby rhythm of his heart; he hugged his knees and buried his head in them for warmth. And so he hardly registered the verdict announced in Byrum Waters's cracked whisper ("De island never cast you out, Mr. Prince") nor did he even hear the resultant argument ("Dat all you goin to tell him?" "De mon have a right to hear his fate!") except as a stupid hypnotic round which dazed him further and increased the chill, then turned into ghostly laughter. And he did not notice for quite a while that the chill had lessened, that the light filtering through his lids was yellow, and that the laughter was not voiced by spectral fires but by ragged drunks packed closely around him, sweating, howling, and slopping their drinks on his feet. Their gap-toothed mouths opened wider and wider in his dimming sight, as if he were falling into the jaws of ancient animals who had waited in their jungle centuries for such as he. Fat moths danced around them in the yellow air.

Prince pushed feebly at the floor, trying to stand. They laughed louder, and he felt his own lips twitch in a smile, an involuntary reaction to all the good humor in the room.

"Oh, damn!" Maud slammed the flat of her hand down on the counter, starting up the bar flies and hiccuping Freddie Fender's wail. Her smile was fierce and malefic. "How you like dat, Mr. Prince? You one of us now!"

He must've passed out. They must've dumped him in the street like a sack of manure! His head swam as he pulled himself up by the window ledge; his hip pocket clinked on the stucco wall . . . rum bottle. He fumbled it out, swallowed, gagged, but felt it strengthen him. The town was dead, lightless, and winded. He reeled against the doorway of the Dream and saw the moldering shanties swing down beneath running banks of moonlit cloud. Peaked and eerie, witches' hats, the sharp jut of folded black wings. He couldn't think.

Dizzy, he staggered between the shanties and fell on all fours in the shallows, then soaked his head in the wavelets lapping the shingle. There were slippery things under his hands. No telling what . . . hog guts, kelp. He sat on a piling and let the wind shiver him and straighten him out. Home. Better than fighting off the rabid dog at the Hotel Captain Henry, better than passing out again right here. Two and a half miles across island, no more than an hour even in his condition. But watch out for the purple fires! He laughed. The silence gulped it up. If this were just the drug doing tricks . . . God! You could make a fortune selling it in the States.

"You scrapes off de color and dass what you smokes," he sang, calypso style. "De black coral takes, boom-boom, just one toke."

He giggled. But what the hell *were* those purple fires?

Duppies? Aliens? How bout the purple souls of the niggers? The niggers' stinging purple souls!

He took another drink. "Better ration it, pilgrim," he said to the dark road in his best John Wayne. "Or you'll never reach the fort alive!"

And like John Wayne, he'd be back, he'd chew out the bullet with his teeth and brand himself clean with a red-hot knife and blow holes in the bad guys.

Oh, yeah!

But suppose they were spirits? Aliens? Not hallucinations?

So what!

"I one of dem, now!" he shouted.

He breezed the first two miles. The road wound through the brush-covered hills at an easy grade. Stars shone in the west, but the moon had gone behind the clouds and the darkness was as thick as mud. He wished he'd brought his flashlight . . . That had been the first thing which had attracted him to the island: how the people carried flashlights to show their paths in the hills, along the beaches, in the towns after the generators had been shut down. And when an ignorant, flashlightless stranger came by, they'd shine a path from your feet to theirs and ask, "How de night?"

"Beautiful," he'd replied; or, "Fine, just fine." And it *had* been. He'd loved everything about the island—the stories, the musical cadences of island speech, the sea grape trees with their funny, round, leathery leaves, and the glowing, many-colored sea. He'd seen that the island operated along an ingenious and flexible principle, one capable of accommodating any contrary and eventually absorbing it through a process of calm acceptance. He'd envied the islanders their peaceful, unhurried lives. But that had been before Viet Nam. During the war something inside him had gone irreversibly stone-cold sober, screwed up his natural high, and when he returned their idyllic lives had seemed despicable, listless, a bacterial culture shifting on its slide.

Every now and then he saw the peak of a thatched roof in silhouette against the stars, strands of barbed wire hemming in a few acres of scrub and bananas. He stayed dead center in the road, away from the deepest shadow, sang old Stones and Dylan, and fueled himself with hits of rum. It had been a good decision to head back, because a norther was definitely brewing. The wind rushed cold in his face, spitting rain. Storms blew up quickly at this time of year, but he could make it home and secure his house before the worst of the rains.

Something crashed in the brush. Prince jumped away from the sound, looking wildly about for the danger. The tufted hillock on his right suddenly sprouted horns against the starlight and charged at him, bellowing, passing so raw and close that he could hear the breath articulated in the huge red throat. Christ! It had sounded more like a demon's bellow than a cow's, which it was. Prince lost his balance and sprawled in the dirt, shaking. The damned thing lowed again, crunching off through a thicket. He started to get up. But the rum, the adrenalin, all the poisons of his day-long exertions roiled around in him, and his stomach emptied, spewing out liquor and lobster salad and coconut bread. Afterward he felt better—weaker, yet not on the verge of as great a weakness as before. He tore off his fouled shirt and slung it into a bush.

The bush was a blaze of purple fires.

They hung on twig ends and leaf tips and marked the twisting course of branches, outlining them as they had done at Maud's. But at the center of this tracery the fires clustered together in a globe—a wicked, violet-white sun extruding spidery filaments and generating forked, leafy electricities.

Prince backed away. The fires flickered in the bush, unmoving. Maybe the drug had finished its run, maybe now that he'd burned most of it out the fires could no longer affect him as they had previously. But then a cold, cold prickle shifted along his spine and he knew—oh, God!—he knew for a certainty there were fires on his back, playing hide-and-seek where he could never find them. He beat at his shoulderblades, like a man putting out flames, and the cold stuck to his fingertips. He held them up before his eyes. They flickered, pulsing from indigo to violet-white. He shook them so hard that his joints cracked, but the fires spread over his hands, encasing his forearms in a lurid glare.

In blind panic Prince staggered off the road, fell, scrambled up, and ran, holding his glowing arms stiff out in front of him. He tumbled down an embankment and came to his feet, running. He saw that the fires had spread above his elbows and felt the chill margin inching upward. His arms lit the brush around him, as if they were the wavering beams of tinted flashlights. Vines whipped out of the dark, the lengths of a black serpent coiled everywhere, lashed into a frenzy by the purple light. Dead fronds clawed his face with sharp papery fingers. He was so afraid, so empty of everything but fear, that when a palm trunk loomed ahead he ran straight into it, embracing it with his shining arms.

There were hard fragments in his mouth, blood, more blood flowing into his eyes. He spat and probed his mouth, wincing as he touched the torn gums. Three teeth missing, maybe four. He hugged the palm trunk and hauled himself up. This was the grove near his house! He could see the lights of St. Mark's Key between the trunks, white seas driving in over the reef. Leaning on the palms as he went, he made his way to the water's edge. The wind-driven rain slashed at his split forehead. Christ! It was swollen big as an onion! The wet sand sucked off one of his tennis shoes, but he left it.

He washed his mouth and his forehead in the stinging salt water, then slogged toward the house, fumbling for his key. Damn! It had been in his shirt. But it was all right. He'd built the house Hawaiian style, with wooden slats on every side to admit the breeze; it would be easy to break in. He could barely see the roof peak against the toiling darkness of the palms and the hills behind, and he banged his shins on the porch. Distant lightning flashed, and he found the stair and spotted the conch shell lying on the top step. He wrapped his hand inside it, punched a head-sized hole in the door slats, and leaned on the door, exhausted by the effort. He was just about to reach in for the latch when the darkness within—visible against the lesser darkness of night as a coil of dead, unshining emptiness —squeezed from the hole like black toothpaste and tried to encircle him.

Prince tottered backward off the porch and landed on his side; he dragged himself away a few feet, stopped, and looked up at the house. The blackness was growing out into the night, encysting him in a thicket of coral branches so dense that he could see between them only glints of the lightning bolts striking down beyond the reef. "Please," he said, lifting his hand in supplication. And something broke in him, some grimly held thing whose residue was tears. The wind's howl and the booming reef came as a single ominous vowel, roaring, rising in pitch.

The house seemed to inhale the blackness, to suck it slithering back inside, and for a moment Prince thought it was over. But then violet beams lanced from the open slats, as if the fuming heart of a reactor had been uncovered within. The beach bloomed in livid daylight—a no-man's-land littered with dead fish, half-buried conchs, rusted cans, and driftwood logs like the broken, corroded limbs of iron statues. Inky palms thrashed and shivered. Rotting coconuts cast shadows on the sand. And then the light swarmed up from the house, scattering into a myriad fiery splinters and settling on palm tops, on the prows of dinghies, on the reef, on tin roofs set among the palms, and on sea grape and cashew trees, where they burned. The ghosts of candles illuminating a sacred shore, haunting the dark interior of a church whose anthem was wind, whose litany was thunder, and upon whose walls feathered shadows leapt and lightnings crawled.

Prince got to his knees, watching, waiting, not really afraid any longer, but gone into fear. Like a sparrow in a serpent's gaze, he saw everything of his devourer, knew with great clarity that these *were* the island people, all of them who had ever lived, and that they *were* possessed of some otherworldly vitality—though whether spirit or alien or both, he could not determine—and that they had taken their accustomed places, their ritual stands. Byrum Waters hovering in the cashew tree he had planted as a boy; John Anderson McCrae flitting above the reef where he and his father had swung lanterns to lure ships in onto the rocks; Maud Price ghosting over the grave of her infant child hidden in the weeds behind a shanty. But then he doubted his knowledge and wondered if they were not telling him this, advising him of the island's consensus, for he heard the mutter of a vast conversation becoming distinct, outvoicing the wind.

He stood, searching for an avenue of escape, not in the least hopeful of finding one, but choosing to exercise a final option. Everywhere he turned the world pitched and tossed as if troubled by his sight, and only the flickering purple fires held constant. "Oh, my God!" he screamed, almost singing it in an ecstasy of fear, realizing that the precise moment for which they'd gathered had arrived.

As one, from every corner of the shore, they darted into his eyes.

Before the cold overcame him, Prince heard island voices in his head. They ranted ("Lessee how you rank with de spirit, now! Boog man!"). They instructed ("Best you not struggle against de spirit. Be more merciful dat way"). They insulted, rambled, and construed illogics. For a few seconds he tried to follow the thread of their discourse, thinking if he could understand and comply, then they might stop. But when he could not understand he clawed his face in frustration. The voices rose to a chorus, to a mob howling separately for his attention, then swelled into a roar greater than the wind's but equally single-minded and bent on his annihilation. He dropped onto his hands and knees, sensing the beginning of a terrifying dissolution, as if he were being poured out into a shimmering violet-red bowl. And he saw the film of fire coating his chest and arms, saw his own horrid glare reflected on the broken seashells and mucky sand, shifting from violet-red into violet-white and brightening, growing whiter and whiter until it became a white darkness in which he lost all track of being.

The bearded old man wandered into Meachem's Landing early Sunday morning after the storm. He stopped for a while beside the stone bench in the public square where the sentry, a man even older than himself, was leaning on his deer rifle, asleep. When the voices bubbled up in his thoughts—he pictured his thoughts as a soup with bubbles boiling up and popping, and the voices coming from the pops—and yammered at him ("No, no! Dat ain't de mon!" "Keep walkin, old fool!"). It was a chorus, a clamor which caused his head to throb; he continued on. The street was littered with palm husks and fronds and broken bottles buried in the mud that showed only their glittering edges. The voices warned him these were sharp and would cut him ("Make it hurtful like dem gashes on your face"), and he stepped around them. He wanted to do what they told him because . . . It just seemed the way of things.

The glint of a rain-filled pothole caught his eye, and he knelt by it, looking at his reflection. Bits of seaweed clung to his crispy gray hair, and he picked them out, laying them carefully in the mud. The pattern in which they lay seemed familiar. He drew a rectangle around them with his finger and it seemed even more familiar, but the voices told him to forget about it and keep going. One voice advised him to wash his cuts in the pothole. The water smelled bad, however, and other voices warned him away. They grew in number and volume, driving him along the street until he followed their instructions and sat down on the steps of a shanty painted all the colors of the rainbow. Footsteps sounded inside the shanty, and a black bald-headed man wearing shorts came out and stretched himself on the landing.

"Damn!" he said. "Just look what come home to us this mornin. Hey, Lizabeth!"

A pretty woman joined him, yawning, and stopped mid yawn when she saw the old man.

"Oh, Lord! Dat poor creature!"

She went back inside and reappeared shortly carrying a towel and a basin, squatted beside him, and began dabbing at his wounds. It seemed such a kind, a human thing to be so treated, and the old man kissed her soapy fingers.

"De mon a caution!" Lizabeth gave him a playful smack. "I know dass why he in such a state. See de way de skin's all tore on his forehead dere? Must be he been fighting with de conchs over some other mon's woman."

"Could be," said the bald man. "How bout that? You a fool for the ladies?"

The old man nodded. He heard a chorus of affirming voices. ("Oh, dass it!" "De mon messin and messin until he half crazy, den he mess with de *wrong* woman!" "Must have been grazed with de conch and left for dead.")

"Lord, yes!" said Lizabeth. "Dis mon goin to trouble all de ladies, goin to be kissin after dem and huggin dem . . ."

"Can't you talk?" asked the bald man.

He thought he could, but there were so many voices, so many words to choose from . . . maybe later. No.

"Well, I guess we'd better get you a name. How bout Bill? I got a good friend up in Boston's named Bill."

That suited the old man fine. He liked being associated with the bald man's good friend.

"Tell you what, Bill." The bald man reached inside the door and handed him a broom. "You sweep off the steps and pick up what you see needs pickin, and we'll pass you out some beans and bread after a while. How's that sound?"

It sounded *good*, and Bill began sweeping at once, taking meticulous care with each step. The voices died to a murmurous purr in his thoughts. He beat the broom against the pilings and dust fell onto it from the floorboards; he beat it until no more would fall. He was happy to be among people again because . . . ("Don't be thinkin bout the back time, mon! Dat all gone." "You just get on with your clean dere, Bill. Everything goin to work out in de end." "Dass it, mon! You goin to clean dis whole town before you through!" "Don't vex with de mon! He doin his work!") And he was! He picked up everything within fifty feet of the shanty and chased off a ghost crab, smoothing over the delicate slashes its legs made in the sand.

By the time Bill had cleaned for a half hour he felt so at home, so content and enwrapped in his place and purpose, that when the old woman next door came out to toss her slops into the street, he scampered up her stairs, threw his arms around her, and kissed her full on the mouth. Then he stood grinning, at attention with his broom.

Startled at first, the woman put her hands on her hips and
018 looked him up and down, shaking her head in dismay.

"My God," she said sorrowfully. "Dis de best we can do for dis poor mon? Dis de best thing de island can make of itself?"

Bill didn't understand. The voices chattered, irritated; they didn't seem angry at him, though, and he kept on smiling. Once again the woman shook her head and sighed, but after a few seconds Bill's smile encouraged her to smile in return.

"I guess if dis de worst of it," she said, "den better must come." She patted Bill on the shoulder and turned to the door. "Everybody!" she called. "Quickly now! Come see dis lovin soul dat de storm have let fall on Rudy Welcomes's door!"